GIRL OF LIES

CHARLES SHEEHAN-MILES

Books by Charles Sheehan-Miles

Thompson Sisters
A Song for Julia
Falling Stars
Just Remember to Breathe
The Last Hour

Rachel's Peril
Girl of Lies

America's Future
Republic
Insurgent

Nocturne (with Andrea Randall)

Prayer at Rumayla
A Novel of the Gulf War

Saving the World on Thirty Dollars a Day:
An Activist's Guide to Starting, Organizing and Running a Non-Profit Organization

GIRL OF LIES

5-3-14

Christy

Thank you so much!

If you enjoyed this book, please share it with a friend, write a review online, or send feedback to the authors!

www.sheehanmiles.com

ISBN-13: 978-0-9898688-6-0

Printed in the United States of America
Cincinnatus Press
www.cincinnatuspress.com

v12182013

Dedication

for Andrea

Acknowledgements

Thank you to Andrea. For your heart, your courage, your love. Lori Sabin, you've been a wonderful editor for most of the Thompson Sisters books and Nocturne. Thank you.

Thank you to my fantastic beta reader team: Brett Lewis, Jackie Yeadon, Tanya Spence Hall, Kristen Teaff, Emma Corcoran, Kathy Harshaw Baker, Wendy Neuman Wilken, Dimitra Fleissner, Laura Wilson, Bryan James, Michelle Kannan, Sarah Griffin, Amy Burt, Jennifer Mirabelli, Stacy McDowell Grice, Kirsten Papi, Beth Suit, Rita Jenkins Post, Kelly Moorhouse, Kirsty Lander and Sally Bouley.

Thank you to Ashley Wilcox and ACS Tours for organizing the blog tour.

Jillian Dodd, Tiffany King, Tara Sivec, Michelle Pace, Les Pace, Maggi Myers, Jenn Sterling, Melissa Perea, Michelle Warren and Priscilla Glenn form part of my professional network of authors: all gave advice and suggestions regarding the cover, blurb and more through this process. Thank you.

Cast of Characters

The Thompson Family
Richard Thompson
Adelina Thompson
Julia Wilson (Thompson)
— Crank Wilson
Carrie Thompson-Sherman
— Ray Sherman
— Rachel Sherman
Alexandra Paris (Thompson)
— Dylan Paris
Sarah Thompson
Jessica Thompson
Andrea Thompson

The Wakhan File
Roshan al Saud
Leslie Collins
Mitch Filner
Vasily Karatygin
George-Phillip Patrick Nicholas
Chuck Rainsley

Diplomatic Security
John "Bear" Wyden
Leah Simpson

The Washington Post
Anthony Walker

Prologue

Andrea Thompson

Andrea Thompson shivered as Javier's hands slid up the back of her shirt, his fingers curled, raising goose bumps and sensation as they ran down her spine. She gasped a little as his lips touched her, his stubble rough against her neck.

"*Te quiero*," he said as her back arched, pressing her chest against him. I want you.

"No," she replied. "*Abuelita* expects me home."

He sighed, lifting his head. His eyes were dark, too dark, easy to get lost in. "You know you're the only girl I want, ever."

She put her lips to his ear, the faint, aquatic smell of his cologne gratifying her senses. "You say that because your *verga* is hard and I'm in the car with you. You want every girl you see, Javier. Take me home."

He smiled, his full lips curving up a little more on the right side, and said, "*Sí*, Andrea."

One second later, she felt the buzzing of her phone in her pocket, and then the ringtone that represented her sisters.

He sighed, and broke away from her, his smile wistful. She returned the smile as she dug in her jacket pocket for her phone. As Javier started the car, she got the phone out. *Mierda!* She wasn't in time.

"Which one of your sisters is it?"

"Carrie," she said as she unlocked the phone. "She lives in Washington, DC."

As Andrea dialed the phone, she counted the hours back. It was close to ten pm in Calella, so that would make it about four in the afternoon in Washington. She hadn't expected to hear from Carrie. Truthfully, she hadn't expected to hear from any of her sisters. Julia, the oldest of her sisters at thirty-two years old, was the only one who called her regularly.

"Hello?" Carrie's voice. A little breathy.

"Carrie? It's Andrea."

"Andrea! Thank you so much for calling back so quickly! Your number didn't show up on my phone."

Andrea shrugged. International calls could be weird sometimes. "How are you? How's the baby?"

Silence. Just long enough that Andrea sat up straight in her seat, her eyebrows scrunching together, and then she said, "Carrie? What's going on? How's the baby?"

Andrea felt a shiver down her spine at the sound of a sniffle from Carrie. Carrie, the foundation of her family, the daughter who'd always taken care of all of them. Carrie, who lost her husband to murder and tragedy less than a year ago.

"Andrea...I need help. Rachel needs help."

"Anything," Andrea said without thinking.

"Can you come? To Washington?"

Andrea swallowed. "I have school..."

"Andrea. Rachel is very sick...she needs a bone marrow transplant. And I'm not a close enough match. I just...will you come get tested? *Please?*"

Andrea had seen little Rachel's pictures on Facebook. A beautiful, tiny, five-week-old baby. Carrie and Ray's daughter, who would never know her father.

Carrie couldn't take any more pain.

"Of course I'll come."

Andrea shivered at the sound of a sob on the other line. She looked up and met Javier's eyes. He raised his eyebrows, and she mouthed the words *llévame a casa*. Take me home.

Javier nodded and put the car in gear. A moment later, he was driving through the narrow streets of Calella. "I'm going home now, Carrie. I'll talk with *Abuelita* and get a flight home right away, okay? I promise." As she spoke the words, she couldn't help but see in her mind how much of a mess her sister had been eight months ago. Everything had been a disaster. Her husband Ray was in the hospital alongside their sister Sarah, both of them badly injured in a car accident that turned out to be intentional.

Murder. That's what it had been. Ray, her brother-in-law who she barely knew, had been brutally murdered. And now his daughter was sick.

Andrea sighed. She would figure out something for school. Right now she needed to make arrangements to get back to the United States.

Javier turned the car onto Carrer Diputatio, the tiny one lane street two blocks from the beach. Abuelita, her grandmother, had her flat here, a third floor apartment above the don Panini snack bar. The snack bar was still open when Javier pulled the car to a stop in front of it, and patrons were crowded into the open restaurant and spilling out onto the sidewalk. Bared midriffs, short skirts, coverall dresses, sweat and carnal intentions. Loud music blasted out of the Isard restaurant and pizzeria across the narrow lane. A car came to a stop behind Javier's and the driver immediately honked the horn as more traffic backed up behind it.

"You're going away?" Javier asked, ignoring the honking.

She signed. Then nodded. "I have to go to the United States."

"You'll be careful?"

She thought the question seemed odd. Of course she'd be careful. "I'll be back soon. My niece needs a bone marrow transplant. I'm probably not even a match. But I have to go to my sister."

The driver behind them honked his horn again, shouting obscenities out the open window. The street was too narrow for him to drive around unless he went onto the sidewalk in front of the *Gaviota* bar, which had a crowd of twenty or more people crowded outside.

"I have to go," she said.

"*Te amo*," he said softly.

Andrea shivered, even though she knew he didn't mean it. Because...what if he did? She leaned forward and kissed him goodbye.

"*Despedida*," she said. *Farewell*. Then she slipped out of the car, shutting the door behind her.

The driver behind Javier, an angry, frustrated man in his mid thirties with a remarkable mustache, had laid on the horn, letting it continuously sound. She gave mustache-man a scornful look, slapped her left bicep with her right hand and raised her left fist in an obscene gesture. Then she slipped into her grandmother's apartment building.

Part One

CHAPTER ONE
Hairy Chest

1. Andrea. April 28. 11:30 am EST

"**Is** Washington your final destination?" the man asked. He wore a black suit with a white shirt, the collar open. Medium brown skin with a hairy chest, Andrea thought he looked Arab, possibly from Egypt or Saudi Arabia. His eyes danced a little, from her face to the swell of her breasts, and he spoke too loud, even over the whine of the jets. A creeper, probably. He wore cologne, too much of it, and Andrea was disturbed to notice that it was the same scent as Javier's, but not *exactly* the same. The man next to her smelled earthier, almost musky. Disturbing.

She shifted in her seat, hoping the questions were friendly, but not too friendly. She didn't relish an eight-hour flight with someone hoping to get lucky.

"It is," she said.

"Business? Vacation?"

"Personal," Andrea answered, looking him straight in the eye. "I don't have any business, I'm sixteen. My father's an American diplomat and I'm flying home."

The creeper swallowed. "I'm headed that way for business," he said. Then his eyes darted to her legs.

Damn it. Her sister Julia had made her travel arrangements, and she was flying first class. So far as she could see there weren't any other first-class seats, and as much as she didn't want to ride all the way to the United States with this guy checking her out, she also didn't want to ride in the back of the plane, jammed in like commuters on a Tokyo subway.

She reached into her purse and took out a paperback guide to backpacking in Italy, which she was planning to do that summer. More importantly, the book would act as a shield, hopefully fending off a too friendly conversationalist. Once the flight was in the air, she would switch to her laptop. She wanted to research *beta thalassemia major*, a rare genetically linked condition that could result in severe anemia. Failure to thrive. Bone malformation. Early death.

Rachel had it.

How was that even possible?

She certainly didn't know of anyone in the family with thalassemia. What little she'd had time to read while waiting for the cab to take her to the airport hadn't reassured her. The lifetime prognosis wasn't good unless they could find a matching donor.

She tried to bend her mind away from her niece's health condition and back to the book. Her creeper kept his distance while she read. Or pretended to. Her mind wasn't really focused on the intricacies of the youth hostels of Italy, and what she really wanted to do once the plane was in the air was put her seat back and take a nap. She'd barely made the last non-stop out of Barcelona and would arrive in Baltimore late in the afternoon. But if she caught a short nap now, she'd be able to stay up most of the flight. Or... something. Jetlag was hell.

In any event, within half an hour the flight was in the air, the seat belt signs were off, she had cup of tea and her laptop was open, earbuds plugged into her phone and music playing.

Her first stop was Wikipedia, where she began reading about genetic blood disorders. She found it interesting that Queen Victoria of England had apparently spontaneously carried hemophilia as a mutation, which she'd then passed on to her children and ultimately several European royal houses in Russia, Spain and Germany. *The Royal Disease,* it had been called. Thanks to all the inbreeding. But thalassemia was primarily seen in people with Mediterranean and Asian backgrounds, which of course the sisters shared through their mother Adelina. And while it didn't have the immediate life-threatening properties of hemophilia, the longterm effects were just as severe.

She pressed pause on her music, shifting in her seat. Time to make a stop in the facilities.

"Excuse me."

Andrea jerked in her seat, looking up from the computer. It was her next door neighbor in first class, Mister Hairy Chest.

"Yes?"

"I couldn't help but noticing you were researching medical conditions. Are you a medical student?"

That was just...strange. Why would he ask that? She'd already told him she was only sixteen. She didn't want to be a giant bitch. But something about him set off all her alarms. "No," she replied. "I'm in secondary school. I'm reading...actually my niece has a genetic blood disease...I'm going to Washington to help my sister."

"Ahhh," he said. "I see. I only ask because I've considered going to med school."

Andrea let a breath out. Something about this guy rubbed her completely the wrong way. But Abuelita hadn't raised her to be impolite to anyone.

"Are you a student?" she asked.

"I am...*Universidad Autònoma de Madrid.*"

"I see. And you study...?" One of the several schools she'd looked into had been UAM.

His teeth gleamed in a broad grin. "Mechanical engineer. I'm in my third year."

She swallowed, feeling an odd tightness in her chest. "Well. That's nice. Excuse me just a moment."

She slid her laptop into the leather pocket of the seat in front of her and folded back the table, then slipped out of her seat. Heart thudding a little, she made her way to the restroom at the front of the cabin, stepped inside and closed and locked the door.

Something was wrong. She'd spent two days touring the University and had met with the science and engineering faculty there. He was a lot older than his twenties. And UAM didn't have a major in mechanical engineering. Which meant Hairy Chest was lying.

Why?

2. George-Phillip. April 28

"**S**ir? A moment please?"

George-Phillip looked up from his desk, raising his ample eyebrows. There were only two people in the Special Intelligence Service...four people in the entire country...who could walk into his exquisitely decorated office and interrupt him without an appointment. As the Chief of the SIS he controlled the British government's foreign intelligence service. Thousands upon thousands of people and billions of pounds dedicated to tracking the enemies of the Queen. And friends, of course.

George-Phillip—formally known as *Prince* George-Phillip, Duke of Kent—had served in the SIS since 1986. Unlike his father, who had been content to waste the family's fortune on fast cars, drunken parties and inappropriate women, George-Phillip had decided immediately on his father's death that he would spend his life in service to his country. And he had done so, for more than thirty years. One could almost say he had his position in spite of his heritage—members of the Royal family, even those so far removed from the throne that assuming it would be inconceivable, simply did not rise to high ranks in the *civil* service.

George-Phillip, however, ended up with a fairly unique career. Starting with a brief stint as a special aide to the ambassador in Washington, DC, he'd attended Sandhurst, the Royal Military Academy, and then entered the SIS. That career had taken him to places as diverse as Afghanistan and China, Istanbul and Paris and finally here, at the nerve center of the intelligence world.

George-Phillip's role in the intelligence world was well known by the public—after all, he often appeared in testimony before Parliament or in meetings. He was clearly recognizable in public by his unusual height and his bushy, over expressive eyebrows. George-Phillip had eyebrows that were unruly, often out of control, acting out their own soliloquy regardless of his audience or his desires. It was his eyebrows that kept George-Phillip honest. It was his eyebrows (or, as the *Times* always said, his *unibrow*) that provided the media with plenty of entertainment fodder.

SIS Chief Raises Eyebrow Over Improprieties, said one headline on the front page of the *Mirror.* He was still convinced, two years later, the picture had been manipulated in Photoshop.

George-Phillip took such things in stride. His job didn't require that he be popular with the British public, nor did it require a movie-star reputation. It *did* require credibility, and that George-Phillip had. His credibility had led him unerringly to the job of Ambassador to the United Nations, followed by his current position as Chief of the Special Intelligence Service.

At the door was Oswald O'Leary. O'Leary was as unlikely an aide as one could ever expect the Chief of Intelligence to have. He was Irish, for one thing. Small, with beady eyes and the flattened nose and hanging jowls of a pug, O'Leary always looked as if he wanted to grab the nearest person and just *shake* them.

He was also brilliant, incredibly loyal, and therefore the recipient of some of the most unusual assignments George-Phillip could hand out.

"Sir, I have some information on the Wakhan file."

George-Phillip winced inwardly. Then he beckoned O'Leary forward.

"What is it?"

O'Leary laid the file on his desk and George-Phillip opened it. His eyes widened.

"Andrea Thompson," O'Leary said. "This is the youngest daughter of Ambassador Thompson."

There was no mistaking who she was, even though she was much older now. A much younger twin to Carrie Thompson, her older sister. Dark hair, pale blue-green eyes, fair skin, remarkable height.

"What's the situation with the Thompson children?"

O'Leary shifted. "It seems she lives in Spain with Ambassador Thompson's mother-in-law, and has little contact with the family. She did briefly visit the United States last summer during the Dega Payan court-martial, then returned home."

"So what takes her home now?"

"It seems that she's to be tested as a possible donor match."

George-Phillip raised his hand to his mouth, covering it. He closed his eyes and sat, motionless, for several seconds. Finally, his eyes opened and darted to O'Leary. "It is imperative you keep me informed, O'Leary. This is a matter of the highest national security. You understand?"

O'Leary looked back at George-Phillip with grim eyes. "I understand, sir."

3. Andrea. April 28. 4:35 pm

As always, Baltimore-Washington International airport was a chaotic mess of people. Andrea moved through the crowds, grateful that she finally shook Hairy Chest at Customs. Her U.S. Passport took her into a separate line, and that was all it took. Now, as she walked to the ground transportation area to catch her ride, she also kept an eye out for his return. Her backpack was slung over her shoulder and she wheeled a larger suitcase behind her.

The terminal smelled like machine oil and body odor, and every few minutes overhead speakers burst out in mechanical sounding voices, making announcements in half a dozen languages. Finally she found her way to the baggage carousel. Her last two flights into Washington, DC had taken her through Dulles airport, and her unfamiliarity with this one made everything just a little bit more difficult.

On top of that, her mobile wouldn't boot back up. The black screen mocked her repeated attempts to turn it on. She supposed the battery was dead, but now, once she found her luggage, she was going to have to find a pay phone. If such a thing even still existed.

Finally. Ahead, near the taxi entrance, a man stood holding an iPad with the name "Andrea Thompson"displayed with glowing white letters.

"Hello!" she called, waving to the man. He was tall, in his mid-thirties, with a blonde crew-cut and blue eyes. He didn't look like a limo driver...he looked like a bodyguard.

Of course, if Julia had sent him, he might well be a bodyguard.

"I'm Andrea," she said.

He flashed a mouthful of glowing white teeth at her. "Nice to meet ya, Miss Thompson. I'm Dan. This way to the car...you got any luggage? Just that?"

He reached out a hand and took her suitcase. She turned to follow him, then said, "Wait..." and walked, slowly toward the newspaper stand next to the exit.

The *Washington Post* was displayed prominently, and caught her eye, because her father's photograph was splashed across the cover. The headline was a shock. *Ambassador Thompson tapped for Defense Secretary.*

She didn't realize her father was planning to come out of retirement. And Secretary of Defense?

The driver—Dan—paused, failing to hide his irritation. Andrea shrugged. That didn't matter to her. And what was the idea of sending a driver to pick her up anyway? She wasn't close to her family, but it felt awfully impersonal to send a hired driver.

Then again, her mother was probably there, and Adelina Thompson was Queen of the impersonal.

Andrea pulled the top paper off the stack and handed over her debit card, hoping it would work in the United States. She held her breath for a moment. It did. Then she turned and followed Dan to a black Lincoln Town Car. He opened the back door and she slid inside. The back seat was wide, leather. Cool and comfortable. A moment later the car shuddered as he tossed her bag into the trunk and closed it.

As he slid into his seat, she said, "Do you have a USB phone charger? Mine's dead."

Dan grunted, then leaned over and dug in the glove box. "I've got one, but the only plug is up here."

"Do you mind plugging this in?" she asked, and then passed her phone forward.

"Sure."

A horn honked somewhere behind them. Dan glanced in the rearview mirror. For a second she thought she saw a flash of worry in his eyes, but it was gone as quick as it came. Then he looked away and put the car in gear.

Where the car sat now, it was dim, one or more layers of road and parking deck above them. Taxicabs and shuttle buses surrounded them, the sound of horns and engines overriding everything except the occasional jet engine, the smell of diesel fumes heavy in the air. She was glad the window was up as she leaned back in her seat and said, "How long will it take to get to Bethesda from here?"

The driver shrugged. "Depends on traffic." He turned away from her and began to drive, turning the radio on and flooding the car with the sound of too-loud and too-excited disk jockeys.

Andrea felt tension tighten the muscles in her neck and shoulders. At the very end of the ground transportation area stood Hairy Chest. His eyes scanned the traffic, looking for his ride. He didn't have any bags, just a small backpack. Odd for an international flight. At least she was done with him. She leaned forward in her seat a little to look at her phone, laying on the dashboard. It hadn't taken enough of a charge to start yet.

Dan muttered, "Can you sit back please?" Then she jerked in her seat as he suddenly swing the car over to the curb, directly in front of Hairy Chest.

Before she could speak or say anything, Hairy Chest opened the door and jumped into the front passenger seat. "What the hell?" she cried, reaching for the door handle.

It pulled, but the door didn't open. She yanked at the handle again, as Hairy Chest shouted, "Go! Go!"

Dan, the driver, hit the gas, the car accelerating rapidly away from the airport.

CHAPTER TWO
AMBER Alert

1. Sarah. April 28. 4:50 pm

Sarah Thompson leaned her head against the steering wheel, trying to contain her frustration. The sound of cars and shuttle buses echoed off the roof above her, and she could smell gasoline and diesel fumes in the air. The text message from her little sister Andrea was clear enough. She was waiting at the Terminal C, near ground transportation, at the first exit from the terminal.

That's where Sarah was. That's where the cop waving her on was. But Andrea was nowhere in sight.

She double-checked her phone, and then sent a reply.

I'm here ... where are you?

This time there was no response at all. *What now?*

Sarah had turned eighteen years old just a few weeks before, and she was a bundle of walking contradictions. Dressed in grey and black, her hair was cut off in jagged, rough edges at her collar, died black with bleached white highlights shifting as her head moved. Dark eyeliner and mascara set off pale blue eyes that scanned the terminal for her sister.

The cop waved her on again. His face was growing tense.

She checked her phone again. Still no answer. Had Andrea's battery died? What the hell?

A loud rap on the window. She jerked in her seat.

"You can't sit here." The cop...actually TSA...looked cranky. His face was a little round, a little red in the cheeks. Late forties, balding, a good-sized paunch. But the gun on his hip and the badge he wore were real enough.

Sarah rolled down the window. "I'm picking up my little sister."

"Go back around, and wait at the cell phone lot until she calls you." The cop's demeanor was agitated.

Feeling her face flush, "She *did* call me. I'm confused, she says she's at Terminal C at the first exit."

The cop frowned. "Well, is she?"

Sarah shrugged. "No! I don't understand, look, here's the text from her." She showed him the phone, with Andrea's message. **I am Terminal C, next to first exit.**

The cop shook his head. "She must be confused. How old is your sister?"

"Sixteen," Sarah responded.

The cop frowned, looking at the text. "And when did she send you this text?"

"Five minutes ago? I tried to call her back and she's not answering now."

He stood there for a moment, as if undecided whether or not to take this seriously. Then he looked back at Sarah. "All right, I want you to pull ahead, down there to the end of the terminal so you aren't blocking traffic. I'll meet you there in two minutes."

Sarah nodded, her pulse throbbing in the arteries in her neck. She knew it was nothing. Andrea was in one of the other terminals, and her battery had died, or something else. Andrea was fine.

But sometimes, even when you thought things were fine, they weren't. She'd learned that the hard way. It still felt like yesterday. She'd been sitting in the back seat of Carrie's Mercedes, arguing with Jessica, when a jeep came out of nowhere, slamming into the car. Instantly her life had changed. Everything changed. When she woke, her brother-in-law Ray was dead, killed in the accident.

Not accident. It was murder. It took away the life of her sister's husband. Sarah herself had nearly died, and undergone major surgeries leaving her left leg scarred with what looked like huge shoe laces running up the outside of her calf up to her thigh. She spent weeks in the hospital, months in a wheelchair, and still went to physical therapy twice a week.

That wasn't the worst part. The worst part was the panic.

It snuck up on her, always. She'd think about Carrie and the pregnancy, or Rachel after she was born, or her twin Jessica, and a tiny tendril of fear would work its way into her chest. Her muscles would tighten up, her breath quickening, and soon she felt as if her throat were closing and she couldn't breathe.

She hadn't told anyone about the panic attacks. She hadn't told anyone that sometimes she thought she was going to die. But moments like this, her muscles would tense, and the pain in her chest would bloom like some hideous flower, and the tears would be just below the surface ready to burst. Sometimes she felt a tingling in her fingertips and in her throat, as if she'd been electrified.

Now, she swallowed the rock in her throat as she pulled the car up to the sidewalk just past the terminal. The cop jogged over to her, then leaned in to her.

Sarah tried to slow her breathing.

"All right...by the way, I'm Officer Harmon. Let me get some details from you, and we'll find your sister, okay? First, what's her name?"

"Andrea Thompson."

"Age?"

"Sixteen."

"Traveling alone?"

"Yes...she flew in on, um...American Airlines flight 3663 from Madrid."

"Spain?"

"Yes..."

"Why was she traveling alone?"

"She lives there with our grandmother...she flew in because our niece is sick...and may need bone marrow transplants. We're all being tested."

The cop nodded. "I see. Description?"

"Um...I haven't seen her in a few months." She felt a sharp pain in her chest as she said the words. The last time she'd seen Andrea, Sarah was still in the hospital, out of her mind with grief and morphine. "She's um...tall. Six feet. Dark brown hair. Green eyes. Not sure what she's wearing."

"All right. And she definitely got off the plane from Madrid."

"You saw the text," she replied.

Officer Harmon grimaced. "Yeah. All right, hold still, I'm calling this in. The airport will page her, and we'll alert TSA and the police to look out for her. She's in the airport somewhere, all right? She's probably in the bathroom or something, and you guys will get a big laugh out of this in a few minutes. You got a picture of your sister? On your phone?"

Sarah nodded, trying to contain the panicky feeling bubbling up in her chest. She flipped through her photos as quickly as she could, but she couldn't find any recent pictures of Andrea. *Wait.* She went online. Andrea had updated her profile picture just a few days ago.

"I've got it."

"Can you text that to me?" Officer Harmon gave her the number.

A moment later, Harmon stepped away and began speaking rapidly into the microphone at his shoulder. She barely heard the words through the rushing sound in her ears. "White female... sixteen years old...unaccompanied minor...did not meet sister at ground transportation..."

Sarah stared at the steering wheel. Her chest was twisting tighter and tighter, so much that she felt a sharp pain in her sternum. She put a fist to her chest, trying to breathe.

"You all right, miss?"

She tried to answer, but couldn't, just nodded her head, tears welling up. In her head, the thoughts kept running through her mind. *Please be okay. Please be okay. Don't let her be hurt too.*

Hands shaking, she picked up her phone and sent another text message to Andrea.

Call. Me. Please.

No reply.

Flashes of her hospitalization ran through her mind. The bizarre dreams she'd had of walking through the ghostly hospital with Ray. Waking up to find her leg cut open from ankle to thigh, swollen to triple its normal diameter, shoelace-sized sutures crisscrossed over the surgical wound, her brain fuzzy from heavy doses of morphine.

In her dream she'd made a promise to someone. Ray? Her sisters? She couldn't remember what the promise was, and it terrified her.

"Miss?"

Jerked back to the present, she looked up at Officer Harmon. "Can you come with me? One of the other officers will keep an eye on your car."

"Yeah," she said. The shaking threatened to burst into the open, and the one thing she would not do, the one thing she *refused* to do, was give in to the slightest weakness in front of anyone else. There would be no fucking tears. No fucking shaking. No panic. No *nothing*.

She opened the car door and stepped out. The cop got his first good look at her and his eyes went a little wide. She wore a grey t-shirt with the *Yellowcard* logo emblazoned across it. Whenever it wasn't too cold she stuck with shorts and miniskirts, hiding none of the extensive scarring on her left leg. Right now she wore black shorts, and the crisscrossed pattern of scars on her leg stood out above her black leather combat boots.

With one look at Sarah's leg, Officer Harmon was thrown way off balance. In some ways, that helped her regain her own. She said, "Where to?"

Harmon didn't kid around. Taking long strides, he led her through the clean, well lit terminal. She had to run to keep up, and a moment later he stopped at an unmarked door and swiped an access card.

Behind the door was a hallway. It was utilitarian, the walls the dull beige of a public school or hospital, the floor scuffed and cracked tile. Outside was the public area, brushed with veneer of polished wood and glass, an exfoliated and cosmetic covered skin disguising an aging, sickly infrastructure the public never viewed. Inside, the debilitated condition lasted right up to the door of the security suite.

Security, here as everywhere in the United States, was well funded, portly, even corpulent. Inside, the equipment was new and expensive, the product of more than a decade of continuous budget priority. Half a dozen uniformed TSA officers sat at desks with security camera feeds in front of them. Three large displays on the wall cycled through various security camera feeds all over the airport, and the security center as a whole had a high-tech, well funded appearance.

A tall African American man approached her. "You're Miss Thompson?"

"Sarah."

"Lieutenant Aaron Miller. I'm with the Transportation Security Administration. I understand your sister texted you a few minutes ago?"

Sarah nodded, fumbling with her phone, then handed it over to Miller.

His brow furrowed, and he said, "Your sister lives in Spain? Is her English okay?"

"Yeah, of course," Sarah responded.

"This text...it's oddly worded." He passed the phone back to her, and she read it. **I am Terminal C, next to first exit.** Miller was right. It was strangely worded. Not like teenaged text-speak, but like someone who didn't know the language. She slowly nodded. "What's going on?"

"Just one second...we've got an image of her coming through Customs, can you verify it's actually her?"

Miller nodded to one of the cops. An image appeared on the leftmost screen. She expected the stereotypical grainy security camera image, but this was digital, in focus, and very clear.

The image was of Andrea standing in a Customs lane, holding her passport out to the inspector. She was smiling, wearing a knit sweater that revealed one shoulder, her hair slightly longer than shoulder length. She was taller than the Customs inspector.

"That's her."

"What about this...do you recognize either of these two men?"

On the other two screens, images appeared. In the center was a tall, well built man with short blond hair. The image was slightly blurry, but it was clear enough. He carried an iPad with her name on it, and was smiling directly at Andrea, who walked directly toward him in the photo.

The other picture showed a man in his thirties, dark hair, shirt open halfway down his chest with extensive chest hair, getting into a black Lincoln Town Car.

"No," Sarah said, panic suddenly rising in her voice. "I don't recognize those men. And I was supposed to pick her up, not some random driver."

Officer Harmon and Lieutenant Miller met each other's eyes.

"Miss Thompson, can I get your parents' phone number?"

"Yes," she said. Her father would be at the Pentagon right now, or maybe on Capitol Hill, but he was at least in the same time zone. She quickly gave his number to the police, and then sank into a chair, the rushing in her ears too loud to hear much of anything else. But some words came through. *AMBER Alert. Possible abduction. FBI.*

She exhaled forcefully. She had to keep it together. She scanned the room. Miller stood there, giving orders. An officer was talking into a phone, reading the license plate of the Town Car to someone on the other end. Officer Harmon was on another phone. With her father? Maybe. She took another breath. She needed to make some calls.

2. Andrea. April 28. 4:52 pm

"**W**ho are you? Where are you taking me?"

"Shut up," said Crew Cut. "I told you to keep your mouth shut." *Dan*, he'd said. Whatever his real name was. Deep furrows on either side of his mouth marked a lifelong frown, and sweat dampened his crewcut, demonstrated his current worry.

The clock on the dashboard showed 4:52 pm. 32 minutes had passed since they'd picked her up. *Kidnapped* her. Crew Cut had passed an automatic pistol to Hairy Chest moments after they left the airport. And then he held another pistol up in his right hand, displaying it for her appreciation.

"Don't try anything funny. I don't much care whether you survive this or not."

The words sent chills down her spine, but not as much as moments later when Hairy Chest said, "Give me your purse. And your passport."

She had no choice. What was this? Who were these people? Terror twisted her guts when she passed the purse, with her identification and passport, over to the man in the front passenger seat. Last year she'd done a report on sex trafficking for school. And too often it happened like this. Passports and documents seized, young women carried off from airports or bus stations.

The back door latch didn't work; she'd tried that at the airport. Surreptitiously, she'd tried the power windows. They didn't work either. Child-safety locks? She didn't know. Whatever the mechanism, she was trapped in the spacious leather back seat, with two armed men in the front, in a car moving at high speed down the highway.

She swallowed, keeping her fear in check. She needed to stay alert and pay attention to her surroundings. She'd been watching the road, a circuitous route that had taken them around Baltimore and now onto Interstate 70 West. She needed details. If she managed to get to a phone, she'd send a text message, anything. She watched the road closely.

A sign. Exit 80, for Sykesville Road in Clarkesville, Maryland.

4:56 pm. She was getting further by the minute from the airport, further from her family, further from safety.

She took a deep breath. Maybe she could try negotiation. She leaned forward in her seat slightly then said. "My father is wealthy. He'll pay a big ransom."

Crew Cut rolled his head to the left for just a second, his jaw tightening, the powerful muscles in his neck going tense. She didn't anticipate the sudden violence, as he lashed out with his right fist. Her vision went white as his fist connected and she cried out, her mouth flooding with blood. She'd bit her tongue, hard.

Hairy Chest shook his head and chuckled. He glanced over his shoulder at her, and then said, "Don't mess her face up too much. I want to break her in before we get rid of her."

Andrea's entire body shuddered. She'd taken self-defense. More than one course, in fact. *Abuelita* had always been insistent that Andrea be able to defend herself in any situation. She knew how to fight, how to draw blood, how to run away. But fighting in real life was a completely different undertaking than in the control of the classroom, or even kneeing an obnoxious drunk in the balls. Plus, But there were two of them. And they had guns.

"Yeah, well right now, every second fucking counts," the driver said. "We need to get off the road."

"How far?"

"Twenty minutes. No way they'll have an alert out that fast, but we can't kid around. Keep her fucking quiet back there."

She sniffled then ground her teeth. She wasn't giving up. No matter what. Hairy Chest met her eyes, then said in a conversational tone, "I fuck you so hard you scream."

The words froze her in place, all panic and fear gone. She was ice cold. And if she'd held a knife in her hand at that moment, she wouldn't have hesitated to slide it right between his ribs.

As it was, she needed to think, and quickly.

There was nothing in the backseat she could use as a weapon. Normally she carried a can of mace, but she couldn't take that on an airplane. *Fuckers.* Heavy floor mats lined the backseat floor. They wouldn't make much of a weapon, though she might be able to use one to blind the driver for a moment. And cause the car to crash. At the moment the speedometer rested at 74 miles per hour. She might be killed if they crashed, but she thought her odds would be better in a high speed collision than whatever else these two had in mind.

Her eyes moved back to Hairy Chest, still watching her, and she intentionally breathed in deeply and made her lower lip tremble. "I'll cooperate. Please don't hurt me."

She said it in as meek a voice as she could muster. But she was going to fucking hurt him if she got the chance.

And that's when she saw it. The driver braked a little, as a state patrolman pulled out onto the highway three lanes over.

Without thought or preparation or hesitation, she reached down with her left hand and grabbed the floor mat.

Hairy Chest shouted. "What the—"

He was too late. The floor mat swung wide and caught Crew Cut right in the face. The car lurched to the left, away from the police car, and skidded onto the median. The ride suddenly went rough as the car ran partly onto the gravel and grass, bumping this way and that, and then hitting a pothole with a wrenching thud that jarred her brain in her skull.

"Fucking bitch!" shouted the driver as he fought to get the vehicle back under control.

She reached both hands forward and grabbed Hairy Chest from behind, digging her nails into his face. He let out a scream and forced his way out of her grip, then spun around and lunged blindly, just missing her with his fist as she scrunched back as far in the seat as she could get.

That got the response she wanted. The squeal of a siren, then a flash of blue light, as the cops responded to the highly visible fight inside the Lincoln.

"Motherfucker!" shouted the driver. Hairy Chest reached for his gun, and she grabbed at his arm, but screamed as the driver punched her in the head. Once. Twice. Her vision narrowed to black and she lost her grip on Hairy Chest's arm. The driver accelerated, and Hairy Chest moved in nightmare slow motion as he raised his pistol. She dived down behind the seat as far as she could go, and then heard an explosion of sound.

Hairy Chest leaned out the window and fired his pistol at the pursuing police car.

3. Sarah. April 28. 4:58 pm

"**What** the hell?" shouted Lieutenant Miller into a phone. "Can someone please tell me how the daughter of the Secretary of Defense came through my airport...and was abducted...and I wasn't notified? What the hell is wrong with you people?" A long pause. "I don't give a damn if he hasn't been confirmed yet. You people dropped the ball, and now there's a sixteen-year-old girl who's been kidnapped!"

Sarah groaned and stayed low in her seat. She didn't want to remind them she was here, because right now, she had some clue what was going on. If they made her leave, she'd lose that. For the last ten minutes she'd been sending text updates to her sisters: Carrie in Maryland, Alexandra in New York, Julia in Los Angeles and Jessica in San Francisco. Jessica hadn't responded, but then again, she didn't much lately.

Carrie had reminded her in a message that their father, recently called out of retirement by the President, was on Capitol Hill today preparing for his confirmation hearings. He wouldn't take any phone calls, but Carrie thought she could reach him through the Pentagon.

"Lieutenant!" one of the cops called. "State patrol spotted the vehicle. They're in pursuit."

Miller covered the receiver of the phone he'd been shouting into. "Any visual?"

The cop shook his head. "Audio only."

"Put it up."

Sarah shook. She couldn't breathe. She couldn't think. She started to send another text message to her sisters.

The room filled with sounds from the state patrol dispatchers. A lot of unrelated radio chatter. Then a loud, strong voice calling, "Shots fired, four-four-four, shots fired."

More voices, calling in locations, more cars responding.

Miller hung up on whoever he was talking with, and Sarah dropped her phone. The glass front of the phone shattered.

4. Andrea. April 28. 5:02 pm

Andrea felt her stomach lurch as the car swerved left, right, left again. Hairy Chest was yelling now, cursing in Arabic at the following cars. She stayed hunched down as tightly as possible, ignoring the rushing wind, the stomach churning swaying of the car, the sound of the tires screeching—she was focused only on survival. Terror threatened to paralyze her as she thought of never being able to see Javier again, the thought of losing her sisters, of not being there for them.

Then it happened. Hairy Chest's body jerked, then spasmed. Blood splattered on the windshield in a splotchy pattern, and he fell awkwardly against Crew Cut, who swerved again, shoving him away. Hairy Chest's face was dark with blood, his lips swollen, as he fell between the seats. Hairy Chest's head came to rest right next to Andrea, who let out a scream as blood poured from his mouth.

The scream was cut short a second later when the driver fired a shot, unaimed, a wild shot, right through the seat. At her.

She jerked up behind the seat, powered by adrenaline and fear, grabbing his gun hand from behind and covering his eyes with the other. He screamed and she did too as he lost control of the car and then he pulled the trigger once, twice, three more times. The bullets flew randomly, all of them missing her. The sickening screech of tires grew lower in pitch, the car moving sideways now, threatening to roll. As the car reached a stop she realized her mistake. The police were behind them, but there was nothing to prevent the son of a bitch from shooting her right now.

In desperation, she leaned forward, over his shoulder, and sank her teeth into his cheek. She felt her teeth break the skin, salty, copper tasting blood spurting into her mouth as he jerked and howled in pain, and then it happened. His hand released the pistol.

Instantly, she grabbed it, diving into the back seat.

And then the driver was gone, running, the front door of the car swinging open.

She sagged into the seat, spitting out her kidnapper's blood, and dropped the gun. Her eyes went to Hairy Chest. His bloodshot, dead eyes stared up at the roof of the car. Did he wonder what had happened? Did he wonder how two armed men managed to lose control of their prisoner, a sixteen-year-old girl?

Well, fuck him.

She flinched at the sound of gunshots outside. A lot of shots, followed by silence.

A few seconds later, a police officer appeared in the window, shouting, "Step out of the car now!"

She exhaled slowly, exhaustion sinking fast into her bones. Then she called out, "I can't open the back door!"

She *didn't* say that there was no way in hell she was crawling over the body of Hairy Chest to get to the front door. They could figure that out on their own.

Seconds later, the door opened, and she staggered out of the vehicle.

CHAPTER THREE
Bear

1. Andrea. April 28. 5:20 pm

"It's just a precaution," the police officer said. "We've got orders to make sure you get to the hospital safely and get checked out."

Andrea sighed. She knew it was necessary, especially since she'd gotten an unfortunate amount of blood in her mouth from the driver. But a helicopter?

Whatever her objections, the bright red air ambulance was coming in for a landing, the rotors throwing up a wash of dirt and dust all over the highway. Westbound traffic on Interstate 70 was stopped, and police directed frustrated and angry commuters to alternate routes. Half a dozen police cars, two ambulances, a fire truck and a swat team truck had converged on the site.

The need for that level of force had already come to an end. Fifteen seconds after exiting the car, Crew Cut, or *Dan*, or whatever his name was, opened fire on the police, then died from half a dozen gunshot wounds. The police were quite thorough making sure he wasn't getting back up.

The police had refused to allow her to retrieve her phone or purse. *Evidence*, they said. It might be evidence, but her passport was in there. Her frustration about that situation lasted right up until the moment she stood up to walk to the helicopter. After a brief argument with an EMT who wanted her to be strapped down on a stretcher, she squeezed herself into a crew seat and they buckled her in.

She stared out the windows as the twin engines roared to a high pitch and the helicopter lifted into the sky. To the east stood Baltimore, a city she'd never actually been in other than passing through the airport. Toy buildings, tiny cars, the hazy horizon, all contributed to her sense of unreality and isolation. Was it only two days ago she'd said goodbye to Javier? To her grandmother?

She wanted to go back home. She shivered, looking out at the harbor on the right side of the helicopter as it sped toward its destination.

Damn it. She didn't even know Javier's number. Or any of her friends from school. And if she got a replacement phone, it wouldn't do any good, because her backup was on her laptop, in the trunk of the stupid car.

Who the hell were they? What did they want? It didn't make any sense. Sure, her father had been nominated for some job with the US Defense ministry or whatever they called it. But that had nothing to do with her. And her attempt at negotiation wasn't exactly honest. For all she knew, her parents wouldn't lift a finger to ransom her. She barely knew them, and had been raised primarily by her grandmother. Her mother and father were remote figures on another continent.

The only one of her sisters she was close to was Julia, the oldest. At thirty-two, she was double Andrea's age. But she'd also been the one sister who consistently visited her in Spain. She was the sister she could count on.

It had been eight months since she'd seen Julia. That was a long time. They'd sat in the park together near Carrie's condo in Bethesda, Maryland, the day after Ray Sherman's funeral.

"Why don't they want me home, Julia?"

She had asked the question, not really expecting an answer. What possible answer could there be when your parents don't want you there?

"Of course they want you, sis," Julia said.

Andrea shook her head. "No...they don't. When I told Mom I wasn't coming home for Christmas last year, she didn't even argue."

Julia flinched. "Mother and I...I've never understood her."

Andrea said, "There's nothing to understand. They're both awful. She's crazy and he's an icebox. I'm *glad* Abuelita raised me. At least I know I'm loved."

Julia sniffed. "They love you...our parents are just screwed up. They don't know how to show it. And...we love you. Your sisters."

"You say that, but you know as well as I do that except for you, I barely know the others. Carrie might as well be a stranger."

Julia shook her head. "That's not true. She practically raised you."

"Until I was what...six? I don't even remember."

"I feel like we failed you."

Andrea sighed and sniffed. "I'm sorry. I didn't mean to...I just...sometimes I'm so lonely, you know?"

She'd cried that day, and Julia held her. Two days later, she flew back to Spain. She and Julia talked on the phone twice a week, whether they had anything to say or not. She called once every two weeks to check on Sarah and Carrie. Sarah was recovering from her injuries and Carrie was going through her pregnancy.

Her mother rarely asked to speak to her during those calls. That loneliness pervaded her.

The helicopter circled the hospital, a low bass vibration rising up through the soles of her feet. Bright light sparked out in the harbor, sunlight reflecting off the waves.

The crew chief sat across from her. "We're going to land in a minute...they're going to want to do the full VIP work-up on you. Keep your chin up, okay? I know it's going to suck, but they just want to cover their asses and look out for your best interests, okay?"

The unexpected kindness caught her off guard. Andrea nodded. The crew chief touched her shoulder and said, "Did you get any of *his* blood on you?"

"Yeah," she said at a whisper. He couldn't hear her, but he could see her shudder.

"You're gonna be all right, kid. This is just about the best hospital in the country. They're gonna do all the tests and make sure you're good to go. You got nothing to be worried about."

She sniffed. She wasn't used to being called *kid* and having someone reassure her. She wasn't used to needing other people. But something about the crew chief reminded her of her Uncle Luis, and before she could stop herself, she said it. "I'm scared."

She hated herself for saying it. He smiled kindly then squeezed her shoulder.

"Here we go," he said. He stretched up a little, wrapping his hand around a handle mounted above the door. The helicopter landed gently.

"You ready, kid?"

She nodded. "Thanks."

2. George-Phillip. April 28

"**D**addy, I love you."

"And I love you, darling."

George-Phillip leaned close to his daughter and kissed her on the forehead, then tucked her in. Jane was six years old, raven haired with green eyes. Creative. Mischievous.

Trouble.

His lips turned up in a half smile at the thought.

"I'm turning out the light, Jane."

"No…" she said.

He said, "I'll leave the door cracked?"

"Thank you, Daddy."

He smiled, switched the light out and stepped out into the hall, leaving the door open six inches.

Adriana Poole, Jane's nanny, sat reading a book in the room down the hall. "She's down," he said.

"For now," Adriana replied. "I'll be here, sir."

"Thank you."

He sighed, walking down the hall. He left the overhead lamp off in the study, choosing to only turn on the small desk lamp that lit one spot in the center of his desk. He turned on his computer and looked out at Belgrave Square.

Department security had warned him repeatedly about the wisdom of having his study facing the square. But Dukes of Kent had occupied this home for more than a hundred years. Princess Alexandra had been born in this house in 1936. Grudgingly, SIS security had installed additional equipment, bulletproof glass and a twenty-four hour security detail on the premises. And George-Phillip kept his study where he could see into the square.

The Wakhan file had been troubling him ever since O'Leary brought him the news of Andrea Thompson's travel to the United States. It was one of the oldest files he'd worked on. One of the most explosive, on a personal and international level.

It haunted him. He unlocked his desk and slid the top drawer open, taking out the file marked with seals labeled *CONFIDENTIAL* and *EYES ONLY*. He opened the file.

As always, it was the photos that caught him first. The bodies, laying where they'd fallen, twisted, bloated.

Many of them had been children.

He closed the file. He wouldn't find any answers in there tonight, any more than he did ten years ago or twenty years ago.

Thirty years since the photos had been taken. *Thirty years.*

He sighed then slid the folder back into his locked drawer. In the morning, he would instruct O'Leary to increase the surveillance on everyone related to the Wakhan file. But for now, he needed to get some sleep.

That, of course, was when the phone rang. Not his personal phone. The official phone.

He lifted it to his ear. "This is the Chief," he said.

"O'Leary, sir."

"What is it?"

"Wakhan file, sir. It's heating up."

"Tell me."

"Andrea Thompson was abducted on arrival at Baltimore Washington airport."

George-Phillip stood up, suddenly, his chair rolling back on its casters.

"What?" he cried.

"That's right, sir. We didn't have any assets on the scene, unfortunately. She was able to overpower her abductors, though. Both of them are dead, and she's en route to Johns Hopkins Hospital in Baltimore."

"How serious were her injuries? Any idea who they were?"

"Not serious, sir, and we've got a lead on one from the surveillance video. This one's getting massive attention from the Yanks though, so I've not put anyone too close to the investigation. One of the kidnappers looks like Tariq Koury. Saudi born, he's been around ISI and CIA and a bunch of other three letter agencies for decades."

"Three letter agencies...like SIS?"

"He did a couple jobs for us in the early 90s. Nothing since then that I can tell. He works for the highest bidder...not reliable. But he's a killer. He spent most of the last five years working for Blackwater."

George-Phillip shook his head. "And a sixteen-year-old girl *escaped* from him?"

"Not just escaped. As best as I can find out, she killed him. I'll get more info as soon as I can."

"We need to know who hired him, O'Leary."

"Working on it, sir."

"Put some serious assets on it. I want to know who was behind the abduction, O'Leary."

They hung up, and he stared out the window. George-Phillip thought about what he knew of Andrea Thompson, which amounted to virtually nothing. The idea that a sixteen year old girl had fought—and killed—two trained intelligence agents simply defied credibility. But then, nothing about this case, from the very beginning, had made sense. Especially not the contents of the file, which he didn't need to have open to see its contents. The twisted and darkened bodies. They haunted his every thought.

3. Bear. April 28. 6:30 pm

It was long past six o'clock when John "Bear" Wyden closed the briefing folder and walked it down the hall to the Classified Materials Officer, who signed for the documents and gave Bear a receipt. Temporarily, Bear occupied a desk on the sixth floor at Main State. For the last three years, he'd been assigned as the deputy Regional Security Officer in Pakistan for the Diplomatic Security Service. An insanely challenging job, where he'd supervised dozens of agents in one of the largest and most strategic field offices.

In two weeks he'd be taking over as an assistant deputy at the FBI's National Joint Terrorism Task Force. Bear was forty-three years old, with dark hair starting to turn grey. But he was fit, weighing in at little more than the one hundred eighty pounds he'd carried the day he entered Diplomatic Security twenty years ago. Back then he'd been called Bear because of the thick hair covering his arms, legs and chest, a fact which had embarrassed him for years.

For now, he had a couple of weeks to kill, and Tom Cantwell, the head of Diplomatic Security, had given him several ongoing files to work with. Busy-work, really, reviewing findings of existing investigations and raising questions and holes. He didn't mind. Bear Wyden liked to stay busy.

For now, though, it was time to go home.

Bear had rented a studio apartment not far from DuPont Circle and walking distance from the office. He didn't have many needs these days. Leah left with their two dogs and three kids and everything he'd owned two years before. He couldn't blame her. They'd often worked together, and as colleagues, they were good to go. Not so much as husband and wife. So now he had his apartment and his books, a laptop computer, and way too much time on his hands, and she had a new husband, a new house, and had cut back her hours.

He locked his temporary desk, and put on his jacket, preparing to leave the office. There were no personal touches—no point, considering he'd be leaving soon anyway.

The phone rang, and for five seconds he considered ignoring it. It was Cantwell.

"Bear Wyden," he answered.

"Cantwell. Can you come up for a few minutes, Wyden? We've got a hot one."

Bear raised his eyebrows. Cantwell was normally dull, tired, uninterested. He described potential crises as "synergistic opportunities," not as "hot ones." Something was definitely odd here.

"I'll be right there."

Five minutes later he'd ridden the temperamental old elevators up to the seventh floor, the inner sanctum. Secretary Kerry had his office here, as had predecessors throughout his career: Hillary Clinton, Madeleine Albright, Colin Powell, Condoleezza Rice. It might be a little old fashioned and hokey, but Bear was a believer. He was a believer in democracy. He was a believer in his country. And sometimes he was a little bit in awe of the stature of the place he worked, when he wasn't overwhelmed by the bullshit. Whenever his work took him to the seventh floor at Main State—not very often—he felt that sense of awe.

Cantwell did not awe him. A political functionary, appointed to the job after the shakeup following the Benghazi attack, Cantwell did little to offend and little to inspire. He occupied his desk, let the department work underneath him, and periodically testified on Capitol Hill.

Bear supposed there could be worse people sitting in this chair.

"Bear. Good, I'm glad you were still in the building. I need to brief you in on a case, and it's one with potentially serious implications."

"Yes, sir."

"All right. Do you happen to know Ambassador Richard Thompson?"

"The new Sec Def? Of course. I ran the security detail for the Embassy in Brussels when he was there. We had to provide protection for the entire family, along with some of the other high profile people, if I remember correctly."

"What's your impression?"

Bear tilted his head. His impression had always been that Richard Thompson was a cold fish, and a dangerous one, and that his wife...*what was her name?* Something Spanish, he thought. She was way too young for Thompson, way too passionate. It was a bad match, he thought. But Diplomatic Security agents weren't paid to have personal opinions about their charges.

"I can't really give one, sir. That was more than twenty years ago. I knew the Ambassador and his wife, and I arranged for their security detail."

"Anything unusual?"

Bear shrugged his shoulders. "Not really. There were some specific threats against his family, if I remember correctly. They had two...no, three little girls. I think the oldest was ten or so at the time."

"What sort of threats against the family?"

Bear shrugged. "The usual. It was all stuff out of the Middle East...remember this was about a year after the Gulf War. What's all this about?"

Cantwell sat back in his seat. "Ambassador Thompson ended up having six daughters. The youngest was abducted this afternoon."

"Son of a bitch," Bear muttered.

"Exactly. Sixteen years old. She escaped. But we've already got indications there may have been a foreign power involved."

"What? Who?"

"Tariq Koury was one of the kidnappers. We've got a positive ID, though he came through with fake papers. He flew to the States right next to her in first class, and then they grabbed her plain as day. It was dumb luck and quick thinking on her part that got her free."

Tariq Koury. That was...odd. He was a low life, a mercenary, and an opportunist. Bear had encountered him a number of times in the course of his work in Pakistan. Koury wasn't driven by ideology or religion or political loyalties; his only desire was money. But he typically didn't get involved in serious wet-work, and kidnapping the daughter of an American cabinet member was as serious as it got.

"Who else was involved?"

"We're still trying to identify the other perp."

"All right. Who's running the show?"

"Who isn't? Fucking Pentagon wants a piece of this. FBI, maybe Secret Service. But the Secretary talked to the President and Ambassador Thompson half an hour ago. DSS is running the show. I want you to head the investigation. I'll get Joyce Brown or someone to run the back office stuff. You get out there while things are hot and find out what's what."

"I want to talk to the girl, if I can."

"They're flying her to Johns Hopkins."

"Is she seriously hurt?"

"No, just a precaution, from what I understand. Everybody wants to close the barn door now the horses have escaped."

Right. Just like Cantwell. He grimaced and checked his watch. It could easily take two hours to drive to Baltimore from downtown DC at this time of day. He'd requisition a uniformed officer and official car with lights and sirens, and hopefully that would shorten the trip. In the meantime, he'd scramble Leah and have her get a protective detail organized. She'd be just thrilled.

"All right. I'm on it."

Twenty minutes later, Bear Wyden was in a car, speeding up the Baltimore-Washington Parkway.

CHAPTER FOUR
Talk to your therapist

1. Andrea. April 28. 8:00 pm

Andrea Thompson was losing her patience. For nearly two hours she'd been poked, prodded, examined, and exhausted. She'd been questioned by the police, subjected to a host of blood tests, x-rays and a CT scan. "Just as a precaution." She'd drawn the line at a rape kit, finally threatening to call the police if they touched her any more.

Finally the first round of doctors backed off, replaced by a trauma therapist. Dirty Blonde drifting to grey, with a salt and pepper beard, he shoved his way past the other doctors, nurses, hospital administrators and the morbidly curious, then forced them all out with a few well chosen obscene comments.

Against her will, Andrea immediately warmed to the man, if only for running off the med students who had been gawking at her. She breathed a sigh of relief as the room cleared out.

"I'm Will Fisher," he said.

"Andrea Thompson," she replied. "Thanks for...clearing them out."

"It won't last," he said. "The police are outside clamoring to get in too. For now I've got you on restricted access."

She scrunched her eyebrows close to her nose. "My family?"

"Of course your family can come in. And I expect you'll be out of here in a couple more hours."

"What's left?"

"Let's just talk for a moment."

"About?"

Will gave her a warm, crooked smile, his teeth flashing white behind the beard. "How are you *feeling?*"

"Are you a priest?"

He coughed. "I'm a psychiatrist."

"I don't need a psychiatrist."

"I'm sure you don't," he said. "You're a resourceful young lady. But this is part of what we have to do. It's kind of like getting a chest x-ray, but for your brain."

She blinked. "No. It's not. You can see the results of an x-ray. Your examination consists of nothing but supposition and your own biases."

Will's eyes widened and he grinned. "Humor me, then. Because in order to get you out of here quickly, I have to reassure the hospital administration that you're fit to go and you aren't a danger to yourself."

Andrea crossed her arms over her chest and said, "All right, then. Psychoanalyze me if you must."

Will laughed and gave her a sideways grin. "Tell me about your mother, then."

Eye roll. "My mother sent me off to Spain when I was six, and I see her on holidays whether I like it or not."

He frowned. "I was actually joking, but...you've really lived in Spain since you were six? Who with?"

"My grandmother," Andrea replied. "We have a flat in Calella... it's a small town on the beach, about half an hour from Barcelona."

"What brings you to the States?"

"My sister Carrie...her daughter needs a bone marrow transplant. I'm supposed to be tested to see if I'm a match."

He grimaced. "Leukemia?"

She shook her head. "Thalassemia."

He frowned. "It's been a while since my straight med school days, but my recollection is thalassemia isn't life threatening, at least not in the short term."

She shrugged. "It can be. Depends. If she can't find a donor, she'll be dependent on blood transfusions the rest of her life. The typical prognosis is pretty poor."

"You're a pretty smart girl for sixteen."

She shrugged her shoulder. "I'm a freak."

"I wouldn't say that."

"How else do you explain it? Why didn't my parents come pick me up from the airport, then? Why do they pack me off to live in Spain? The only reason I'm here is for my sister. The minute we know if I'm a donor or not, I'm on a plane back home."

Will nodded. "Tell me about your sister and her daughter."

Andrea shrugged. "I barely know her." Her tone was sharp-edged, bitter.

He raised his eyebrows. "But you fly thousands of miles to undergo a potentially painful medical procedure to help her daughter."

Andrea blinked. Then she said, "I didn't have much a mother as a child. But what mothering I got was from Carrie." She choked up a little, and then said, "I'd do anything for her. And she's had an awful time."

"How so?"

Andrea shrugged. "Husband murdered last summer. Surely you read about it in the papers."

He sat back and studied her. She could almost see the wheels working in his brain, as he put together the names Carrie Thompson, the fact of Ray's murder and her mention of the papers. Then his eyes widened just a little bit. Yep. He got it. Ray Sherman, Carrie's husband, had been falsely accused and brought before a war crimes court last summer. Exonerated by the court, he was murdered by another soldier.

Will thought that through, then said, "Your brother-in-law was murdered. Is there any possibility that the kidnapping attempt was related to that?"

She shrugged.

"Did your kidnappers say anything to you? Were you scared?"

She swallowed and thought of Hairy Chest, staring her in the eye as he said, "*I fuck you so hard you scream.*" She closed her eyes, her mind resting on the death in his eyes. It was terrifying. But it was also oddly impersonal. Hairy Chest and the driver—the best way she could put it was, they didn't seem to be emotionally engaged in their work. This was just that. They'd been hired or ordered to kidnap her. It wasn't personal for them.

But it was damn personal for her, and for that reason, she was glad they were dead.

There. She'd settled on her answer. "I'm glad they're both dead," she replied.

Will nodded. "How do you feel about that?"

"About the fact they are dead?"

"Yes."

She gave him an ironic grin. "I'm delighted. It's like someone bought me an iPhone for Christmas, I'm so excited."

"You don't sound excited."

"You don't sound very intelligent."

He rubbed a hand along his forehead, briefly massaging the bridge of his nose. "Andrea, I'm here to help you."

"Then sign whatever papers it is you need to sign, and let me go. I didn't commit the crime here. I didn't kidnap anyone. I didn't hurt anyone. I didn't threaten to rape anyone. I didn't assault anyone. All I did was fly to help my sister. So there is absolutely no reason for me to be here anymore. If you wish to have me arrested, call the police. Otherwise, I'm leaving."

Andrea stood.

"Andrea, please. I'm very concerned about trauma."

She stared at him for a solid thirty seconds. Then she blinked her eyes, and said, "You should talk to your therapist about that."

She ostentatiously stepped around him and opened the door.

The first thing she saw was two Maryland state troopers blocking the door. They wore crisply pressed khaki shirts and matching hats, and both of them had the look of too many cases of beer in between lifting weights.

Beyond them, to the right, stood a large man grey suit that looked as if it had been used for a pillow. A leather folder, folded outward, displayed a badge at his pocket. She looked close enough to see he was from the Diplomatic Security Service.

To the left stood two of her sisters.

Carrie Thompson-Sherman might have been an older twin to Andrea. Dark brown hair, cut almost savagely short, framed a pert face with blue green eyes. Like Andrea, she was more than six feet tall, with narrow features, high cheekbones and unusually pale skin. Andrea did the math in her head...Carrie was born in 1985, so she must be 29 now. She didn't look close to thirty, but she didn't have the fresh look of eighteen anymore either. Worry and strain had given her new lines around her eyes and in the center of her forehead.

Next to her...and considerably shorter than either of them...was their pixie-like sister Sarah. She was a few inches over five feet, and since Andrea saw her last, Sarah's leg had healed into a permanent and startling network of scars running up her calf to her thigh. The scarring looked like shoelaces. Sarah had dark hair, dyed black with white streaks, and strikingly pale blue eyes and a nose ring that matched her eyes perfectly. She was still the same girl Andrea had last scene in a hospital bed in August, but something inside of her had changed. Her eyes were cold and distant, as if she'd seen too much.

Andrea pushed her way past the police and walked to her sisters, silently pulling them both into an embrace.

"Oh my God, Andrea," Carrie whispered, her tone fierce. Sarah, almost comically, put her arms around both of them, like a child around both parents.

"Are you okay?" Sarah asked.

"Yeah," Andrea replied. "I'm all right. Just...can we get out of here?"

"Miss Thompson." The voice was deep, unpleasant.

Andrea looked up. It was the large man in suit that desperately needed dry-cleaning. She sighed.

"I'm Bear Wyden. Diplomatic Security Service. Before you go, I need a few minutes of your time."

For just a second, Andrea wanted to cry. She just wanted to get out of this hospital, get away from all these people, and curl up under a blanket.

Carrie saw her reaction and said, "Mr. Wyden, is this necessary right now? I think she's exhausted."

"It is, unfortunately," he said. "At this point we don't know who was behind the kidnapping, so there are significant concerns about your security."

Andrea said, "The kidnappers are dead." But then she thought back to her earlier conclusion that the kidnappers were hired. She swayed a little on her feet. It was long past midnight at home, and she'd had little sleep the night before.

Wyden said, "We'll make this quick."

"Fine."

He led the way down the hall. "In here, please, the hospital's provided a meeting room."

"We're staying with our sister," Carrie said.

"No problem." He held the door open and waved them forward. Then he said, "Are you Julia or Carrie?"

Carrie jumped a little. "What?"

"You won't remember me, you were too young. But I was in charge of your family's security detail in Brussels in the early 90s."

"Oh... I'm Carrie."

He frowned quickly. "I'm sorry for your loss. I didn't have much of a chance to brush up on the files before I drove up here, but I did read the *Post's* coverage of Sergeant Sherman's court martial."

Carrie was never off balance. Poised. Intelligent. Brave. But now she recoiled almost, and Andrea felt a flash of rage. *How dare he?*

"We're done here." Andrea said it at the exact same moment Sarah said, "Will you just leave her alone?" Sarah's face was flushed and angry.

Bear looked between the three sisters and froze in place. Then he looked at Carrie and said, "My apologies. I...I'm very sorry."

Carrie sighed then said, "It's okay. It's just...very fresh."

"I understand." His voice was soothing. "Please. Have a seat."

The three sisters sat, Andrea and Sarah flanking Carrie.

"Let's start over. And again, my apologies. My name's Bear Wyden, and I'm a special investigator for the Diplomatic Security

Service. Until three weeks ago I was assistant regional security officer at the Embassy in Pakistan.

"Three weeks ago?" Sarah said. "Were you fired for insensitivity?"

Bear smiled wryly. "Maybe I should have been. In fact, I'm moving on to the Joint Terrorism Task Force. But in the meantime, I'm heading the investigation into your kidnapping, Andrea."

She shrugged. "I don't know if there's much to investigate. They gave the impression it was some kind of human trafficking ring?"

"Oh?" he said. "What gave you that idea?"

She thought back. Then said, "At some point one of them...the hairy one...said he was going to rape me before they...disposed of me."

Carrie reached out and gripped Andrea's hand.

"I see," Bear said. "Why don't we start at the beginning, then? Just tell me everything you remember. When did you first see the kidnappers?"

"Well, the hairy one, he was on the plane."

Bear nodded. "Tariq Koury."

"That's his name? He claimed he was a student."

He shook his head. "He's no student. I can't really say anything more."

"Koury...he's middle eastern?"

"Saudi," Bear answered. "Had you ever met him before this flight?"

Andrea shook her head. "No. Neither of them."

Bear asked her a series of questions. When did she first see him on the flight? He took her through everything Koury said on the plane, then back through it a second and then a third time. Then they moved on. The car. She described how she'd passed her phone up to the front of the car.

"Wait," Sarah said. "I got text messages from you when you got off the plane. I was waiting at Terminal C."

"You didn't get any text messages from me," Andrea said. "My phone was dead. In fact..." She froze. How could she be so *stupid?* "Wait. I went off to the bathroom pretty early on the flight. And left my phone in the seat. It was dead when I got back."

Bear made some notes. "It sounds like Koury may have switched batteries or SIM cards, then sent the texts to Sarah to keep her unaware of what was happening."

"This was all planned, then," Carrie said.

Bear met Carrie's eyes. Then he nodded. "I think it best that we assign a security detail for now."

Andrea's eyes widened. She didn't need or want that. "I'm only going to be here a few days. It's not necessary."

"I think it is," Bear said. "And I'm certain your father will agree."

This provoked nothing more than a sneer from Andrea. "I'm not terribly concerned about my father's opinion. May I go?"

Bear sat back. "Fine. Let me ride along behind, for now, until we've got the security detail in place."

Carrie gave him the address, while Andrea stood there rolling her eyes and wishing she could just go back to Calella.

2. Carrie. April 28. 8:50 pm

Carrie Thompson-Sherman looked in the rearview mirror at her much younger sister Andrea. Andrea sat in the middle row of seats, staring vacantly out the window. Her mouth was slightly open, as if she were suffering from exhaustion and shock. Which she probably was.

Carrie understood shock and exhaustion. She put the Suburban in reverse, slowly backing out of the too small parking space and into the main area of the parking deck. Up until last summer, for years she'd driven a restored 1976 Mercedes 280S. Gleaming black, fully restored, she'd loved that car until it was destroyed in the same collision that killed her husband and nearly crippled her sister Sarah.

When she finally got back on the road, her newfound fear of accidents drove part of her buying decisions. She'd purchased a new black Chevy Suburban. It felt like it weighed five thousand pounds. She felt safe behind the wheel, and it wasn't often these days that Carrie felt safe.

The clock on the dashboard said 8:55 pm. She glanced back at Andrea again. The poor girl was traumatized and exhausted. To Carrie's right, Sarah didn't seem to be in much better shape. Sarah liked to push herself and act like she could do anything, and, in fact, she could. But sometimes she pushed herself too much. Her injuries in the accident that killed Ray were severe, and it had taken months before she was even able to walk again. Today had been a very long day for her.

"Tomorrow can you give me a ride back out to the airport to pick up my car?" Sarah asked.

"Sure. Or we can send someone to get it." Carrie didn't want to say that she thought Sarah was much too tired to make the drive in the morning.

"So..." Sarah turned to Andrea. In a completely deadpan voice, she said, "How was your flight?"

Carrie held her breath for a moment, as silence descended on the car for just a moment. She swallowed. Then she looked in the rearview mirror. Andrea stared at Sarah in shock, her eyes wide. Then Andrea's eyes darted over to Carrie. One second of eye contact was all it took. Andrea burst into laughter, and then all three of them were laughing.

"Oh my fucking God," Andrea said. Carrie bent over in her seat, resting her head against the steering wheel. Then a loud belly laugh burst out, uncontrollably.

Gasping for air, she said, "Andrea, I was so worried about you."

"I was scared," Andrea said, sobering a little. Then, in a mock-serious tone, she raised her left eyebrow. "Tell me, please. How was your flight?"

All three of them rocked with laughter again. Carrie felt tears running down her face, at first slow ones, then quickly. She hiccoughed then laughed again.

"Carrie?" Sarah had stopped laughing, and was leaning toward her now.

"I'm okay," Carrie replied, waving a hand in the air. "I just...it's been a long time since I laughed." She sniffed then chuckled again, at the same time as she fiercely wiped away tears. "Sometimes I just...I needed to laugh, okay?"

She felt a slender hand touch her shoulder as she put the Suburban back in gear. "It'll be okay, Carrie. Rachel will be okay."

Andrea's voice was soothing. But Carrie knew the dangers of soothing voices, the dangers of putting faith in anything you couldn't see, the dangers of believing miracles could happen. Miracles didn't happen. Not in a world where your husband could be exonerated the same day you told the doctors to pull the plug and let him die.

So she got them out of Baltimore and onto 95 South headed for Washington. It was late enough they'd likely make it to the condo in forty minutes. And then Carrie could deal with the next big question of the day.

Where the fuck was their father? And why hadn't he come out to Baltimore the moment he learned of the kidnapping?

3. Andrea. April 28. 9:05 pm

Carrie, who sat in the seat in front of Andrea, gripped the steering wheel so hard that her knuckles were white. Her hands shook every time she let go of the wheel, the occasional traffic light catching off her wedding ring with tiny tremulous sparkles. She was bordering so close to hysterical that Andrea almost wished Sarah would take the wheel. But Sarah herself wasn't in the best of condition.

The last time Andrea saw Sarah was the day after the funeral. Andrea went to the hospital and spent half an hour with her. At the time she'd been laid up in the intensive care unit. Her left leg had been crushed in the accident, and the doctors had performed a fasciotomy to prevent tissue death. But leaving an open and draining wound for days at a time had its own dangers, and she'd fought a days-long battle with an antibiotic-resistant staph infection which kept her in the hospital for nearly two months after the accident. It was a miracle, really, that she was up and around.

Andrea knew for sure she wasn't capable of driving. She'd been awake far too long and had one too many shocks. Right now it was all she could do to keep her eyes open, and the longer they drove, the more she had to fight the heaviness of her eyelids.

She lost that battle. She didn't know how long she was out, or when she fell asleep, but when she woke up, they were sitting at a red light in Bethesda, Maryland, and their parents' condo was straight ahead of them. Andrea was groggy, her head still cloudy from confusing, messy dreams. Dreams featuring her father and Hairy Chest, dreams where she was being choked.

She shook as Carrie pulled the Suburban to a stop in front of the doorman.

It took Andrea's brain several seconds to register that half a dozen news vans were parked in front, a line of reporters along the sidewalk.

Carrie looked around, and Andrea followed her eyes. Several police officers were blocking the sidewalk, preventing the reporters from coming any closer. But that didn't stop Bear Wyden, who had pulled up behind them, from approaching the vehicle. One of the county police ran to him, but Bear held up a badge. After a few words, the cop turned away and Bear knocked on the window.

Carrie slid her window down.

"I'll escort you up, and the cops will keep the reporters from coming any further. All right?"

Sarah looked a little panicked.

"Don't worry," Carrie said. She put a hand on Sarah's. "You'll be fine. Andrea? You okay?"

Her eyes met Andrea's in the rearview mirror. Andrea felt panicked. She didn't want to deal with reporters. That was never in the plan. But there was nothing she could do about it now.

"I'm good," Andrea replied.

"Come on, then," Bear said.

The three of them burst out of the vehicle. Andrea and Carrie moving at a very fast pace. Sarah, who had to come around from the passenger side, and who was so tired she'd begun to move with a painful limp, was slower. The reporters began to shoot pictures of her, one of them shouting, and Bear quickly moved to her.

"Put your arm on my shoulder," he said, wrapping a sizeable arm around her waist.

With his assistance, they crossed the ground to the doorman quickly.

"Upstairs," he said.

"Let me be clear, Mr. Wyden," Carrie said. "This is my home. I appreciate your concern, but I'm not sure we're going to accept security guards from the State Department."

"Doctor Sherman," he replied. "You're a smart woman. We don't know who tried to kidnap your sister or why, but I know Koury. He doesn't come cheap. Whoever wanted her kidnapped or dead still does."

Carrie swallowed and took a deep breath. "Very well."

She turned and walked to the elevator, her sisters following.

The four of them rode up the elevators in silence. Andrea felt her eyes wanting to close again, and she had to force them open. Finally, the bell rang and the door opened to the eighteenth floor and they were moving down the hallway.

She remembered the condo, of course. Her earliest memories were here, when she was three, maybe four years old, before they went to Moscow for a year. Over the years she'd come back a few times, when the family had visited Washington, and most recently she'd slept here during the two weeks she'd been in Washington last summer. When Ray and Sarah were injured, and Ray died.

So it didn't come entirely as a shock, when they walked in the door and she saw her father standing at the mantel, his eyes apparently resting on an ancient copper head. He turned around as they came in, and then he closed his eyes and said, "Andrea. Thank God."

A confused rush of emotions overcame her. For one thing, where was Jessica? Sarah's twin. Or their mother?

She looked at Sarah and asked, "Where's Jessica?"

Sarah shrugged, but her face guarded something, and Andrea didn't know what it was. "California with Mom."

"She's not coming?"

Carrie looked sad and Sarah rolled her eyes. "I don't know," Carrie replied.

Andrea looked back at her father. It was so confusing. To find him here, with his arms out like he meant it. To find their mother just...*gone?* It didn't make any sense. She had thought Jessica and her father had gone back to California together. Everything was mixed up, and no one had told her anything.

Richard Thompson stood for a moment more, then put his arms out stiffly in front of him. "Come here, my daughter. Welcome home."

She shook her head and gave him a look of disdain. Then she brushed past him and down the hallway.

CHAPTER FIVE
Home is Calella

1. Andrea. April 29. 12:10 pm

Andrea Thompson was awakened by a shout, and she didn't know if it was real or a dream.

She lay in the unfamiliar, too-soft bed, eyes open and fixed on the ceiling. Her heart was thumping, adrenaline flooding her system, her pulse urgent at her throat.

From the angle of the sun in the brightly lit room, it was nearly noon. She lay there, letting her heart calm down, listening. Listening. A murmur of voices from beyond the bedroom door, but no shouting. Whoever it was, sounded calm. Engaged.

A dream, then.

She sat up, eyes falling to the clock at her bedside. Noon or so. Six in the morning back home. She generally didn't have problems with jetlag—Andrea traveled far too frequently for that. But given what she'd had waiting for her on her arrival in the United States this time, it was no wonder she'd slept so long.

Foggy, she stood, eyes scanning for her bag, before she remembered that her bag was in the custody of the police. She'd have to go shopping today, because she couldn't wear the same clothes every day. In the meantime, she'd ask Carrie for something to wear. They were close enough to the same size.

When she walked out of the bedroom and down the hall, she immediately identified the voices. Carrie. Sarah. And another voice, a woman, clipped and professional.

Andrea listened for just a second, then walked out into the living room.

Carrie and Sarah sat on a couch, facing the mantel and fireplace. Carrie looked serious and attentive. She was a scientist, a systems ecologist working on infectious diseases at the National Institutes of Health. She hadn't gone back to work yet after her pregnancy, but she always dressed elegantly and professionally.

Sarah, on the other hand, was busy outlining the crosshatch scars on her legs with black eyeliner. She'd already outlined her eyes in the heavy black eyeliner curling up in cat's eyes. The very pale blue of her eyes was startling against the dark circles around them. Her clothes were all black: a torn t-shirt, black Dockers shorts and combat boots. The scars on her left leg stood out in stark relief underneath the black outlines.

The woman was across from them in another chair. Khakis, combat boots which ironically matched Sarah's, and a black t-shirt with the logo DSS in gold letters across the left breast. Her tanned face was framed by dirty blonde hair. Somewhere in her early forties, she looked competent and probably deadly. Her wedding ring was a plain gold band. She stood up when Andrea entered the room.

Andrea came to a stop, and the woman said, "Good morning. I'm Leah Simpson, with Diplomatic Security Services."

"Andrea Thompson."

"I'm in charge of your family's security detail."

"Not Bear?"

Simpson smiled at the use of the nickname. "Bear...uh...Mr. Wyden's overall in charge of the investigation, among other things. You'll be seeing a lot of both of us, I'm afraid."

Andrea nodded unhappily. Right now she wanted nothing more than to get on a plane and fly back to Spain. Instead, she had to deal with investigations into her *kidnappers*, parents who seemed to be missing—*at least that was normal*—and everything seemed to be out of control. She closed her eyes and said, "How long does this go on? When will I be able to go home?"

Leah looked over to Carrie. Then she said, "I don't know how long your family business will take, but unless we receive orders otherwise, a protective detail will accompany you back to Spain until we're sure the danger is past."

Andrea closed her eyes. She tried to imagine Abuelita's response to a bunch of armed agents in her flat. Then she snickered a little. Federal agents or not, Abuelita was a fierce old woman. She'd tear them to pieces.

"Let me get some coffee," Andrea said. "Then we can discuss all this?"

"Of course," Leah said.

As gracefully as she could, Andrea made her way to the kitchen. A pot of coffee was already on the counter, still half-full. As she poured it, Carrie walked in.

"Sorry we couldn't warn you first. I figured you needed the sleep."

"I did." Andrea mixed sugar into her coffee as she spoke. "It's okay, this isn't your fault."

Carrie smiled uncertainly. Then her eyes darted away at the sound of crying.

"Rachel's awake." Carrie hesitated a moment, as if she needed to stay and reassure Andrea.

"Go, I'm fine," Andrea said. She opened up the refrigerator in search of milk for her coffee as Carrie slipped out. Carrie looked tired...exhausted really. The good news was, she had help—a full time nanny their father paid for. Undoubtedly that helped. But it didn't take away the worry gnawing away at her soul. It didn't take away the trauma of her husband being murdered.

Andrea didn't want to be here. She didn't want to be dealing with the police, the feds, and whoever it was who had attempted to abduct her. But no matter what, she'd be there for her sister.

She stepped back into the living room. Sarah was still intently drawing a detailed outline around the lines of the scarring on her left leg. Andrea walked over, sipping her coffee and watched her sister. Hair draped over Sarah's face, almost hiding it. Her eyebrows were scrunched together, a vertical line of concentration centered in between them.

"Is it getting better?" Andrea asked.

"I can walk again. That took months."

Andrea swallowed. "What about the scarring?"

Sarah leaned her head back and met Andrea's eyes. "Mom wants me to see a plastic surgeon next month to start talking about repairing it. For a while they thought I was going to lose the leg."

Leah Simpson sat forward in her seat. "This happened when Sergeant Sherman was killed last summer?"

Sarah nodded. "Ray."

"You were in the back seat?"

"Yes," Sarah said. "I woke up two days after the accident. Ray died a few hours later."

Andrea lowered herself into her seat and sipped her coffee. Her emotions were roiling, confused. She had only met Ray Sherman once while he was alive. She'd flown to New York last summer for Alexandra's wedding to Dylan Paris. Alexandra, the third eldest sister of six, had fallen in love with a boy who eventually ended up in the Army. Dylan and Ray were best friends and had married sisters in ceremonies two days apart.

She thought back to that ceremony, and the reception that followed. Alexandra standing up, hand on her sister's shoulder, and saying words that spoke of loyalty and love and intense, passionate sisterhood. Andrea suddenly wondered how Alexandra was doing? They hadn't spoken in months. Nor had Andrea talked with Jessica, currently at their childhood home in San Francisco finishing her senior year in high school. She didn't know how either of them were doing. She found herself wishing she'd talked with Jessica more. They'd been close once.

Sitting here now, watching Sarah outlining her scars in black, she wished she knew them. All of them. She wished she'd been there to comfort Carrie after Ray died. She wished she'd been there for the thousands of big things and small things that had happened in their lives, and she wondered, for the ten thousandth time, why her parents had taken that away from her.

Leah's eyes shifted to Andrea like a pair of searchlights. "And you live with your grandmother? In Spain?"

Mind your own business.

Instead of vocalizing the thought, she said, "Yes."

"It must be beautiful."

Andrea shrugged, a short gesture devoid of any meaning.

"Why do you live there?"

The eyeliner pencil froze in Sarah's hand, and her eyes swiveled up toward Leah. Andrea shook her head. "I don't know. I used to go for summers, then they got longer and longer. When I was about six or seven, my mom sent me to live there permanently, and then I visited here on the holidays."

Leah Simpson looked troubled, her face reflecting ill-formed emotions. Andrea looked away. She didn't need or want anyone's pity. The one thing she was grateful for was Abuelita. Her grandmother didn't just raise her. She filled her life with love. Abuelita made sure, every day, that Andrea knew she was loved, no matter what was wrong with her parents.

"When was the last time you came home?"

"Home is Calella. Spain."

Simpson nodded. "Of course. I meant to say, when was the last time you visited the United States?"

"Last summer. After the accident."

"Not the holidays?"

Andrea rolled her eyes, but not quick enough to hide the sting.

She remembered the phone call. A week before Thanksgiving, last fall.

"Hello?" her mother had said.

"Mother, it's Andrea."

"Andrea, dear, how are you?"

Andrea had leaned back at the question, staring at the ceiling, and said, "Bueno, mother. And you?"

"I miss you, darling."

"I'm sure." Her mother didn't react to the sarcasm.

"Mother..." she said.

"Yes, dear?"

"I think I want to stay in Spain for the holidays this year. Carrie is still grieving and I have final exams in January. I think I just need some down time."

Silence at the other end of the line. Her mother didn't react. She didn't say, *no, you have to come home*, or even *no, please come home*. She didn't say that she'd miss Andrea. She didn't say *anything*.

"Mother?" Andrea had said.

Adelina Thompson's tone of voice had been uninterpretable. "I see. Well, then." She had fallen silent again.

A few weeks later, Christmas had come. Andrea spent Christmas Eve with her grandmother and two of her cousins in the old town centre, walking around the *Nacimiento*, a massive Nativity scene spreading over nearly the entire square. The town centre was heavily decorated with colorful fruit and flowers, candles in windowsills, Christmas trees and along the edge of the town centre, a bustling Christmas market. Across from the market, the *Hogueras*, a Christmas bonfire celebrated the shortest day of the year. Shortly after sunset the bonfire was lit. Later, some daring young people would jump over the bonfire. Javier would be among them, laughing and strutting.

As the stars rose that night, families all over town lit oil lamps in their windows, leaving the entire town sparkling with the lights. She'd ended up spotting Javier that night, kissing a girl in the alley. She wasn't jealous—Javier was someone to have fun with, and a good friend. But he wasn't boyfriend material, no matter what he thought.

At midnight, Abuelita served a Christmas turkey with truffles and a variety of other dishes. Both of Andrea's uncles were there. Miguel—forty years old, married to the flighty and vain Maria Carmen. Their two children, both pre-teens, threw fits when Andrea wouldn't let them play in her closet. Luis, her younger uncle, was thirty-five. Single, nattily dressed, he wore an easy smile and had a confident gaze as he talked of building his advertising business in Barcelona. They all talked and laughed until the early hours of the morning.

Christmas morning was spent primarily at the parish church of Santa Maria in old town. The front of the building, with its rounded arches and tower, was faced with old tan and brown brick, and dominated the intersection of three narrow streets. The three alleys were decorated with lights and candles, creating a magical scene.

Later, she spoke on the phone with Carrie, still silent and wounded from the loss of her husband, saving strength for the coming birth of their child. Sarah, on the phone, had been snappy and irritable, and her parents distant. Julia had been in Boston, and Jessica sounded stoned. In the end, Andrea decided that the magical Christmas she'd experienced was far preferable to the cold, often quiet holidays she'd grown up with in San Francisco with her parents.

Staying in Spain for the holidays had been the right decision. Increasingly as she'd come closer to finishing secondary school, she'd felt that Calella was home and the United States just a place she visited sometimes. Last Christmas hadn't just reinforced it...it had solidified it. After discussion with Abuelita, she'd struck the American colleges off her list, confining her search to universities in Spain, Paris and London.

Now, answering Leah Simpson's questions, she felt awkward, unsure of herself. How do you explain to a stranger the hurts and rejections that you can barely even admit to yourself? Somehow she had the feeling this self-confident, mature woman who wore a sidearm wouldn't be sympathetic to the sometimes overpowering sense of loneliness and grief Andrea felt.

Whatever she felt, Simpson at least mimicked feeling some empathy. Her eyes softened, and she said, "As I'm sure you're aware, Bear and his team are working to investigate your kidnappers.

But...can you remember anything about them that might give us a clue what they were after? Is there anyone you've angered? Anyone have a reason to hurt you?"

Andrea shook her head. "No...I...I don't have any enemies. Nothing like that."

"When did Tariq Koury first approach you?"

"He was in the seat next to me on the flight. He was...creepy. I knew something was wrong because he lied to me about where he was going to school, and he was too old for that anyway. But I figured he was just a creep...not a kidnapper or whatever."

"Koury was much more than a kidnapper." Simpson shifted in her seat, as if debating how much to say.

"Don't hesitate," Sarah said. "Andrea needs to know what she's up against. *We* need to know what we're up against."

Andrea flashed a grateful look at her sister.

Simpson said, "Koury's fairly well known. He's Saudi born. Not religious, he's been involved in various sorts of intelligence work for a long time."

"Spy stuff?" Sarah raised her eyebrows.

Andrea frowned. What did that kind of thing have to do with her?

Simpson nodded unhappily. "More often mercenary. Koury did some contract work in Iraq, Afghanistan, plenty of other places not all that safe for Americans. We're not sure who he was working for in this case."

"But you're certain he was working for someone?" The words came from Carrie, who had returned to the room with a baby clutched to her chest.

Andrea's eyes were drawn instantly to the small figure in Carrie's arms. Tiny. She stood up and moved to Carrie in deliberate motions.

Carrie met her eyes and smiled. "Andrea, this is Rachel."

Andrea swallowed. Her chest was tight, stomach clenched, throat closed up to the point she felt as if she was going to have difficulty breathing. She whispered. "May I...may I hold her?"

"Very carefully. Have you held a baby before? Cradle her head."

"I have," Andrea replied. Carrie wouldn't know, of course, but Andrea had spent much of the last four years babysitting for two young couples in her building. She knew how to handle babies.

But this was different.

She took baby Rachel in her arms, sliding her left hand up behind Rachel's head. For just a second, Rachel's face began to go red, and her toothless mouth opened. Andrea pulled her a little closer then rocked on her feet.

Rachel quieted. Her skin was very pale, like Carrie and Andrea's, and her eyes were a faint blue. A diaphanous fringe of hair showed on her head.

"She's beautiful." Andrea said it in a reserved voice, not demonstrating any of the storm of emotions she felt. Inside, it was as if a gale had been unleashed. Her emotions on holding the infant were confused, conflicted. More than once she'd sat at home in Calella and felt a cold knot of resentment in her stomach. Not for her parents, who she knew were shits. But for her sisters, who knew it too, but who didn't seek her out. Except for Julia, she knew about the rest of her sisters' lives through Facebook, or in Carrie's case, through the newspapers.

She didn't want to feel that way. And this infant drew her in. Instead of disdain, or separation, or anger, what she felt was fierce protectiveness. She looked in those eyes and knew that if it came down to it, she'd give her life to protect that baby. It was a difficult, confusing emotion, and her eyes flooded with tears as she thought about it. She looked up at Carrie, and saw in Carrie's expression the mirror of what she felt. Except that Carrie wasn't looking at the baby. Carrie was looking at *Andrea*.

She swallowed. That naked protectiveness and love felt raw and dangerous. She held Rachel out to Carrie, her hands suddenly shaking.

Carrie took the baby without hesitation. "Are you all right?" she asked. Her eyes dropped to Andrea's shaking hands.

Andrea nodded. In her peripheral vision, she saw Leah Simpson stand.

"I'll be going. For the time being, until we have more permanent arrangements made, two uniformed officers are stationed in the lobby and one at your door twenty-four hours a day. If you need to go anywhere, please talk with the officer outside so you'll have an escort."

Andrea nodded, desperately wanting to get out of that room.

"Here's my card," Simpson said. Andrea reached out and wordlessly snatched it. She needed this woman to leave. She needed to step out of this room.

Sarah was staring at her frankly now, eyes filled with curiosity.

"I...I need to...I'll be back."

Clutching the card in her hand, she ran down the hallway to the bathroom and slammed the door behind her. She barely made it to the toilet before the nausea forced her to her knees.

2. Leslie Collins. April 29. 12:30 pm

Leslie Collins looked around the relative darkness of Assaggi's on Bethesda Avenue and took a bite of his tortelli di zucca. Organic whole grain fresh pasta filled with pumpkin and glazed with a butter sage sauce, it was surprisingly good. Despite the fact that his job frequently forced him to eat in sometimes inconvenient and occasionally downright awful locations, Collins preferred to eat at home, with his wife.

Today that wasn't an option. For one thing, the planned topic of discussion would ruin her appetite.

Filner was late. Again. Collins would have preferred to have met somewhere more discreet, or not at all. Or if he'd never been forced into his uneasy business relationship with Mitch Filner in the first place. He often wished none of this had ever happened.

But since it had, he had no choice but to see it to the bitter end. He took a sip of his Dewar's and Soda, breaking yet another of his own informal rules. He didn't drink in the middle of the day. But then again, he'd never ordered the kidnap and murder of a teenage girl before, either. No matter what most Americans thought—especially the liberals and conspiracy theorists—his agency was scrupulous about law virtually all of the time. Unfortunately, this was one of those times when extraordinary measures became necessary.

Filner seethed as he scanned the headlines on his tablet. *Daughter of Secretary of Defense escapes abduction attempt.* That was the front page of the Washington Post. The New York Times said *Police Identify Suspect in Kidnap Attempt.* This was a real shit-show, one that had been turning Collins's stomach all morning. It took the feds no more than an hour to identify Tariq Koury. One hour. His identification was bound to lead to plenty of uncomfortable questions to several agencies in Washington Koury had freelanced for at one time or another. Not to mention the private military contractor where he'd found a home.

Collins was relatively sure nothing would find its way back to him. But relatively sure wasn't good enough. Too much rested on Wakhan staying buried forever. Anything threatening to bring it out in the open needed to be dealt with.

Mitch Filner arrived fifteen minutes late. Collins spotted him walking up the street from the direction of the Apple Store, then crossing Bethesda Avenue behind a gaggle of mothers with drooling and bubbling children in their strollers. When Filner crossed the street, he was hidden from view for a moment, but Collins knew he would reappear.

Collins mentally catalogued once again the people who knew about Wakhan. Thompson...soon to be Secretary of Defense. Roshan al Saud, the head of the Saudi Arabian Intelligence Agency and brother to the King. George-Phillip Windsor, the appallingly nosy busybody who saw himself as an intelligence professional and found himself in a game he couldn't have imagined. Windsor was a dilettante, a distant cousin of Queen Elizabeth who owed his position as Chief of the Special Intelligence Service to his family name. Senator Chuck Rainsley, retired Marine Corps Colonel and now Senior Senator from Texas. Before the Marines had their heads handed to them in Beirut in 1983, he'd been a nobody, an obscure man assigned to an obscure position. Somehow he'd turned the massacre of his own troops into political capital that fueled his powerful career in Washington. Finally, there was Vasily Karatygin, who had disappeared for much of the 90s, only to turn up as a prominent "businessman" after the Northern Alliance swept the Taliban out of Kabul.

Karatygin could be eliminated without anyone knowing or caring. But the rest were prominent in their own countries and agencies. With the exception of George-Phillip, they all owed their careers to maintaining their secrecy. And Windsor knew the consequences of letting the secret out would be especially dire.

Another variable he couldn't control was Thompson's children. The moment Collins received the report that all of the children were getting genetic testing to find a match for the baby, he scrambled. The results of those genetic tests were going to raise questions which might fuck everything up. If Collins could have gone back in time and retroactively sterilized Thompson's slut of a wife, he would have done so without hesitation.

Filner appeared in the doorway and made his way through the restaurant, scanning everyone in the crowd. An Army veteran, he'd been with the CIA Directorate of Operations through most of the 90s and into the early part of the 2000s. Filner was a bit of a roughneck and didn't fit in well with the buttoned-down Ivy League culture at CIA's headquarters in Langley, Virginia. But he'd been an ace at some of the ugliest operations, until a rape accusation in Singapore ended his agency career.

Collins had been forced to personally break the news in 2008. Filner had been quietly booted from the agency. Since then, Filner had transitioned into a world even more shadowy than the Agency. He was a private contractor, sometimes providing services via contacting outfits like Blackwater, but sometimes directly.

Right now he was on a private assignment. Off the books.

"Collins."

"Filner."

Filner's eyes scanned the room again then looked at Collins's half-finished plate. "Sorry I'm late."

Collins's eyebrows pulled together. He leaned forward and said, "I'm not concerned that you're late, Filner. I'm concerned about the situation with Richard Thompson."

Filner shrugged. "It was unexpected."

"It's a disaster. I give you the job of quietly making that girl disappear. Instead, we've got a massive media fiasco. How the hell did Koury end up dead?"

"Dumb luck, Collins. You know that happens sometimes. The cops saw something they didn't like and pursued them."

"You sent two seasoned killers to pick up a sixteen-year-old girl, and somehow she not only gets away, but also kills both of them."

"She didn't kill them. The cops did."

Collins waved his hand. "Semantics. And here's the thing. She's under the eye of the media now, and Diplomatic Security is lining up to give protection to the entire family. You fucked up, Filner. You blew it."

"We can still take her out."

Collins shook his head. "Too late. It was one thing for her to disappear. It's another thing for something to happen now with the entire world watching. We're going to have to wait and see. I expect you to pull together whatever assets you need. Every member of that family needs to be watched. Where the fuck is the mother?"

Filner shrugged. "Don't know. Nobody seems to. Wherever she is, she hasn't used her credit cards in the last few days."

Collins muttered. "And the other twin is with her?"

"We assume so."

"Has MI-6 moved on this?"

"Not that I'm aware of. My source there says there's nothing he knows of related to this. But you know how it is. It's all compartmentalized. England probably has more spies in the U.S. than Russia."

"We need someone closer to Windsor. He's the one person who could blow everything."

Filner nodded. "Normal rates still apply?"

Collins leaned forward, spearing another fork of pasta and turning it over, examining it before he placed it in his mouth. He chewed for a few seconds before answering. "Emergency. I don't care what assets. I don't care how many hours. Your mission in life is to make sure Richard Thompson's secrets never come to light, Filner. At all costs. This was all supposed to be nice and quiet, and now it's not, and it's your fault. I want it fixed. I want it to go away. Am I clear? If this problem doesn't go away, then *you* will."

"You're clear, Collins. But let *me* be clear. You better have some contingency plans in place. If you'd taken care of this problem fifteen years ago, no one would have noticed. A simple house fire would have wiped them all out. Now you've got Thompson up as the next Secretary of Defense and one of his daughters is married to a rock star. Anything happens to them and it's visible."

Collins shook his head. "I can manage Thompson. And rock stars die in plane crashes all the time. You worry about the rest."

CHAPTER SIX
Classified

1. Andrea. April 29

It took Andrea several minutes to compose herself, rinse her mouth and wash her face. Her heart was racing, and she felt tension in her chest, but she forced herself to calm down and focus.

Once she was calm, she opened the medicine chest in hopes of finding a hairbrush. Instead, she was faced with a shelf of medications. Zoloft. Andrea felt a morbid fascination and didn't want to touch it or look, because it was none of her business. But she couldn't stop herself, and she turned the bottle. The prescription was two weeks old and was written for her sister Carrie.

She tried to imagine what it must be like for Carrie. Andrea hadn't known Ray well, but she'd been impressed with him. A handsome and tall soldier, he'd been brave, incredibly brave, and that courage had directly resulted in his death. When Andrea flew into Washington last summer, she'd had little opportunity to speak with the devastated Carrie, lost in the debris of a life Andrea knew nothing about. They'd barely spoken half a dozen words, Carrie overwhelmed by the stress of the accident and the court martial. It was all just too much. Way too much.

Was this stuff even safe to take during a pregnancy? Andrea didn't know, but presumably the doctor did.

Whatever the answer was, Andrea wasn't going to second-guess or judge. She took out the hairbrush and carefully brushed her hair, then put it away, the brush and the medicine now out of sight.

Finally composed, she stepped out of the bathroom and walked back toward the family room. As she walked down the hall, she heard a phone ringing in the kitchen. She stopped in place and sagged against the wall, overcome by a wave of exhaustion. It hadn't even been a day since she landed in the United States. Not even twenty-four hours since two men had attempted to kidnap and possibly murder her. She didn't know why. But, despite the presence of federal security guards at the door, she felt afraid like she'd never felt before.

The phone stopped ringing, and she heard Carrie's voice. Quiet. Words, then more words, unclear, out of focus. Then, "Andrea! Phone!"

Andrea swallowed. Was it one of her sisters? Her mother? Julia and Crank were in Los Angeles this week, she knew that. Crank's band, *Morbid Obesity*, was recording a new album. She had no idea what was going on with Alexandra or Jessica.

She walked into the kitchen and promised herself one thing. She was going to get to know all of her sisters. She was fed up with secrets and isolation.

Carrie had the baby on one shoulder and the phone at her ear. "Sí," she said nodding. "Sí." Then in terribly accented Spanish, she said, "Adios." Grinning, she passed the phone to Andrea.

"Hello?"

"Andrea! Como estas?"

"Luis!" she replied, delighted. Uncle Luis owned a growing marketing design firm in Barcelona, and often visited with his mother, and therefore Andrea. Over the last three years he'd become a trusted figure in her life. A father in many ways.

"Andrea, why didn't you call me? I wake up this morning to the news that thugs kidnapped you? Mother will have a heart attack when she watches the news."

Andrea whispered, "Does she know yet?"

"No," he said. "She thinks her television is broken, no thanks to your resourceful uncle. I should be at work today, but the minute I saw the news I got on the road to Calella."

Andrea breathed a sigh of relief. Then she said, "It was scary, Luis. But it's over. I'm all right. There's no need to tell Abuelita."

"I see how it is, Andrea. You want the old women at Church to tell her, and then she'll say, *Luis, why do you keep secrets from me?* No. No. Who were these thugs?"

"The police here are investigating. And they've given me body-guards."

"It's because of your father? I saw in the paper he's to be the new Defense Minister."

"It might be that," Andrea said. "I don't know."

"You should come home," he said.

Andrea swallowed. "I will soon, Uncle, I promise."

"Okay. And next time you tell me when you're leaving the country, and if you're planning to mix it up with kidnappers. You understand?"

She giggled, feeling tears forming at the edge of her eyes. "I promise."

"Okay, *Muñequita*. Let me talk to my sister, por favor."

Andrea blinked and said, "She's not here."

"What? Your mother isn't there? Where is she?"

"I...I don't..."

Luis muttered a series of curses, and then in an angry voice, said, "What about your father? No doubt he's off saving the government instead of taking care of you."

She didn't want to lose it. She didn't want to respond that way. She didn't want to do anything. But involuntarily, Andrea burst into tears. "I don't know!" she cried. "He was here last night, but not this morning. I don't know where he is."

"*Muñequita*," he said in a quiet voice. "I'm sorry. I didn't mean to upset you."

"It's not *your* fault," she replied.

"No, it is. Maybe not my fault your parents are no-good, but it's my fault I lost my temper. Andrea, just...I know your parents are loco, but they love you in their own way. And more importantly, I love you, little doll."

She sniffed back tears. Then said, "Thank you, Luis."

After she said goodbye, she stood there, looking at the counter, a growing rage spreading in her chest. *Where was her mother?* Why the hell had she left her to be cared for by her brokenhearted and injured sisters? She didn't care if Carrie were thirty or fifty. She'd lost her husband and had a sick daughter. Sarah was technically an adult now, but she'd only been eighteen for four weeks.

All of which took Andrea back to the same question again. Where the hell was her mother?

She walked out of the kitchen into the living room. Sarah was still sitting, staring out the glass at the balcony, arms wrapped around her legs. Carrie rocked the baby in her arms, a nursing cloth draped over her shoulder.

The phone rang again. Carrie stirred, and Andrea said, "I'll get it."

Carrie gave her a relieved smile, and Andrea picked up the phone.

"Hello?"

"Hello, this is Sergeant Gorman, with the security detail. We have a couple of people here to visit. Dylan and Alexandra Paris. Okay to clear them in?"

"Yes!" Andrea cried.

2. Carrie. April 29

Oh, *thank God*, Carrie thought.

The minute the AMBER Alert went out the night before, Carrie had called Alexandra and Julia, and kept them updated during the terrorizing ninety minutes before Andrea was found again. Both had agreed to come as soon as possible. Alexandra and Dylan were coming in on the train from New York, and Julia on a flight from Los Angeles later in the day.

"I didn't know they were coming," Andrea said.

Carrie frowned. "Of course they are. We're your sisters."

Andrea gave her a weak smile. A doubtful smile. "I just assumed they were all busy."

Carrie sighed. She couldn't stand up easily, Rachel was still breastfeeding, but as she shifted in frustration, Sarah unfolded herself and stood. She looked almost comical as she reached her arms up to her much taller sister. But her expression was fierce. "We take care of each other, Andrea."

Andrea looked doubtful. And really, why shouldn't she? It's not like they'd done anything to seek her out. Carrie had planned to last summer. She'd even talked with Ray about it. Then everything in her life went horribly wrong. And it was just exhausting, because she *wanted* to watch out for Andrea. She wanted to know why she'd spent most of the last years in Europe. She wanted to be there for her. But she couldn't be *everywhere*. She couldn't be the only one. Especially not now, when she had a young daughter to care for. She'd been a surrogate mother at one time or another to every single one of her sisters but Julia.

It was time for someone else to pick up that mantle. She was a real mother now, to a helpless little girl—Ray's daughter—and she'd be damned if she'd let *anything* interfere with that.

Sarah and Andrea both walked to the door of the condominium when they heard the knock. Then, a moment later, Sarah opened the door.

Outside, in the hall, stood twenty-two-year-old Alexandra and her husband Dylan Paris. Alexandra looked weary. Her honey-brown hair was windblown, a little tangled, and she had circles under her green eyes. Carrie sat up a little at the sight of her. This wasn't a night's lost sleep. Alexandra looked like she'd been going without rest for a while.

Dylan was in worse condition. His eyes were bloodshot, hair unkempt, several days' growth of beard on his chin and neck.

The worst part was that Dylan and Alex weren't touching anywhere. A solid inch of space divided them, but it might as well have been a mile. Neither of them seemed conscious of it.

Alexandra's eyes teared up at the sight of Andrea, and then they were embracing.

Dylan gave a wry smile to Sarah. She returned the smile, then said, "Hey Dylan, show me your scars later?"

He shrugged. "Only if you show me yours."

They hugged, then all four of them moved back into the apartment.

Objectively, Dylan looked awful. Carrie had a sinking, dreadful feeling tied up in her throat. Dylan had been a heavy drinker in high school, but he quit. But the last couple years had been tough on him. Wounded in Afghanistan, then his best friend murdered.

She watched him closely, worried. She'd never seen him looking this disheveled.

Dylan approached Carrie. She studied him. She was assuming too much. Exams at Columbia would be in another week or two. Dylan and Alexandra were probably just tired. This was Alexandra's last term at Columbia—she would be graduating in a few weeks.

Rachel had fallen asleep. Carrie smiled then whispered, "Give me just a second to put her down." Very carefully she unlatched the baby, covered herself, then stood and carried Rachel into the bedroom and lay her in the crib.

She felt Dylan's presence behind her. He was silent, as was she, but his eyes were on Rachel. Carrie looked over at him. He was somber. Dark circles under his eyes were accentuated by the growth of stubble all over his face. It had been several months since she'd seen him. His hair had grown down well past his collar, and she couldn't help but wonder if he'd had a haircut since Ray died.

She swallowed. Ray had loved Dylan. Brothers, in so many ways.

He whispered, "She looks like both of you. She'll be like ninety feet tall when she grows up."

She gave him a crooked smile, and then backed out of the room, switching out the light. "She'll stay out for a couple hours," she said.

Dylan followed her back down the hall. "How is she doing?"

She shrugged, moving down the hall. As she passed by the living room, she saw Andrea, Sarah and Alexandra huddled near each other on the couch talking. She paused for just a second. Even there, on the couch, she could see the separation. Sarah and Alexandra sat close to each other. Andrea was a few inches away...just enough that they didn't accidentally touch.

Carrie sighed. She couldn't fix everything. But she'd keep trying. She kept on going into the kitchen.

"Coffee?" she asked, taking down a mug for herself.

"Please."

She took down a second mug and busied herself pouring coffee. Dylan knew where the sugar and cream were. He'd been here often, both before and after Ray's death.

Dylan repeated his question. "How is she doing?"

Carrie shrugged. "Rachel? Or Andrea."

He gave her a gentle smile. "Both, I guess. Rachel first."

Carrie crossed her arms over her chest, the coffee mug in her left hand. "She's not in any immediate danger. We have a blood transfusion scheduled for next week...she'll have to get them weekly for now."

"And...finding a donor?"

Carrie shook her head. "I've been tested and I'm not a match. But I'm close. Neither is Sarah. We should have Julia's and Alexandra's results back today, and Andrea gets blood drawn tomorrow."

"I'm surprised she didn't get the testing done in Spain," he said.

Carrie shrugged. "I asked her to come. And then...well, you know what happened."

"No one could have predicted that, Carrie. Give yourself a fucking break."

She bit her lip and looked away. Abruptly, she set the coffee cup down, spilling a little on the counter. "*Damn it,*" she said. She reached for the paper towels, but Dylan grabbed her wrist.

"Carrie. You don't have to shoulder everything, okay?"

Horrified at herself, a sound escaped from her throat, some-where between a hiccough and a scream. She covered her mouth, but said through her fingers, "I have to stay strong for Rachel."

"Christ," he muttered. Then he pulled her to him, wrapping his arms around her in a warm hug that locked her in like a vice.

She kept her arms across her chest, in between her and Dylan, shielding herself somehow. "I can't. If I let go of control I'll never get it back together."

"I know," he said, his voice raw. "It's okay. I miss him too. But you gotta know he's out there somewhere looking out for you and Rachel."

She sobbed. "*Stop*," she said.

"Carrie, we're here. I'm here, and Alex, and your other sisters, and we won't let you fall."

Carrie nodded viciously. And then dropped her arms and wrapped them around him. "Thank you," she whispered. "I miss him so much sometimes."

And then she felt other arms on her shoulders. Andrea had squeezed beside her, wrapping an arm around her. She whispered in Carrie's ear, "We'll take care of you, Carrie. I promise."

3. Bear. April 29

Bear Wyden had spent his entire career in the Department of State, and had always thought the large four-winged building at Foggy Bottom was a huge, messy maze.

It had nothing on the Pentagon. He'd shown up fifteen min-utes early, and needed that much time just to clear security. It troubled the Pentagon employees mightily that an investigator from the Department of the State would actually have a sidearm. After all, interagency cooperation only went so far, and arming diplomatic personnel was akin to arming the enemy. Several phone calls to increasing levels of seniority later, he'd finally been cleared into the building, and provided an escort to get him through the maze to the Secretary's office.

Forty-five minutes after his arrival, he was escorted into the office of the Secretary of Defense. It was a large office, nearly fifty feet along one wall, with plush blue carpeting. A nine foot long teak desk faced the room. Behind it, an equally ornate and large credenza was the Secretary's workspace. Two computers, three separate phones, and a scattering of papers. Above the desk, huge portraits dominated the room. On the left, General Dwight Eisenhower, on the right General George Marshall. In between, a family portrait showed Richard and Adelina Thompson, surrounded by their six daughters. To the left and right, the desk area was flanked by an American flag and the flag of the Department of Defense.

Bear wanted to study the portrait—he had experience with all kinds of families, including broken ones. A good look at the portrait might have shown him something—they often did. Sometimes, when he looked at the photo he and Leah had taken about six months before the divorce, he could see it. The disappointment and anger had been right there in her eyes. But, back then, he'd been too blind to see it.

So Bear tried to get a good look at the Thompson family portrait. But he didn't get a chance. Richard Thompson approached him; hand out, a smile on his face.

"Mr. Wyden, a pleasure to meet you." Bear snorted internally. Thompson wasn't one to forget a face—much less the face of the man who had once provided the protective detail for his own family. This was nothing more than a display of how important Thompson had become.

"Mr. Secretary."

"Come in, please."

Thompson led him to a round, highly polished round table with four seats near the desk. Wyden understood that Thompson was a career diplomat. A politician, really. But the smile seemed off. His youngest daughter had been kidnapped. The wide smile somehow seemed inappropriate.

The two of them took seats at the table. It was mahogany, with ornate carvings around the edge, and polished so much Bear could have safely shaved in the reflection.

"What can I do for you Mr. Wyden?"

Bear shifted uncomfortably in his seat. "Sir, as you know, I'm the lead investigator in the kidnapping of your daughter. I need to ask you some questions."

"Please, however I can assist the investigation. Can you tell me what you've found so far?"

"We're still early in the investigation."

"I know that. But I do know the identify of one of the suspects is known. A Saudi named Koury?"

Bear nodded. "There are some things I obviously can't discuss as of yet, Mr. Secretary."

"I'm sure you are aware I have security clearance, Mr. Wyden."

"Of course, sir. But this is an ongoing investigation. That said, you are correct, Koury was involved in your daughter's kidnapping."

"Who was behind it?"

Bear swallowed. "We don't know that yet."

Thompson leaned forward. Any traces of a political smile were gone. "Why the hell not?"

"Mr. Secretary, I'm sure you're aware both suspects died. It takes time—"

"Don't talk to me about time!"

Bear shook his head. "Sir, I need to ask you some questions. If you want us to resolve this, then you need to answer them."

"Fine. What do you need to know?"

"First, why does your youngest daughter live in Spain?"

Thompson waved his hand, as if swatting away a fly. "Her mother felt it was best."

Bear was stunned. That was it? "And you had no opinion?"

"Of *course* I had an opinion. What relevance does this have to the investigation?"

"Koury flew over here from Spain, sir. In the seat next to her. This was a sophisticated operation, launched on a moment's notice, with people involved from multiple countries. Who do you know who has the resources to pull off something like that?"

"Not many criminals," Thompson replied.

"That's right. Now, is there *anyone* you can think of on a personal level that might be involved? Enemies?"

Thompson shook his head. "Of course not. I'm a career diplomat, of course, and I've dealt with some unsavory characters over the years. We did, after all, require a protective detail for some time."

"I remember," Bear said. Interesting that Thompson thought he needed to remind Bear about the protective detail. Was it some kind of subtle one-upmanship? Thompson pointing out that he was so important that he didn't even remember who had been in charge of protecting his family?

Something was very wrong here.

"Mr. Thompson," Bear began. Thompson didn't respond, even though Bear deliberately violated protocol by not addressing him with his title. "Where were you last night? When your daughter was at the hospital?"

"I was on Capitol Hill all yesterday afternoon. My daughter Carrie went to pick up her sister because she could get there quicker than I could. And we agreed to meet back at the condo."

"I see. And your wife? Why wasn't she there?"

Thompson rolled his eyes. "You're asking a lot of irrelevant questions, Mr. Wyden."

"Wives are never irrelevant, sir, mine would have told you that, at least before she left me. Where is Mrs. Thompson?"

"If you must know, our daughter Jessica has been...problematic of late. My wife is in San Francisco with her."

Bear sat back in his seat. *What?* That just didn't make any sense. "Prob65lematic how?"

Thompson coughed. Then muttered, "Drugs. Teenage issues. Nothing life threatening, but Adelina felt it necessary to take her on some...prayer retreat, some days ago. I really can't tell you any more, except that she's out of touch."

"You have no way of getting in touch with her?"

"That's correct."

"Sir...that's...don't you think that's a little odd?"

Thompson raised an eyebrow. "How so?"

Bear sat forward, finding himself unable to control the tone of his voice. "Sir, don't you think it a little odd that your wife and one of your daughters is somewhere you don't know and out of touch? Don't you think it's odd that your youngest daughter was *kidnapped* and you didn't even bother to go to the hospital to check on her?"

Thompson glared at Bear. "How dare you? Are you here to investigate a crime or not?"

"Mr. Thompson, have you ever encountered Mr. Koury before?"

Thompson frowned.

Bear sat back in his seat. "You have, haven't you?"

Thompson sighed. "It's classified, unfortunately."

What the hell is wrong with this man? "Mr. Thompson, I have the clearance."

Thompson sighed. "Well, then. You may or may not be aware that following my retirement I did a significant amount of consulting, including a diplomatic mission to Iraq in late 2002. It was a last minute attempt to get Iraq to back down and reveal their weapons of mass destruction to avert war. Mr. Koury was part of the security team for our mission in Iraq."

Bear held his breath. "He was part of the security team?"

"Yes. I believe he was the second in command? Possibly."

Bear thought through the implications of this. "Did you personally have dealings with Mr. Koury?"

"The mission was three weeks. Of course I had dealings with him."

"What do you remember about him?"

Thompson's lips curled unpleasantly. "He was an uncouth man. Barbaric really. Fond of pornography. He routinely used foul language."

"Did you ever suspect any criminal activity?"

"I wouldn't doubt it."

Bear sighed. He'd been involved in investigations for many years. He'd dealt with criminals and terrorists. He'd dealt with distraught parents and panicky corrupt officials. But he'd never held an interview as frustrating as this one. He actually found himself wondering if Thompson was a sociopath. No one was this dispassionate about his daughter's kidnapping. He knew Thompson was a cold fish, but no one was *this* cold. Thompson was hiding something.

"Mr. Thompson...when was the last time you had any contact with Tariq Koury?"

Thompson thought for a moment then said, "Koury held a contract for the coalition provisional authority in Iraq from 2003 to 2005. I dealt with him on a fairly routine basis then."

"I wasn't aware you were in government at the time, Mr. Thompson."

"I was officially retired. But I took on occasional contracts."

"And some of those contracts took you to Iraq?"

"Among other places."

Bear nodded. "Were these places classified?"

"They were."

So Koury knew Thompson. That was unexpected, and in some ways might change the direction of the investigation. But he didn't really know how. Bear studied the man, eyebrows pressing together.

Thompson looked at his watch.

"I'm aware we're running short of time, Mr. Secretary. But I have a few more questions."

"Please proceed."

"When did you learn Andrea would be coming to the United States?"

Thompson answered the softball question immediately. "Two nights ago. Right after Carrie made the call to Spain."

"I see," Bear said. "And...your wife is in California right now. How tall is she?"

Thompson's eyes widened. At 5 feet 10 inches, he was the average height for a man. The anger on his face was unmistakable. "She is five foot three inches, Mr. Wyden."

Carrie and Andrea were both taller than six feet. They looked very similar to each other...and significantly different from the rest of their sisters.

Bear could only come to one conclusion. He stared at the Secretary of Defense and said, "Sir...who is Carrie and Andrea's father?"

CHAPTER SEVEN
Play Nice

1. Bear. April 29

Sir...who *is Carrie and Andrea's father?*

Bear Wyden felt the temperature drop in the room when he asked the question. It was the sort of question that could infuriate people. The sort of question that could end careers. After all, he wasn't asking some deadbeat in Chicago this question. He was asking the Secretary of Defense.

The second the words left Bear's mouth, Secretary Thompson's eyes narrowed and he stiffened in his seat. His face went slightly red and Bear thought Thompson was going to show his teeth. "How dare you?"

"Sir, where is your wife?"

"This interview is over."

"Mr. Thompson, this is a federal investigation into your own daughter's kidnapping, and you seem more concerned—"

"Mr. Wyden, you won't be concerned with this investigation or any other for very much longer. Now get out of my office."

Thompson stood and walked toward his desk. Wyden stood too, ignoring the feeling that he'd just stuck his bare hand into a wasps' nest. "Mr. Thompson. Your daughter was kidnapped. I need answers to my questions."

Richard Thompson wasn't answering any further questions. He lifted a phone to his ear.

"Sir—"

"Colonel Richardson, please have armed guards remove this... *person*...from my office immediately."

Bear leaned over the desk, right arm extended, index finger pointing at the photo of Thompson and his family. He knew he wasn't acting rationally. He knew his behavior was neither professional nor was it really accomplishing anything. But when he thought about that girl, kidnapped and alone, and then when she got out of it neither one of her parents could be bothered to show up at the hospital? He didn't give a shit if you were the President of the United States or a local janitor...you went to your kid in that kind of situation.

The thought of her all alone filled him with rage. "Is all that a sham, then? You don't give a shit about her, do you? That's why you weren't at the hospital."

"Mr. Wyden, I've asked you twice now to get out of my office."

"And I've asked you, Mr. Secretary. Who is Andrea's father?"

The office door opened. Two men stepped inside. Bear couldn't tell if they were soldiers or not. Neither wore a standard uniform—instead, they wore black unlabeled fatigues, combat boots, and wore sidearms. Close cropped hair, tan skin, pistols at the ready. They could be military or police or private contractors. He had no way of knowing.

He did know that there were two of them, and they were armed.

Wyden threw his hands in the air. "Fine, then. I'm gone."

One of them, a blonde haired, blue-eyed former football player who was probably from Texas, pushed forward while the other stood back to cover him. "Lay down on the floor!"

Two more black-dressed quasi soldiers came into the room as he shouted.

"I'm with Diplomatic Security," Wyden said. "Can I reach in my left pocket for my credentials?"

"On the floor!" Blondie shouted.

Wyden rolled his eyes. "Look at my credentials, please." He reached to open his jacket. Unfortunately, that brought attention to the 10mm Sig-Sauer in the shoulder holster on his right side.

The blonde quasi-soldier shouted, "Gun! He's got a gun!"

That changed everything. In fifteen seconds, the four men had Bear on the floor, arms out to his side. Blondie knelt on his back, knee digging into Bear's spine. He'd been disarmed.

In a disgusted tone, Thompson said, "When you've finished removing him, please have someone inform me. I'll be in the JCS conference room."

Once they removed the Sig Sauer from his jacket, Blondie reached around the front and took out the small folder from Bear's breast pocket that contained his State Department ID and Diplomatic Security badge.

"DSS, huh?" Blondie said. "I dealt with enough of your pals before. Here's the deal. We're gonna get up nice and slow, and you're going to cooperate, and then with any luck you can leave today without handcuffs or any holes drilled through you. Got it?"

"Yeah. Play nice. Gotcha. Let me the fuck up, all right?"

Wary, sidearms still out, the four security guards let Bear to his feet, and then escorted him out of the office. Blondie kept a hand on his arm the entire time. Bear shook his head. Sometimes he regretted the fact that he still worked with his ex-wife. Once she got wind of this, he'd never hear the end of it.

2. Dylan. April 29

"**G**ive me one of those." Sarah was slumped back in a cast iron chair as she said the words, her injured leg tucked up in front of her.

"Hell, no," Dylan said as he lit his cigarette, shielding the lighter from the wind. He took a long drag from the cigarette, the coal lighting up, the faint sound of the tobacco burning audibly in his ears.

"I'm eighteen now."

He raised an eyebrow, glancing over at her. After the too intense discussion with Carrie, he'd stepped outside for a smoke, planning on a little solitude. Sarah had followed him out onto the balcony. Twenty stories up, he could see most of Bethesda and parts of northwest Washington, DC spread out below his feet.

"I don't give a shit if you're thirty," Dylan said. "I'm not giving you a cigarette. If you want one that bad, buy your own."

"You're kidding, right? I don't leave the house. I'm a cripple, didn't you know that?"

He slumped into the seat across from her. "You're no more a cripple than I am. Actually your injuries weren't as bad as mine."

She shrugged. "I'm not a soldier."

"Better toughen up, then. What's this about you being a cripple?"

She sneered. "It's nothing. Mom and Dad basically laid down the rule I couldn't ever leave without an escort."

"Alex said you home schooled this year?"

"Tutors, mostly. I can't imagine what it cost. But it's changed everything."

"How?"

She raised her eyebrows. "You went to high school. You know what I'm talking about."

Dylan shrugged and took a drag off his cigarette. "I don't really. My high schooling wasn't exactly normal."

Her eyes widened a little, then she said, "Oh, that's right. I forgot. I remember the night Alexandra told Dad you'd dropped out of school. He was overjoyed."

"I'm sure he was."

Unexpectedly she leaned forward, tilting her head slightly to the right, a serious expression in her eyes.

"You're drinking again, aren't you?"

Dylan froze. For nearly fifteen seconds he didn't move. Then his eyes darted to the sliding glass door.

"What makes you say that?" The question was unnecessary. He knew why she asked. Everything about his appearance made people wonder. Alex wondered. Everyone who knew him did.

"Common sense," she replied. "You lost your two closest friends in two years. You've got no one to talk to. You're up there in New York married to my uptight as hell sister and you're all alone. You look like shit."

"You don't know what the fuck you're talking about, Sarah."

She leaned forward, raising a knowing eyebrow. "I know *exactly* what I'm talking about, Dylan."

"I'm not going to tell Alexandra," she said. "That's your deal. But you need to."

Dylan grimaced. "It's not drinking a *lot*, Sarah. But like you said, I lost my two closest friends. A drink every once in a while is okay."

Sarah's eyes dropped to the floor. "I was afraid of that," she said.

Even though she wasn't looking at him any more, Dylan still felt defensive. Sarah was Alex's younger sister by several years, but she always seemed to see right through him. And somehow the experience of the accident last summer formed some kind of bond for her with Ray. It didn't make any sense. It didn't have to. But when she looked at him with sad, knowing eyes, Dylan felt like Ray was looking at him.

He didn't like the way that felt.

Dylan looked at Sarah. "Listen, Sarah. We're not discussing this any more. I've got it under control, and Alex is already freaked out enough about Ray and you and Andrea and the baby...she doesn't need this on her plate, all right? In the greater scheme of things, me grabbing a drink every now and then is not that big of a deal. But freaking out Alex is."

Sarah shook her head. "You're fooling yourself, Dylan."

He closed his eyes and sighed, then took another drag off his cigarette. The breeze up here felt cool. Calming. He remembered the first time he'd been on this balcony. Just over a year ago, after he and Alex had rushed to take an overnight train to DC in response to Carrie's call. Staff Sergeant Martin had testified at the preliminary hearing, and then called Ray that night, threatening suicide. Then he shot himself while still on the phone with Ray.

They stood outside, right here on this balcony, Ray's eyes still red, dark circles under his haunted eyes. *They're talking bridesmaid's dresses,* he had said. *Thank God you woke up.*

I'm not so good at asking for help, Ray had said.

Sometimes you have to, Dylan had responded. *You're the one who taught me that.*

The problem was, you could know something, and you could tell other people, but still not believe it in your soul. And sometimes

Dylan just couldn't get his mind around the fact that his two best friends were dead in two years.

He looked back at Sarah. "Sarah, thanks for your concern. I promise, I'll be okay." The words felt hollow, brittle as he said them.

3. Andrea. April 29

Andrea looked out the sliding glass door. Dylan was slumped in his seat, smoking a cigarette. Sarah was out there with him, gesticulating as she spoke. It was a beautiful spring day. She could tell a breeze was blowing outside, because every few seconds Sarah and Dylan's hair blew in the wind.

She turned. Alexandra looked unhappy as she and Carrie exchanged small talk. *Small talk*. Final exams. Train and plane schedules. What was Columbia University like now versus ten years ago. Pretty soon they were going to start talking about the weather or something.

Their voices were like *buzz buzz buzz* in her ear, and for a second Andrea wanted to just throw some heavy object across the room. Something serious was obviously going on between Dylan and Alexandra—normally they were two of the most affectionate people she'd ever seen. Now they didn't look at each other? They didn't touch? Carrie was on the verge of falling apart every moment, and the help she got from a part-time nanny was wholly inadequate. Their mother and father were among the missing, Jessica was—who knew where—and there were armed guards right outside the condo to *protect them* from terrorists or kidnappers or whatever.

Yet, they sat here engaged in small talk.

She wanted to scream just to get their attention. Instead, she sat down on the couch across from them. Back straight, shoulders back, and legs crossed at the ankle, just as their bitchy mother taught her all those years ago before outsourcing Andrea's upbringing. Then she stared at Carrie. She didn't say a word. She just stared.

It took about 40 seconds before Carrie broke off her sentence and looked from Alexandra to Andrea.

"Are you all right?"

Andrea shrugged. She tilted her head, looked toward Alexandra, and took a deep breath. Even though she'd brought on the question, she felt suddenly frozen. A tightness in her chest, her throat closed up.

Alexandra's eyebrows pushed together, and she sat forward in her seat, leaning toward Andrea. "Hey…are you okay, hun?"

Andrea started to speak, and found her hands suddenly flapping, the words colliding in her mouth like a ten car pileup on a two-lane highway.

"Breathe," Carrie said, reaching out and taking her hand.

"When do I get tested?" Andrea blurted.

"Tomorrow morning," Carrie replied.

"Why…" She stared at her sisters, her face going pale. Then she said, "Never mind," and started to pull away.

"Whoa," Carrie said. "Wait."

"No, really, never mind," Andrea said.

"Stop," Alexandra replied. "Tell us. Whatever it is. You're safe here. We're your sisters."

Andrea stood up, her eyes swiveling back and forth between the two of them. Then she voiced the words. The words she'd never said out loud, the words that expressed every doubt and fear and insecurity she'd ever had.

"Are we?"

"What?" Alexandra asked.

"Are we sisters?"

Alexandra visibly recoiled a few inches. "Of course we are," she said.

Andrea shook her head. "I know *we* are," she said, gesturing between herself and Carrie. "That's obvious to anyone. But...why else would they send me away? Why?"

Carrie said, "I thought you wanted to go."

"*What?*" Andrea said.

Dylan and Sarah, both sitting on the balcony outside, slid open the sliding glass door. "Is everything okay?" Dylan asked.

"I said, I always thought you wanted to live with Abuelita. I mean...you started spending summers over there when I was at Columbia...and...I don't know...I guess I assumed..."

She assumed. That's what you did when you didn't even really care. But then Andrea felt her heart almost stop.

"Mom said, *Andrea doesn't want to come home.*" Carrie frowned as she spoke. "I asked her why, and she said not to pry. She said...I didn't want to get into it. That you'd be happier if I didn't dig into it...and...she said there was nothing but grief there."

Andrea sank into her seat. "I don't know how she could possibly know that. We've barely spoken a word to each other in the last five years. She won't even speak with Abuelita or Luis." She thought back. Trying to remember. Anything. Details.

She shook her head. "I kind of took it for granted. I mean, I started spending summers there when I was five? Six?"

"Something like that. It was the summer after Julia left for Harvard."

"That far back?" Andrea asked. "I don't remember Julia living with us."

"She finished high school in 2000 I think...you'd have been... two? Anyway...you didn't go to Spain for the first time until June 2002."

"You remember the timing pretty well," Andrea said.

"That's because I went with you."

Andrea's eyes widened. "You went with me the first time? I don't remember that."

"I'm not surprised, you were only four."

Sarah approached closely. Her eyes were on Andrea. "Carrie, do you have any pictures from that trip?"

Alexandra shook her head. "This is *bullshit*. We are sisters. Andrea, I'm sorry I haven't been in touch much the last year or two... college has just been...insane. And...well, you know. But we're *sisters*."

Sarah said, "Get the photos, Carrie."

Carrie nodded. Andrea sat and watched her go, feeling dread in her stomach. Why would it be her and Carrie alone who went to Spain? The two sisters who looked different. The two of them who were more than six feet tall and looked almost like twins and *nothing* like their father?

Why did they go to Spain?

Carrie returned to the room a few minutes later. She had a well worn photo album. It had a canvas cover decorated with the word *Spain* in purple letters. Framed on the front cover was a photo.

She flushed a little when she put the book in front of them, and said, "I was a little more girly when I was seventeen."

Andrea felt a chill looking at it. The photograph, taken nearly twelve years before, looked exactly like Andrea, holding hands with a four year old. Except, of course, it was Carrie, holding hands with her. Both of them had smiles on their faces, huge smiles. Andrea's four-year-old face was smeared with what looked like chocolate ice cream.

Andrea, of course, recognized the location. They were standing on Calella Beach...unmistakable, because of the lighthouse above their shoulders and the word CALELLA in twelve-foot high rock letters on the hillside behind them. That would be near the Hotel Esplai. Javier worked there as a busboy in the summer time.

Carrie slid into the seat next to Andrea.

Andrea took a deep breath. "Was this the only time you went?" she asked.

Carrie nodded. "Mother wanted me to go in 2003, after I graduated high school, but we had a huge fight about it, because I was planning on spending my summer with my friends here."

"What happened?"

"I won the argument. I remember Dad was never around much that summer, and at the end, I drove to Columbia."

"You drove?" Andrea said.

"Yeah, with Julia and Crank and Sean. It was fun. I started college a few weeks later. And...well...I think you started first grade in September."

Andrea couldn't keep her eyes off the album. She didn't have many memories of their home in San Francisco when she was younger. She knew she'd attended her first few years of school in San Francisco, but with the exception of a few early memories, everything before ten years old was hazy. By then, she was spending her summers in California and the school year in Spain.

She reached out and touched the book. The fabric felt well used. Loved, even. She almost felt guilty. She loved Luis and Abuelita. Her family. Somehow, wanting to open that album, wanting to open that can of worms of her past, made her feel disloyal.

But Abuelita would understand. Luis would understand. And even if they didn't...she needed to know, didn't she? She needed to know. She needed to know her history. She needed to know who she was. Who her family was. She needed to know *why*.

Andrea reached out and took the album in her hands and flipped it open to the first page.

CHAPTER EIGHT
What makes you tick

1. Andrea. April 29

The first photo in the album showed two sisters, one seventeen, and the other four, flanking their mother. Carrie was frozen in time in that photo. She had braces on her teeth and wore a vintage blue dress with matching heels. She wore a huge smile on her face, and towered over Adelina Thompson.

"You look so happy," Andrea said.

"We were just leaving for the airport. It was my first trip without Mom and Dad."

"Do you remember how the trip came about? Why it was just the two of us?"

Carrie nodded. "Sort of. I had sort of hinted for a long time that I was hoping to take a trip to Europe sometime. I mean, it's not like we hadn't traveled. I remember living in Brussels, more or less, and I was in middle school most of the time we were in China. You were born there."

"In China," Andrea said. She knew that. But somehow hearing it, now, felt different.

"Right. The twins too."

A cloud fell over Carrie's face. Then she said, "Julia knows more about China, of course. She was in high school then."

Andrea sighed. She flipped the page. The first inside pages showed Carrie and Andrea arriving at the airport in Barcelona. Hugs with family members who must have been unfamiliar to Carrie at the time, but who looked very familiar to Andrea: Abuelita, Miguel and Maria Carmen, Luis. Her *family*, or at least the part of her family that had been a significant part of her life the last several years.

Carrie looked at her for a few seconds, and then she moved, wordlessly, onto the couch next to Andrea.

Andrea shifted position just a little. She knew she should be more open to her sister. Carrie, of all people. But something held her back. She shifted so that their bodies weren't touching.

Carrie said nothing about the shift. Instead, she pointed at the album. "How are Luis and Miguel?"

Andrea shrugged. "Miguel constantly complains about how his wife nags him to death. But you can tell he loves her."

Carrie smiled, nodding. "That sounds right."

"Luis started his own advertising firm in Barcelona...three years ago? Four? He loves it. Lately he's busy all the time, I don't get to see him very often."

Andrea flipped the page slowly. A smile spread across her face. The photograph showed Carrie, laying on the beach sunbathing. Luis was in the photo, laying on a towel a few feet away from Carrie, and his eyes were on her. "Oh, my God," Andrea said, laughter in her voice. "He is *so* checking you out in that picture."

Carrie chuckled. "He's not *that* much older than me. Six or seven years? That's still kind of creepy."

Not far from Luis and Carrie, half covered in sand, holding a shovel in one hand and a pair of goggles in the other, was Andrea. Four years old. Huge smile on her face.

Andrea swallowed. In the photo she looked so happy. No sign of the empty gaping loneliness she'd felt in later years.

After that, a series of beach photos. *Abuelita* in a bathing suit! Andrea gasped and laughed. A photo of a crowd of family members around a picnic table. In the foreground, Andrea played with two other children, three or four or five years old. Carrie sat on a picnic table, in avid conversation with a boy who looked remarkably like Javier. His older brother? Andrea supposed it was possible. Aunts and uncles and cousins were in the photo. In the background, near the edge of a picture, stood two men. One of them dark skinned, Spanish. The other, pale skinned, towered over him. Andrea didn't recognize either of the men.

The next several pages showed Andrea and Carrie out and about in Calella. She recognized the front of the Chapel of Santa Maria in one of the photos and smiled. In the photo, Miguel and his wife Maria Carmen were exiting the chapel. He wore a tuxedo, and she wore a garish wedding dress with entirely too much cleavage.

Andrea shook her head. "We were at Miguel and Maria Carmen's wedding?"

Carrie nodded. "Yes. It was a beautiful ceremony."

"She's a complete witch," Andrea whispered.

Carrie snickered. "Yeah. She is."

And that's when Andrea froze. She picked the album up and held it closer to her face.

In the wedding photo, a large crowd was near the plaza and the chapel. The beginning of the market was right there, and hundreds of people shopped there throughout the week.

Standing in the shade, barely visible in the photo, was a very tall, pale man. He stood next to a shorter, darker skinned man.

Both of them were maddeningly out of focus. But it was the same man, she was sure of it.

"Andrea?" Carrie said.

"Wait..." Andrea whispered.

She set the album down, and flipped back to the beach photo. She studied the too fuzzy features on the man's face. Then she flipped forward to the wedding picture.

It was the same man, she thought.

From the photo, he was probably six foot five. Dark hair. Pale eyes, possibly green. Long, aquiline nose, she thought, but it was impossibly difficult to tell with the photo out of focus. But if she squinted her eyes enough, she imagined that the man might just resemble Carrie.

She reached out and pointed one shaking finger at the photo.

"Do you recognize that man?"

Carrie shook her head. "No...should I?"

"What about..." She flipped the album back to the beach photo. "Here."

"That's odd," Carrie said. Her eyebrows scrunched together. She flipped back and forth between one photo and the other.

Andrea looked up and met Carrie's eyes. Both of them stopped breathing.

"Do you think it's possible?" Carrie asked.

Andrea swallowed. "It would explain...a lot."

"But...Dad would have said something. When I started to get blood tests."

"If he knew," Andrea said.

Carrie swallowed. "But Mom..."

"Where *is* she?"

"Mom? Well...it's a long story."

Alexandra said, "I can't wait to hear this."

Sarah rolled her eyes. "It's not that long a story. Mom thinks Jessica's gay or something and took her off to a rehab camp."

"*What?*" Andrea said.

Carrie shook her head. "I don't think so. Andrea, you didn't see Jessica at Christmas this year. She was stoned out of her mind. That's why Mom decided to go back to San Francisco."

Sarah shrugged. "I can't figure Mom out."

"No one can," Carrie said. "She's never treated any of us decently. Especially Julia."

Andrea followed the discussion with a peculiar sense of confusion. For reasons she couldn't fathom, she felt the urge to defend her mother. Because even though over the years Andrea had spent increasing amounts of time overseas, even though she'd seen less and less of her parents, what memories she did have of her mother were warm.

That was part of what made her rejection hurt so much.

"So no one actually knows where she is?" Andrea asked.

She looked at her sisters. Carrie. Alexandra. Sarah. They looked mystified.

"Okay, does anyone know where *Jessica* is?"

Carrie shook her head. She swallowed and said, "Between you and her, sometimes I feel like such a failure."

Andrea and the other sisters sat there, stunned. Finally, Andrea jumped in and said, "What? What the hell are you talking about?"

Carrie closed her eyes. Then she said, "It was...ten years ago? Longer? Julia and I made a pact. That...our mom couldn't take care of us. She was too crazy. But we agreed that none of you would ever feel that loneliness. That we'd take care of you."

A tear ran down Carrie's face. Then another. She sniffed then said, "But we didn't. I couldn't."

"You did!" Sarah said. "You took care of us. Even after you left for college, you called me every week, and I always knew I could call you."

Confusion roiled through Andrea. She remembered the weekly calls from Julia. Every single week, without fail. The visits, every time Julia was in Europe, and sometimes just for the hell of it.

Had they been watching out for her all along, and she just didn't know?

"I couldn't though, after I left. I tried, but I wasn't enough."

Alexandra looked mortified. She stared at Carrie, an oddly resentful expression on her face, but she said nothing. Andrea saw it and took note.

"Oh, all of you be quiet," Sarah said. "Nobody's perfect. But you know what? The biggest hero I ever knew would have said we all do the best we can, and we have to live with that best. So don't beat yourselves up for not being perfect."

Carrie gasped at Sarah's words, and Andrea sat there. Who was she talking about? Ray, Carrie's husband? Dylan, who had remained silent throughout the long exchange between the sisters, swayed on his feet a little, then said, "He said something like that to me more than once."

Sarah continued. "So just, everybody stop. Andrea's right. Where the hell is Jessica? Can we stop with the psychobabble for thirty seconds and track down our sister?"

Carrie nodded. "I think I just took it for granted she was safe and with Mother."

Andrea nodded and then said, "I think what happened to me yesterday means we can't take anything for granted."

"Right," Carrie said. She took out her phone and dialed. "I'll try Jessica, then Mom."

"Who was the last person who talked with her?"

"Dad. A week ago. He told me when I started calling about getting blood tests. That she's at some kind of retreat or camp-ground or something."

Sarah snorted. "What did I tell you?"

Alexandra said, "If Dad says she's at a retreat, then why—"

Andrea cut her off. "I don't have any reason to believe anything he says."

The other sisters were silenced. Not a word. No agreement. No disagreement.

Carrie took the phone away from her ear. "Jess doesn't answer." She dialed the phone again, and said, "If Mom doesn't answer, I'll try Julia. They're leaving Los Angeles tomorrow. Maybe they can make a stop in San Francisco."

2. Anthony Walker. April 29

When Anthony Walker stepped off the elevator, accompa-nied by a giant masquerading as a security guard, he was automatically inclined to be judgmental. People who rented the top floor suites of Los Angeles luxury hotels didn't get the benefit of the doubt in his book. Not in a world where millions starved or died prematurely of disease. Not in a world where war destroyed lives.

Never mind that he knew that Julia Wilson was an active phi-lanthropist. He'd done his homework, and knew she served on the boards of half a dozen nonprofits, the largest of which was the Cristina Center in Detroit, a shelter for young girls who had been trafficked and forced into prostitution.

But this...palace. It was unconscionable. Appalling. Marble floors and crystal chandeliers. A dozen security guards so far.

What he *didn't* understand was where Wilson got her money. During his research for the interview, a friend had managed to pull her tax returns as well as her father's. Richard Thompson was rich, of course. Old money, lots of assets, some of them less savory than others.

But the father had nothing on daughter Julia. If the story he'd been led to believe was true, she'd taken the money earned from her husband's band and invested it in a wide range of businesses all over the globe, and made appalling sums of money. With a net worth well in excess of forty million, she could afford to fund a place like the Cristina Center and not notice the difference.

In Anthony's experience, people didn't make that kind of money unless someone was getting screwed somewhere.

Still, he didn't want to prejudge her. He followed the security guard down the hallway of the suite...*the hallway*...and stopped when the guard indicated. A knock on the door, and then the guard said, "Through here, sir."

Anthony gave the guard a weak smile, then stepped into the office.

He was met at the door by Julia Wilson. Professionally dressed in a dark blue suit and skirt with tasteful heels, she wore pearls at her neck and wrists, and smaller pearls in both ears. Rich brown, curly hair framed a face that highlighted blue-green eyes and full lips. Born December 16, 1981. She was three months older than Anthony, but looked easily five years younger.

That said, she wouldn't look out of place in any executive office in the world. He reminded himself that this woman controlled a company far bigger than the rock band that had started it—she'd built it into a multi-million dollar international business.

"Mr. Walker," she said. "I'm Julia Wilson."

"It's a pleasure to meet you, Mrs. Wilson."

She gave him an insincere smile. "Julia, please. Have a seat."

"Okay, Julia. Call me Anthony."

He took the proffered chair, positioning a digital audio recorder on the desk and taking out the small pocket sized notebook he carried everywhere with him. Anthony had a strong verbal memory and could often recall conversations with near perfect accuracy. Unfortunately he was a disaster with other types of facts: dates, locations, and sometimes even people's faces.

She took a seat behind the desk, across from him. Nice that this hotel suite had a built-in office with an imposing desk: dark stained cherry, green desk lamp, dark paneling throughout the office. It was classic east coast WASP. On the top floor of a LA hotel. He half-expected to see a balding man in a top hat with a cigar walk into the room. Anthony had interviewed enough politicians and bankers, weapons dealers and Senators to recognize the type.

"Drinks will be served in a moment," she said. "In the meantime, why don't we get started?"

"Thank you." He was happy to get to business. This was uncomfortable enough. "Yes, I'd like to get started. Will Mr. Wilson be joining us?"

"Crank may be by in a little while."

Anthony wasn't happy about that. Despite the fact that Julia was infinitely more interesting than her husband, his assignment was Crank Wilson, the lead singer and guitarist of the obnoxiously popular alt-rock band *Morbid Obesity*. Julia was the band's manager.

"I see. Well, then. I guess we'll start with you."

"Actually," she replied. "I'd like to start with *you*."

"Excuse me?"

"I think you understood me perfectly, Mr. Walker. Surely you're aware that I've spent my entire life around the Foreign Service? And that I run a large multinational business? I'm very familiar with your work."

He blinked. "You are?"

"Of course. Which is why I find it difficult to believe that you're here to interview Crank. You're not an entertainment reporter, and I can't see any reason a foreign correspondent would want to interview him. Unless you're digging for information about something else."

Anthony exhaled. She was absolutely correct, of course. He'd made his career covering wars, peace talks and international conflict. He'd covered stories in Afghanistan and Iraq, in Liberia and London. So finding himself suddenly assigned to the *entertainment* section of the *Washington Post* wasn't exactly in his career path. "The short answer, if you must know, Mrs. Wilson, is that I'm in the doghouse."

"Julia, please," she replied, a prim smile on her face. "I'm guessing that's because you went...um...off the reservation...with regard to the sale of the paper?"

He smiled sardonically. That was a mild way to put it. In the summer of 2013, when the *Post* was purchased by rich media mogul, Walker had published a series of editorials criticizing the sale, then gone on television to do the same.

It made for nice headlines. Pulitzer Prize winning reporter criticizes the sale of his own newspaper. On the second day, he'd been suspended.

There the shock began. Anthony, at first, wanted to thumb his nose at all of them. He was a veteran reporter with a national reputation. He'd covered some of the most celebrated stories of the last fifteen years, from the invasion of Iraq to earthquakes in Pakistan. He could work anywhere.

It turned out he couldn't. The *New York Times* politely said no. Chicago and Los Angeles, the same response. Cox Enterprises, which owned a number of newspapers including the Atlanta Constitution, didn't even return his call.

Even the *Washington Times,* founded and owned by the Rev. Sun Myung Moon, only gave him the barest courtesy interview. It didn't help that Anthony had written a lengthy series of articles exploring the relationship between the self-appointed Messiah's religious and corporate holdings and how they effected the news and editorial direction of the *Times*.

Effectively he was blacklisted.

It was verified when his friend Bill Lieby took him out for lunch. Lieby, also a foreign correspondent, bought him a beer, and told him the facts of life. The new owners of the *Post* weren't happy and they made it clear. In an industry where little loyalty existed, Anthony had still managed to cross a line by going public against his own newspaper.

After four months Anthony went back to the editors of the *Post* and asked what it would take to get back to work.

The answer was not a happy one, but it was one he accepted, because he needed to work. Anthony went back to work, but his punishment was ignominy. He would spend the next several months on the entertainment desk covering for a reporter out on maternity leave.

"It's a chance to expand your horizons," Bill had said.

"It's a chance for them to humiliate me," Anthony had replied.

So here he was, faced off with the manager of a rock band, when a year ago he'd been facing off dictators. He looked at her and gave a straight, direct answer.

"I'm in exile on the entertainment desk for six months. As punishment."

"You're not here to sneak information about the court-martial last summer?"

"I'm not. And that story has pretty much played itself out, I think. I won't lie. I find your sister Carrie infinitely more interesting than...Crank. No offense, that's just what I do."

"Carrie is off limits."

He shrugged. "Like I said, there's no story there, now. And my assignment is *Morbid Obesity's* new album. Though I would love to write about you and your growing little empire."

Julia grinned. "I'm just a believer in putting my assets to work. And...I might be willing to work with you on that. But if you touch Carrie, I'll put everything to work against you."

"Mrs. Wilson, you may be rich and run a big company, but even you can't take on the *Washington Post*."

She gave him a wicked grin then said, "Apparently, neither can you."

Anthony chuckled. "All right. Fine. Just let me get one question out of my system."

"I won't answer."

"Fine. Tell me about your sister's kidnapping."

"My official answer is *no comment.*"

"And your unofficial one?" he asked.

"*No comment.* In fact, I don't really know anything yet. I'm flying to Washington tomorrow afternoon. But she's in good hands with Carrie and our other sisters, for now. So, why don't we get started?"

Anthony nodded. "All right. So let me make sure I understand. Rules are, I can't ask about the kidnapping, or the court-martial. Are those the only restrictions?"

Julia raised an eyebrow. "That's it, but I may refuse to answer other questions as we hit them. And I want to know more about what angle you're pursuing with this piece."

"I don't know yet. But I don't want to just cover the album. Everything I've heard, you've been essential to the success of the band."

She shook her head. "Not exactly. Crank and Serena write the music, and they're magic on stage. That's where the success of the band comes from. What I do is logistics and run the business side of things. I make sure they're where they need to be when they need to be there. I make sure their investments keep growing, that the taxes are paid, and that the business keeps growing no matter what happens in the music industry."

"I'd like to start there. I want to know how you built this into such a big business. I want to know what makes *you* tick."

Julia sighed. "All right, then."

CHAPTER NINE
Change of plans

1. Julia. April 29

Julia Wilson couldn't decide what she thought of Anthony Walker.

Even though she was most often described in the media as either an "entertainment mogul" or occasionally simply as a "business savvy band manager," Julia's background was in international relations. She grew up around the Foreign Service, lived in half a dozen countries by the time she was eighteen, and had majored in international business at Harvard University. Her father—former Ambassador, now Secretary of Defense-designee—had been appalled when she chose to forego graduate school and the Foreign Service and instead take up managing her boyfriend's alternative rock band as a career. But Richard Thompson's objections had waned over the years as Crank's musical talent and Julia's business acumen built a multi-million dollar business.

In short, Julia followed international news, both foreign policy and business. She read the *Washington Post* and *New York Times* nearly every day, and consequently, Anthony Walker's name was very familiar to her. Both of his books—one covering the buildup to the Iraq War, and the other covering the savage Iraqi civil war of 2004–2006—sat on the shelves in her South Boston townhouse. She'd read with interest his editorials bashing the decision to sell the *Washington Post* in the summer of 2013. So it was with some trepidation that she'd agreed to this interview in the first place.

The phone call had come via the band's publicist, Mike De-Mint.

"This guy's the real deal," Mike said.

"I know who he is," Julia replied.

"I think you should talk to him."

"But what does he *want?*" Julia had asked. "He's not a celebrity reporter. The only thing I know that might interest him is my brother-in-law's murder. And there's no way in hell I'm talking about that."

"I'll set ground rules with him before the meeting."

"All right," she had agreed.

Now she sat across the desk from a reporter who she'd admired. And her main priority was to protect her sister Carrie, which meant keeping him interested in other things. She knew most people would react by simply ignoring him. Refusing to do the interview. Refusing to have any interaction with him at all. But Julia knew better. Anthony Walker might be in the doghouse with the *Washington Post*, but he remained one of the most celebrated reporters of their generation. If she refused to talk to him, he'd dig in their trash, spy on Ray's court-martial board, hire phone hackers, or God only knew what else.

Far better to keep him close.

"Okay, then," Anthony said. "Let's start with your background. I understand you're the oldest of six daughters?"

"That's right."

"Carrie—Ray Sherman's widow—is the next youngest?"

Julia's eyebrows narrowed in warning.

Anthony's next statement was defensive. "I'm not planning on doing a story about them, all right? But it's important context."

"She's a few years younger than me," she responded.

"Right. And she's a NIH researcher."

"I don't know all the details. She's doing work on infectious diseases and animal vectors."

"Okay. And the next youngest is…" Anthony's voice trailed off.

"Alexandra. She's graduating from Columbia next month."

"Okay. And then…the next two were twins?"

"Sarah and Jessica."

"Sarah was injured when Ray Sherman was murdered."

"Right."

Anthony continued. "And the youngest is Andrea, who is all over the news right now."

"Right," Julia said. "But, as we discussed, Andrea and what happened yesterday are off limits. And I don't know anything anyway."

He held up a hand. "It's fine. Tell me a little about your background."

"Well…I went to Harvard. Majored in international relations and business. My dad kind of wanted me to go into the Foreign Service."

"But you had other plans."

Julia nodded. "I met Crank. We got involved. The band needed a manager, and I needed a new direction. It was a good fit."

"So you took on managing the band."

As he asked questions, he scribbled notes in his pocket notebook. She didn't know exactly what he was writing, but it was *loud*, the point of the pen digging into the paper.

"I did. And never looked back."

Anthony looked up at the last words. His expression, eyes widened slightly, seemed to register surprise. "Tell me why?" he asked.

She shrugged. "Not many people get to build a huge enterprise from the ground up. Every dollar we made in the first three years got reinvested into the band. Into promotion. Better instruments. Honing their skills. We got out there on MySpace when it was brand new and built a major following. The band worked hard, I worked hard. I love this work."

"You started buying unrelated businesses in 2007."

She snorted. "If Crank had his way, I'd have just bought more and more expensive guitars. But this is a big business. We started going into commercial real estate, medical devices, software. My goal was to diversify the business so it could survive anything."

The truth was, there was a lot more to it than that. Her goal wasn't to build stability, or to prove her hand at business, or to diversify the band, or anything so pedestrian. Her goal was to erase the stain of shame her mother stamped on her heart at fourteen years old. Her goal was to use the band, the business, to create wings of success that would carry her out of the abyss of her mother's abhorrence.

In the end, she'd been successful beyond her wildest dreams. Successful enough to eclipse her father's impressive (but inherited) fortune. Richard Thompson knew how to spend money. Julia knew how to *make* it.

But sometime around the time she turned thirty, she realized it was all emptiness. She'd looked around in the fall of 2012, ten years after she and Crank fell in love. In those ten years she'd made millionaires of the band several times over. She'd built a large international business. She'd far surpassed he ambitions of her parents. But it hadn't made any difference. She still felt empty inside sometimes at night when she thought of the things her mother had once said to her. She still felt like she wasn't good enough. Sometimes she still felt like that eighteen-year-old girl sneaking through the halls of Bethesda Chevy-Chase High School as the word *slut* hung in the air, pregnant with contempt.

As Anthony finished taking his notes, she tried to steer the conversation away. But he promptly said, "I'd like to go back a bit. And you can tell me to buzz off if you want. This is old news, and it's not necessarily germane to the story, and if you don't want it mentioned, then I won't mention it. Okay?"

She felt a chill as he spoke. Because she knew what he was about to say.

"When I was doing background research on the story, I came across the series of blog posts by Maria Clawson."

2. Bear. April 29

"**I**n my office. Now."

That was unambiguous. Bear hadn't made it back to his desk yet after returning to Main State from the five-sided puzzle palace across the river. As he walked through the double doors into the Diplomatic Security suite, signed in with the guard, and swiped his access card at the inner doors, Tom Cantwell appeared on the other side of the door.

Bear followed Cantwell into the large corner office. Facing 23rd and C Street, Cantwell's fourth floor office was prime real estate in the State Department headquarters. From the window, the United States Institute of Peace—underfunded, largely useless in terms of real policy—occupied its brand new building overlooking the Lincoln Memorial on one side and the Kennedy Center on the other. Bear would have loved an office like this, but he knew he'd never occupy it.

Cantwell's face was red, and his eye had a slight twitch. He didn't sit down, instead walking around to the far side of his excessively large desk and turning to face Bear. He took a breath and stared, opened his mouth, then closed it.

Finally, he said, "Have you lost your mind?"

Bear blinked. "I don't believe so, sir."

The response, apparently, wasn't what Cantwell wanted to hear. He slammed a bony little fist on his desk and said, "Mr. Wyden, please explain why you had to be escorted out of the Secretary of Defense's office by armed guards!"

"He didn't want to answer questions about—" Bear didn't get a chance to finish the sentence. The door opened, and Mary Bradley, Cantwell's administrative assistant stuck her head inside.

"Sir? The Secretary wants to see...both of you."

Bear grimaced. He met Mary's eyes. They were baleful, wide, sympathetic. That lasted less than a second, and then she looked back to her boss, expressionless.

For the hundredth time, Bear thought Mary just might accept a dinner invitation. She was unattached, always polite, and she'd given him her phone number a year before.

A year ago he was still wound up tight in his divorce, and not ready to even talk with another woman.

Now was not the time for this internal discussion. Cantwell's mouth puckered up as if he'd just drunk spoiled milk. "Well, then, Mr. Wyden. It's on your head. We're going to see Mr. Perry, and there's nothing I can do to help you now."

Well, then, Bear thought. He'd known intuitively that Cantwell was a spineless weasel, but having it proved under this circumstance was unfortunate.

Silently, Bear followed Cantwell down the wide hallways to the bank of elevators.

At the elevator, Bear reached for the button at the same moment Cantwell did. Cantwell jerked his hand back, an annoyed expression on his face. Bear pushed the up button.

"I would appreciate it if you would remain quiet unless asked a direct question."

Bear raised an eyebrow. Then he said, "I presume we're being asked to see the Secretary to deal with my questioning of the Secretary of Defense?"

Cantwell was, for the first time in Bear's experience, speechless. The elevator doors opened, eliminating the need for Bear to talk with his boss for a few seconds, at least.

As he turned around, facing the elevator door, two other people walked into the elevator behind them. Good thing because it delayed, for a little while, open warfare with his boss.

Five minutes later, Bear walked behind Cantwell into the expansive office of the Secretary of State.

Bear had never been in the office. Wide paneled hardwood floors stained a deep reddish brown, stretched across the spacious office. Most of the office was white, with elegant wainscoting, detailed molding and lavish Persian carpets. The room smelled of expensive cigars, gin and privilege. Forty feet away, Secretary of State James Perry sat behind his desk, talking on the phone. He looked up at their entry and waved them toward an ornate couch, covered in sky-blue fabric and gold brocade. Bear followed Cantwell toward the couch. As they reached it, Secretary Perry hung up the phone and stood.

As he approached, Bear's first impression of the man was shock at how very tall he was. At six feet, Bear wasn't short. But the Secretary of State towered over him in his dark blue suit and red tie. His face was gaunt; hollow cheeks below sunken eyes and jowls suggestive of decades of sleep deprivation. Even though the Secretary was a Democrat, Bear had considerable respect for the man who, prior to his career in the Senate and now the State department, had once commanded naval riverboats in the Mekong Delta.

"James Perry," the Secretary said in a bold voice as he approached. He held out a hand toward Bear.

"Bear Wyden, sir," Bear replied. Perry had a confident handshake. Dry and firm, but he didn't engage in a squeezing contest like many less confident men.

Perry nodded toward Cantwell. It wasn't friendly. "Mr. Cantwell."

Cantwell swallowed. "Mr. Secretary."

"Please have a seat, both of you."

Bear took a seat to Cantwell's left on the couch. Secretary Perry sat on a similarly appointed red chair, oriented perpendicularly to the couch.

"I'll get to the point, gentlemen. I had an...unfortunate phone call from the Secretary of Defense this afternoon."

Cantwell literally squirmed in his seat and began speaking in a hurry. "Sir, my sincere apologies. I'm afraid our investigator may have gotten a little bit ahead of himself this afternoon—"

Secretary Perry narrowed his eyes at Cantwell's torrent of words, then held up a hand and cut him off. "Mr. Cantwell, that won't be necessary."

"Sir, if I could clarify."

Perry leaned forward in his seat, just slightly. "I'd prefer you didn't."

Holy shit. Bear was stunned by the exchange. If anything was clear, it was that Perry did not like Cantwell at all. Of course, now that he thought about it, it didn't surprise him that much. Cantwell was brought in after the wholesale and somewhat random firing of top DSS personnel by Secretary Clinton as a result of the deaths in Benghazi. Bear didn't like him either.

Perry turned his attention to Bear. "Perhaps you could explain the direction of your investigation at this point."

Bear coughed a little then said, "Sir, I was asked to take charge of the investigation late last night. Joyce Brown is coordinating the team and I'm lead investigator."

Perry nodded. "Go on."

Bear described his trip to the hospital the previous night and his discussions with the Thompson daughters, and his visit today with Richard Thompson.

"At this point sir, we're still trying to establish the identity of our second kidnapper. I'm particularly concerned because we've run DNA and fingerprints and not established his identity. Nothing. But based on Andrea Thompson's description, he had a clear Midwestern United States accent. Corn husker. There should be some record of this guy. So I went over to the Pentagon to interview the father."

Perry leaned a little, resting his gangly right arm on the arm of his chair, rangy fingers covering his chin.

"I may have been a little aggressive in my questioning, sir."

The Secretary's fingers shifted to cover his mouth. Bear coughed, then continued. "Anyway, sir. I'll be blunt. I'm concerned. Secretary Thompson...did not react like a concerned father. He didn't meet his daughter at the hospital. He didn't pick her up. He didn't stay home with her today. He's spent all of ten minutes with his sixteen-year-old daughter on the day when she was kidnapped by at least one known mercenary. Something is seriously wrong there, sir."

Perry nodded. Then he said, "You're aware Acting Secretary Thompson has been nominated by the President of the United States."

Bear froze a little at the words. Cantwell, the little weasel, chimed in. "Sir, Mr. Wyden's opinions are not the official opinions of this investigation. In fact, I'm questioning—"

"That will be enough, Mr. Cantwell. You may go."

"Excuse me, sir?" Cantwell looked stunned.

"You heard me, sir. But please, let me clarify. I don't wish to hear another word out of you, and I would strongly urge you to start polishing your resume, because your time in this department just became limited. If there is anything I learned about leadership in Vietnam, it's that leaders don't throw their subordinates into the line of fire."

Bear sat up in his seat. All the blood had run out of Cantwell's face, leaving him looking like a pasty-faced reflection of his already pale face.

Cantwell stood, tugging on his jacket and his dignity. "Sir, I hope you will reconsider, I'm merely looking out for the interests of the Department and Diplomatic Security."

"You may go," Perry said.

Cantwell left in a hurry. Bear held his breath.

Perry looked closely at Bear. "Mr. Wyden...Bear. May I call you Bear?"

Letting a breath loose again, he replied, "Yes sir."

"Bear. I'm aware of your suspicions and concerns about Secretary Thompson."

Bear blinked. "You *are?*"

Perry stood and walked to his desk. Then he picked up an inch-thick brown envelope. He laid it on the table.

The envelope was labeled, TOP SECRET-COMPARTMEN-TALIZED. Below that, in bold letters, PERSONNEL FILE/ CLASSIFIED. Handwritten below that, *R. Thompson. FN 542-1342.*

"You'll need to sign for this. Sign along the flap and tear it off. This is a numbered copy. And it will answer some of your questions. Once you've read it, I want you to go see Senator Rainsley."

If a lightning bolt had struck Secretary Perry in his office, Bear wouldn't have been more surprised. "Excuse me, sir?"

Perry handed the file over. "Read it. Go see Senator Rainsley. Get your investigation underway, Bear. And don't cross paths with Richard Thompson again. If you need answers from him, call my secretary and come see me. Am I clear? There are things you don't know."

Bear held up the file. "Are the answers in here?"

Perry raised his eyebrows. Then he said, "No. But maybe it's a step in the right direction."

3. Julia. April 29

"**W**hen *I was doing background research on the story, I came across the series of blog posts by Maria Clawson.*"

When Anthony said the words, Julia immediately interrupted. "I'm familiar with them. That was before she was sued for libel."

Anthony nodded. "I'm aware of that. And again, I don't want you to throw me out. But given the stuff she published about you... there had to have been some fallout. From what I understand, that was the reason Senator Rainsley put a hold on your father's appointment as Ambassador to Russia."

Julia grasped the edge of her desk, forcing herself to not stand up and march out of the room. This was all ancient history. But she knew the moment the President announced her father's nomination that it would come up. It was inevitable. He'd been nominated as head of the largest department of the United States government, in charge of trillions of dollars of assets, hundreds of thousands of people and responsibility for defense of the United States. The Senate, and the media, would be all over it.

Senator Rainsley was still in office, and he was the senior Republican on the Senate Armed Services Committee, which meant he would be in the lead with questioning and objections to her father's nomination. For the second time in her father's career, he'd be faced off with Senator Rainsley, and she couldn't help having the sinking feeling that her own past would have some bearing on what happened next.

She needed an ally, quickly. Regardless of what happened with her father's nomination, she didn't need an old scandal dragging her through the mud. Plenty of bad stuff had been written in the press about her and Crank before, but that, at least, hadn't come up in years. She didn't need it to start.

"Yes," she finally said. "It *was* Senator Rainsley who put the nomination on hold. He never stated a reason why."

"But Maria Clawson spread it far and wide that it had something to do with you."

"Not exactly," Julia replied. "I wasn't even eighteen at the time. She never printed my name."

His response made her stomach twist. "She did publish a photograph."

Her response came out in a hiss. "She did. A photograph that would probably land her in jail for child pornography if she ran it today."

Anthony nodded. "That must have been tough for you."

"Tough isn't the word, Mr. Walker. I went through some very difficult times in high school. Not the party girl Maria Clawson implied, but someone who was ill-used by a much older boy. Clawson's blog ruined my life. I know you've heard all about online bullying these days. We didn't have Facebook back then, but having a national gossip columnist attack you day after day when you're still a teenager...I ended up attempting suicide."

Anthony winced. A hint of both anger and empathy in his voice, he said, "Are you fucking serious?"

"I was a teenager. I wasn't equipped to deal with that back then."

He nodded. Then he said, "You know, I talked with Sylvia Drake. She told me you funded her lawsuit."

Julia nodded. And then she smiled. Because she remembered Sylvia Drake.

Sylvia was a 19-year-old nursing student when she was raped on campus following a football game at the University of Alabama. The suspect? A 21-year-old football player. When Sylvia went on record with her accusation, the vultures descended. Radio commentators and sports newscasters publicly speculated she was aiming for a big financial settlement from Alabama. Bloggers and newscasters alike lambasted her, but an old enemy of Julia's led the charge: Maria Clawson, whose society blog was still the terror of Washington, DC.

Julia took the opportunity to settle an old score. She discreetly donated a quarter of a million dollars to fund Sylvia Drake's lawsuit against Maria Clawson. The result? Clawson went down in personal bankruptcy and shut down the longest running gossip blog on the Internet. Julia counted that as a victory well worth winning.

"Yes," she told Anthony now. "I funded it. I'd do it again, too. Maria Clawson is a snake who makes her living off destroying other people's lives."

"Was," Anthony replied. "She mostly makes her living fending off lawsuits now."

Julia raised her eyebrows and shrugged. She knew she shouldn't be so smug about it, even as her lips curled up in a satisfied half-smile. Her youngest sister Andrea wouldn't have hesitated to lecture her about the need to keep forgiveness in her heart.

It was a lot easier to forgive someone when they no longer represented a threat.

Her phone, laying face down on the desk, rang, vibrating on the desk. She reached forward and flipped it over. A photograph of one of her sisters in the New York City Clerk's office in the arms of a tall Army sergeant in dress blues appeared on the screen of her phone, underneath the name "Carrie."

She picked up the phone. "I have to take this, sorry."

Anthony sat back, a little annoyed. She didn't care. She unlocked the phone and said, "Hello? Carrie?" As she spoke the words, she stood and walked to the window, looking outside and keeping her back to Anthony.

"Julia? Hey, you! It's not just me...I've got Alexandra and Sarah and Andrea here too."

Julia closed her eyes. She badly wanted to be in Washington with her sisters. She'd left a message that morning on Jessica's cell phone, and on her mother's, inviting them to fly east with her. If Jessica flew east with her, it would be the first time the six of them were in the same room since the summer of 2013. All of them were present for Carrie and Alexandra's weddings, but there'd been little opportunity to talk. And technically all of them were in the same city in August after the accident, but Sarah had been hospitalized and Carrie utterly devastated by the loss of her husband.

Julia badly wanted to bring her sisters together. If nothing else, so they could wrap their arms around Carrie and Andrea and love them.

"Julia, listen, when are you planning to fly to DC. Still tomorrow?"

"Yes, tomorrow afternoon was the plan. Though if necessary we can leave in the morning." As she said the words, she studied Anthony's pale reflection in the window. He shifted uncomfortably at the words they might be leaving early. Interesting, she thought. He badly wanted a story with some meat here. She was considering giving it to him, in a way that would keep a grip on the inevitable release of her own secrets and also protect her sisters.

"Well..."

Julia frowned at the long pause.

Finally, Carrie spoke again. "We're worried about Jessica. And Mom. Neither of them have answered their phones in days."

"Well, of course they have," Julia said impatiently. "I just spoke with Mother on...oh. Friday."

She'd spoken with her mother right before lunch. They spoke *every* Friday. It hadn't always been the case. From 2002 until 2005, she'd barely spoken at all with her mother. Holidays and birthdays, and not always even then. But all that time, the thought kept percolating in her head. A statement really, made by Crank's brother Sean after the first time he met her mother. *She loves you,* Sean had said a few days later, when Sean, Carrie, Crank and Julia were in Washington, DC. Followed by the completely inexplicable statement, *She has secrets.*

Carrie hadn't been willing to accept his answer and demanded clarification.

"Come on, Sean," Carrie needled. *"There has to be something behind what you said. Some evidence? Anything?"*

He sat up. *"They never touched each other. Or even looked at each other."*

"Who?" Carrie replied.

"Your parents."

And of course, when Julia thought it through later, Sean was exactly right. *She* couldn't remember her parents touching. At least only on the rarest of occasions, when she was very young. She had few memories of her early childhood, but some of the earliest were of eating meals with both of her parents when Carrie was still a baby. But even then, they'd never been affectionate with each other.

In any event, Sean's comment had worn on her mind, an ongoing nagging worry.

Finally, in 2005, she'd called her mother and invited herself to San Francisco for a week. A week she and her mother spent together. Talking. In a few cases, *screaming* at each other.

Adelina Thompson never divulged her secrets, but Julia came away from that week believing Sean was right. More importantly, she came away from that week believing in forgiveness. She didn't have it yet. She hadn't forgiven her mother, nor forgotten those horrible years in China and right after. But she at least believed it might be *possible*.

Since that week, they'd talked on the phone every single week without fail, with only two exceptions. The first, the week of March 11, 2011. *Morbid Obesity* was in Tokyo for a concert when a tsunami hit the coast of Japan, wiping out entire towns and setting off a nuclear disaster. For several days power in the country was unreliable, along with cell service. For the first few days after the disaster, air travel was also disrupted, and they'd been unable to get clearance to depart until five days after the tsunami. She hadn't spoken with her mother that week.

The second time was the week after Ray Sherman died. For the first time in their lives, Adelina Thompson went into overdrive as a mother, taking care of Carrie and Sarah at a time when both of them needed her. All of the sisters were stunned, most of all Julia, who had borne the brunt of her mother's bizarre behavior over the years.

Those weekly Friday calls had become a mainstay of their relationship. Sometimes she and her mother went through periods of hostility, sometimes through periods where they were cold; but no matter what, they spoke. No matter what.

This past Friday's call had been normal. Julia talked with her about the new album and the process of getting it recorded. They talked about Carrie's week-old baby Rachel, and the diagnosis, which had come as a shock to all of them. Julia had made the arrangements for Andrea's flight to Washington.

Mother and Jessica were supposed to fly east on Wednesday morning. Julia had taken that for granted, until now.

"When was the last time you talked with her?" she asked Carrie.

"A...a week ago?"

Julia made a snap decision. "I'll fly to San Francisco in the morning. But I think we need to consider having someone local go take a look." She held the phone away from her head. "It's almost 5 o'clock...let me see if I can get Bill Lemke to go take a look, just to see if they're home and not answering the phone or whatever."

Sarah, still on the speakerphone, said, "Dad said Mom was taking Jessica off to some religious retreat."

Julia scrunched her eyebrows. Their mother was a devout Catholic, but this seemed...out of character. "I'm not sure I buy that. Either way, I'll check it out in the morning."

They ended the conversation, and she turned her attention back to Anthony Walker. For just a second she studied him. Trying to decide. Could she trust him? The idea of trusting a reporter struck her as foolhardy.

Something told her this was the time.

"Anthony, I've got a chance of plans. I have to fly to San Francisco in the morning then back to Washington, DC. If you want to pursue this, you'll have to fly with us."

"Commercial?"

"No, we've got a jet. You travel as much as we do, it starts to make sense."

"I'm in."

Part Two

CHAPTER TEN
Something weird going on

1. Leslie Collins. April 29. 5:50 pm

Six pm in downtown Washington and traffic was predictably snarled. Leslie Collins sat in the back of a large Chevy Suburban, papers spread across the folding worktable. The SUV was still new, the smell of leather and bulletproof glass. His driver laid on the horn and said, "You want me to go to lights and sirens, sir?"

Leslie Collins looked at his watch, an antique wind-up aviator's watch with a badly scratched glass cover. "Yes, we need to be there in twenty minutes." Even with the flashing lights and sirens it might take another fifteen minutes to navigate to their destination. Collins sometimes thought that certain roads in Washington needed to be reserved for official traffic.

Inside his jacket pocket, he felt his phone buzzing. He reached in and pulled the phone out.

Mitch Filner.

About time. Collins answered the phone brusquely.

"What is it?"

Filner, as always, sounded out of breath. "Calling to report on progress."

The large black Chevy Suburban inched forward in the traffic. The driver leaned forward, gesticulating at what looked to be a thirty-year old lobbyist at the wheel of a Cooper Mini who blocked the intersection at Massachusetts and 30th. Amazing that poor excuse for a car, which could fit in the cargo space of the Suburban, could block three lanes of traffic. The driver jerked back from the noise of the Suburban's siren and horn.

Seconds later the Mini unsnarled itself and traffic began to flow again. For a block or two.

"All right. Go."

Filner coughed in the phone. Bastard needed to quit smoking and maybe he wouldn't sound like such an invalid. "Okay, first of all, the family here in Washington has Diplomatic Security protection now. Three uniformed officers at the Bethesda condo at all times. Secretary Thompson also has protection, but not DSS—his are private contractors."

"Is Thompson still living by himself?"

"Base housing at Fort Myers. From what I understand, he booted some two-star out of his house."

Collins shook his head. "That'll make him popular with the troops."

"Yeah, well, bottom line is, I don't have any assets close to him."

Collins looked to his left. Across the street was the *Islamic Center*. Built of white stone with an ochre tiled roof and crenellations along the top wall, the building had a minaret. A fucking minaret, in Washington DC, fifteen blocks from the White House. Letters in blue lined Arabic covered the front of the building in a line about five archways into an interior courtyard. The entire building, a remarkable piece of architecture if it had been in Cairo or Baghdad, was a giant middle finger erected against the American people. Luckily for the inhabitants, the building had an eight-foot cast iron fence surrounding it.

He focused his attention back on the moment. "What about the daughters?"

"One of the DSS agents is ours," Filner replied.

"All right. Keep them in place, but don't *do* anything yet."

"Right. As I understand it, the sisters here in DC are headed out to a restaurant shortly. Our agent is with the escort."

2. Andrea. April 29. 6:00 pm

"**I**'m ready," Andrea said, walking back into the living room. All of her clothes—along with her phone and laptop—were still in the custody of the police. Luckily, Carrie had lent her a dress, linen with a blue herringbone pattern. It wasn't something Andrea would have chosen to wear on her own—Carrie was a bit too fashionable for her taste—but it fit her.

"Ready?" It was Leah Simpson. Like the others in the security detail, she'd changed from her semi-uniform into nondescript civilian clothing, in her case jeans and a sweater that was probably too heavy for the April weather. It was just heavy enough to cover her sidearm, which was no longer visible at her hip. Her blonde hair, previously tied up in a simple ponytail, was now braided. It looked professional, but not the sort of thing you would wear out on the town.

Sarah and Alexandra were playing gin at the kitchen table, and Dylan stood on the porch smoking again. Carrie was in the nursery giving instructions to her nanny.

"I'm ready," Andrea said. "But it looks like I'm the only one."

Sarah smirked. "Soon as Carrie comes out we can go. Everything takes twice as long when you've got a baby."

Andrea shrugged. She wasn't planning on having any babies. She looked at Leah.

"You're coming with us?"

Leah nodded. "For the foreseeable future, you'll have a Diplomatic Security escort wherever you go."

"When do you go home to your family?" Andrea asked.

"We'll have a rotation in place by late tonight. But my primary concern is your safety."

She sounded like a robot. Andrea thought that Leah Simpson's primary concern was probably her family, her own safety, her career first. Which was completely normal. She didn't particularly care for misdirection.

"Are you married?" Andrea asked.

Leah raised an eyebrow. "I am."

"Kids?"

"Two." She smiled, then slid a well-worn men's wallet out of her pocket. She opened it up. "My son Jim and my daughter Rebecca."

The boy in the photo was four years old or so. If she was completely objective, Andrea thought the boy was pretty ugly. He had too small eyes and a pug nose and uneven teeth that only a mother could love. But the thing was, his mother obviously *did* love him. And that mattered more than anything. Beside him in the photo was a younger girl, maybe two years old. She wore a yellow and red Washington Redskins cheerleading outfit, complete with pompoms and an Indian head logo on the skirt.

Andrea smiled. Then she said, "I think your *first* priority is them."

Leah returned the smile. "True. But your safety is my professional responsibility, and I take that seriously. Jim and Rebecca are with their step-dad tonight. Once we get you settled we'll be on a fairly normal routine."

Andrea nodded. "You...it must be kind of scary, doing this for a living. When you have kids."

Leah shook her head. "Most of the time I do paperwork and stand around. Or we provide security details for boring old dowager countesses."

Sarah and Alexandra looked up, and Sarah stood as Carrie walked into the room. She'd changed into a knee length pleated dress, dark purple with brass buttons down the chest and flat sandals.

"Sorry about that," Carrie said. "Rachel's asleep. Why don't we get going?"

3. Bear. April 29. 6:03 pm

The studio apartment was simple. At three hundred square feet, Bear had enough room for a twin bed, a tiny couch and television, a kitchen table that doubled as a desk, and a small dresser containing most of his clothes. He owned little else.

The folder on his kitchen table, next to the laptop, was a serious enough security violation that he could expect a reprimand in his file if it was discovered. Not because he had it—after all, the Secretary of State himself handed him the file. But the fact that it was on his kitchen table, instead of secured at the office, was a problem. The tall glass of bourbon and Coke next to it also presented a problem, though not as serious as the bringing of classified documents home.

Regardless, he sat down at the table and took a sip of his drink. He felt the pungent liquor slide down his throat and breathed a sigh of relief. Bear was glad he hadn't stayed in the office, where Tom Cantwell was undoubtedly scheming to bring an end to Bear's career.

Sometimes Bear was ready to pack it in anyway. His career hadn't been perfect, but it had been solid, marked by steady promotions and steps up in seniority. But the further he moved up the ladder, the more political his job became. Sometimes it paid to keep your nose down, do your job and not get noticed.

He sighed. Then broke the seal on the envelope and slid the documents out of it.

The first document at the top of a small stack was an application for federal employment. This was a copy of course, showing the original document filled out in 1973. Richard Isaiah Thompson. Born in San Francisco, California, April 23, 1949. Attended Exeter Academy, followed by Harvard University. Exeter, of course, was an exclusive boys' preparatory school on the East Coast, far from his birthplace.

Bear began to make notes. Because the first question had already been raised. Thompson graduated from Harvard in 1971. What did he do the two years in between graduation and applying to work at State? Nothing in the personal file gave a clue, and the application itself was oddly pro forma. Not everything was filled out on the application, but the cover letter was clear enough. In May 1973, Thompson had enough pull to get a personal recommendation from then National Security Advisor Henry Kissinger. No wonder he hadn't filled out the entire application. He didn't need to.

Bear let his mind wander, not entirely focused on the file, letting his eyes scan over the documents as he free-associated.

Behind the federal application for employment was his initial security investigation, marked SECRET and never declassified. Bear began to page through it. Interviews with his college professors and fellow students were included. One interview with his father, Cyrus Thompson.

Still nothing in the file regarding the years from his college graduation in 1971 to his beginning of employment at State in 1973. It made no sense at all. His eyebrows began to work uncontrollably, a line appearing down his forehead. He took another drink, then scanned through the background investigation again.

Thompson was granted top-secret clearance based on a report which including *nothing* of the last two years of his life. It made no sense at all. None.

The phone rang. Bear jerked in his seat, then glanced at the phone and picked it up.

"Bear."

"Bear, it's Leah."

He winced. But he kept his tone professional, as always. "Hey, Leah. What's the low-down?"

"We're en route with the Thompson sisters to Benihanas in Bethesda. But there's something weird going on."

"What?"

"Bear, I think someone has the sisters under surveillance. And it's professional."

Crap. Who? "Professional. You mean like intelligence professionals?"

"I don't know. I haven't pinned it down yet."

Bear turned the report to the last page and froze. He narrowed his eyebrows, for just a second tuning out Leah.

Richard Thompson's background investigation was signed by William Colby.

He shook his head. That didn't make any sense. Diplomatic Security Services conducted the background investigations for State Department personnel.

William Colby, in 1973, was director of covert operations for the Central Intelligence Agency. In September of the same year he took over as Director of Central Intelligence, just a few weeks before Kissinger took over the State Department.

"Bear?"

"I'm here."

"What do you want us to do?"

Bear's heart was thumping. Richard Thompson...suddenly he began to wonder. What was Thompson doing from 1971 to 1973? And why had Henry Kissinger, then the National Security Advisor, written a letter of recommendation for him? Why had a CIA official signed off on his background investigation?

Was Thompson originally CIA? Was he still?

"Bear?" Leah sounded impatient.

"Sorry!" he shouted into the phone. "Listen. Keep an eye out. Don't approach or attempt to apprehend the followers, all right? Don't let them know you've seen them. Try to get pictures. I want to know who the hell they are. Understand?"

"There's only three of us here. We're going to need more backup."

"All right," he said. Yeah. If he was right, backup might be needed right away. "Let me make some calls."

4. Leslie Collins. April 29. 6:16 pm

Collins answered the phone again, annoyed this time. They were now two blocks away from his destination. The downtown traffic along Pennsylvania Avenue was a nightmare and he was tempted to just get out and walk.

"What?" Collins said.

It was Filner. Of course.

"Sir, we've got a problem."

"What is it?"

"The Thompson Sisters...they've got a tail."

"Your people, right?"

"No, sir. I've got two teams following them. But we've got more followers. I'm certain it's surveillance."

Collins rolled his eyes. "Who is it? The Saudis?"

"No. British, maybe."

Collins was angry now. "Give me some goddamn detail, Filner!"

"Sir. Right now the Thompson family...or four of the sisters, plus one of their husbands, are walking together down Bethesda Avenue. They're accompanied by three DSS agents in plain clothes. I've got a positive ID on all three agents. One of them works for us too."

"Okay..."

"We've also got two men, following on the other side of the street."

"You're certain they aren't just pedestrians?"

"Yeah."

"Our guys are anonymous? Run off the pursuers. Then fill me in later. I can't talk on the phone any more."

"What the fuck are you talking about, Collins? You can't stop talking to me *right now*." Filner's voice had an edge.

"Use your best judgment," Collins replied. Some things superseded even a crisis. This meeting was one of them.

The uniformed secret service agent at the gate of 1600 Pennsylvania Avenue approached the Suburban as it rolled to a stop. Collins' driver leaned out to speak with him and displayed ID.

"I'm going into a meeting that can't be interrupted," Collins said, his eyes on the White House.

"Go ahead to the West entrance, sir," the secret service guard said.

Collins' driver pulled forward onto the grounds.

5. Dylan. April 29. 6:16 pm

Dylan Paris had been walking slightly behind the four sisters. Something had set him on edge, and even though they were only walking four blocks to the restaurant, he felt as naked as if he were on patrol in Fayzabad again. A cold breeze, just a slight remnant of winter, blew up the street as they turned onto Norfolk Avenue. The restaurant was two blocks away. It was a few minutes before six-thirty, and the sky was just beginning to dim. Full sunset wouldn't be for another hour.

He scanned the street again. Across from them and slightly behind, two men were walking. Normally it wouldn't have bothered Dylan, but one of them kept eyeing the sisters. Too many times for comfort. Both of them wore nondescript grey suits and one of them spoke on a telephone. Of course the street was crowded with other people: workers leaving their offices, a few scattered soldiers from Walter Reed, men and women headed to rendezvous and happy hours.

He turned and walked backward for a second. He caught Leah Simpson's eye and discreetly pointed toward the men across the street.

She nodded. "Already on it," she said in a conversational tone. "We need to get you guys inside. But slowly. Let's not alert them, all right?"

"Alert who?" Alexandra asked.

The other sisters stalled, and Dylan spoke in a low, even and tense voice, "Keep walking, relax. Don't. Panic. Andrea, can you tell us something funny? Have any good stories?"

Andrea looked frightened for just a moment, and Dylan thought she wasn't going to be able to hold up. But she clenched a fist and began speaking. Her voice started out shaky.

"When I was fourteen, Uncle Luis took me to Rome. That week changed my life. Abuelita always took me to church. But it was different. Rome was *different*."

She paused for just a second. They kept walking as she tried to formulate her words. Dylan found himself scanning everyone on the street. A man in a t-shirt and jeans stood in the doorway of a shuttered Thai restaurant near the Starbucks. He was smoking a cigarette and talking on a phone, running his left hand across the stubble of a buzz cut. Was he a potential kidnapper? Who was it that went after Andrea in the first place? Why were the guys across the street following them? Or were they, even? Maybe they were just checking out the four Thompson sisters—all of them highly attractive—across the street. After all, they stood out. Andrea and Carrie were both six plus feet tall, and Sarah had those bizarre black markings outlining her scars. And Alex...Alex was still the most beautiful thing he'd ever seen in his life.

And right now, Alex and her sisters were potentially in danger. Without even realizing it, Dylan was walking and thinking like a soldier again. Despite his injuries more than two years before, despite the fact that he was long out of the military, now he walked along, his eyes scanning everywhere, ready to act, ready to *move*, when he saw it coming.

Andrea was still speaking. "When I looked up at the ceiling in the chapel...you can't believe how beautiful it is. This was the work...the work people built to raise up to God. To praise him." As she spoke, the enthusiasm clearly shone through her words. This wasn't just a story—she believed in what she was talking about.

The two men across the street. One of them broke off, approaching the guy in the doorway with the buzz cut and the phone.

Buzzcut dropped his phone. He didn't close it, or switch it off—he just dropped it. And his hands kept moving.

Without a moment's thought, Dylan shouted, "Get *down*," then grabbed Alex and Carrie's arms, pulling them low behind a car parallel parked beside the street. Leah Simpson did the same with Sarah and Andrea. As Dylan lowered himself behind the car, Buzz-cut appeared to drive something into the stomach of the approaching man.

Gunshots rang out.

CHAPTER ELEVEN
He's down, isn't he?

1. Bear. April 29. 6:17 ppm

Bear Wyden hung up the phone. Tension filled his body, a need to get up and move. After Leah's call, he'd immediately contacted the DSS offices and dispatched additional agents to Bethesda. But it was highly unlikely they would have anyone on site in time to affect the situation. Whatever the situation was.

Right now he had to wait.

He didn't want to fucking wait. Bear was a cop, not a desk jockey. And that was his ex-wife out there. And whether he liked it or not, he had to sit here and wait. He needed to calm down and focus, not go charging into the situation.

So he turned back to the Richard Thompson file, with new questions. Was Thompson CIA? Or had he been? Had his work at State somehow been cover for something else? He'd retired from the Foreign Service twelve years before. So it seemed likely that he was pursuing a dead end looking through ancient documents, when the most likely reason for all this attention was his appointment as Secretary of Defense.

On the other hand...Secretary Perry had personally handed him these documents. And he wasn't known for doing things on a whim.

So he reviewed the file and immediately saw an unusual pattern.

In Indonesia, Richard Thompson was detailed as a protocol officer for five years—an exceptionally long assignment. Then he was back at Main State for three years, followed by an assignment to Spain that barely lasted eleven months. That was highly unusual, but might be related to the fact that he'd apparently met and married a woman there.

A quick review of her file from 1981 revealed nothing terribly interesting. Adelina Ramos was young when they got married, the daughter of a florist in Madrid.

Thompson had no performance evaluation for his posting to Spain. The next move in his career was a surprise, given that he had a new wife and child. In 1982 he was posted to Pakistan. For... slightly less than two years.

Bear rubbed his forehead. He'd reviewed a lot of personnel files over the years. And he'd almost never seen a pattern like this. Foreign Service assignments were typically three years, exactly. But it fit the theory that Thompson was CIA. During the early 80s, the US Embassy in Pakistan had more intelligence officers than diplomats. Which meant he probably spent most of his time off doing classified work in Afghanistan or God only knew where else. Those years were some of the bloodiest following the Soviet invasion of Afghanistan.

He thought back to the early 90s, when he knew the Thompson family. Ironic that Richard Thompson hadn't recognized Bear, but not that surprising given what he knew about the character of the man. In 1992 Richard Thompson had been a remote figure: arrogant and dismissive. He'd been argumentative too, insisting he knew more about the security arrangements than was normal for diplomats. His wife had been a pain in the ass too, but in a different way, demanding to know intimate details of the security operation. She struck Bear as anxiety prone, worried unnecessarily about details far beyond her purview.

He remembered the oldest daughter, Julia. At the time she was ten years old. Curly brown hair. The loneliest little girl he'd ever seen. When he made the security arrangements, he'd assigned the youngest Marine in the detail to her. The two became fiercely attached, and Bear remembered all too well seeing her tagging along around the Embassy with him, usually in the garage where he'd somehow wrangled the space for three classic cars that he was always working on when off duty. It was an embarrassing waste of manpower to have a US Marine effectively babysitting a ten-year-old girl, but it was also important. The younger daughter, Carrie, also had her own guard.

When the assignment started, Adelina Thompson had insisted on interviewing the personal guards, an hour long ordeal for each of them that left the Marines sweating. She might have been a tiny, young and inexperienced woman, but she'd been fiercely protective of her daughters and made sure the bodyguards knew it.

In retrospect, it was interesting. The order to provide a protective detail to Thompson's family had come from Main State, but Bear couldn't recall the circumstances. It wasn't exactly normal, and Leah had asked him about it. Years before their marriage, she'd been assigned to the protective detail. It was unusual enough she'd asked about it. *Orders from Washington.*

She'd been right to wonder. Security details were routine, but dedicated security details for a specific family? That was unusual indeed. He made a note to look into it.

The phone rang. Bear snatched it up. "Bear."

"Bear, it's Leah!" The words came at a fast-pitched shout and he shot out of his seat. "Shots fired here. We're moving the family back to the condo now."

"Wait. What happened?"

2. Carrie. April 29. 6:17 pm

Carrie didn't, at first, pay much attention to Dylan when he suddenly became alert, walking backwards, scanning the street.

At the time, she was too busy. Too busy listening very closely to her sister Andrea, who was describing her experience in Rome, and specifically the awakening of her faith, in a way that Carrie found almost shocking. Shocking and...attractive?

Carrie was not quite thirty. She was a mother and a widow. She was a scientist. A pragmatist. She'd grown up attending Roman Catholic services when necessity or family obligations required, but that was it. But Andrea...her youngest sister, barely half her age, had a glow in her eyes when she described how she found herself in awe and wonder in the cathedrals of Rome.

So she paid only the barest attention when Dylan said, "Keep walking, don't panic."

But that oblivious stance came to a sudden crashing halt when Dylan shouted, "Get *down!*" and yanked at her arm, pulling her to the ground behind a car.

"What?" she started to ask then froze in place, at the sound of gunshots. First one, a low intense sound, so loud she felt it in her chest. That was followed by a succession of shots, two, then four, then more.

Dylan, her brother-in-law, Alex's husband, *Ray's* best friend... kneeled behind the car, one hand on her back and one on Alex's, holding them down. He muttered, "Motherfuckers!"

A knife shaped icicle pressed in Carrie's chest, as her mind circled around her daughter, Rachel. What if something happened to Carrie? Who would take care of her daughter? She'd promised Ray. She *promised* him. But he died anyway, and now there was no one, and who the hell was shooting and what did they want and *pleasekeepmydaughtersafe* and she felt herself begin to hyperventilate.

"Stay down," Dylan commanded. His eyes scanned the street as he spoke, his face a rictus, a savage mask. For just a second Carrie expected war paint. Ray Sherman—who had, after all, been Dylan's sergeant—was the love of her life. But she'd never seen him with a warlike expression, she'd never seen him threatened in a physical way like going into battle, and the sight of Dylan with that expression raised a clamor of loss and rage of grief all over again.

And then he was *gone*.

"Dylan!" Alexandra shouted as he stepped, suddenly, out from behind the car and ran. Across the street. Toward the shooting.

Alexandra cried out after her husband, and her legs started to straighten, as if she'd lost her mind too and was about to run out into the street after him. Carrie grabbed her arm and said, *"No!"* and a moment later Leah Simpson had her arm on Alexandra.

"Stay the fuck down," the woman said, an expression of rage on her face.

Another gunshot, and Alexandra screamed, and then there was a scuffle followed by a loud thud, and Leah Simpson was up and running too.

"Just stay," Carrie said to her sister, wrapping her arms around her. But for once, Carrie wasn't protecting anyone else but her and her daughter. She grabbed Alexandra selfishly, urgently, because no matter what happened, they needed to take care of each other, no matter what happened. *Rachel* was going to need them both, and Alexandra running after her fool of a husband to protect him from gunshots wasn't going to do any good at all.

Carrie had lost all the family she was willing to lose.

Alexandra struggled more, until finally Leah was standing over them again a minute or a hundred years later, her dirty blonde hair bedraggled and slick with sweat.

"You can let her up," Leah said, but Carrie didn't believe her, and she held on, and then Dylan was back. His face was a mask of concern, but Carrie couldn't see it. What she saw was the violence underneath. The violence they'd committed in Afghanistan, the violence that kept going and going, destroying more lives, the violence that killed her husband.

For the first time in her life, for just a second, Carrie hated soldiers and everything they stood for.

"Carrie, it's okay," Dylan said. "Let her go."

Just the sound of his voice was enough to set Leah Simpson off.

"What the *hell* is wrong with you, Paris?"

Dylan did a double take. Carrie eased her arms off of Alexandra, who finally got to her feet and threw her arms around him.

"You heard me," Leah said. "What the hell were you thinking?"

Dylan only half paid attention to Alexandra's stranglehold as he turned toward the Diplomatic Security office. "What I was thinking," he said, "was that I saw a threat to my family, and no one was doing anything about it."

Leah's mouth dropped open. "So you just charge someone with a gun?"

Dylan shrugged. "He's down, isn't he?"

Leah's nostrils were flared, her eyes two pinholes of fury, as she said, "My job is to *protect* you. We had DSS agents to take care of that."

"Yeah, well I wasn't waiting around for them to get their act together."

At this point Alexandra broke off from Dylan, growing confusion and anger on her face.

Leah pointed at Dylan. "You interfere with anything like that ever again and I'll see to it you spend the night in a jail cell."

He shrugged. "Wouldn't be the first time, lady. Threaten me with something worthwhile, why don't you?"

Leah's shoulders slumped. Then she marched off, her only parting word, "Stay right here."

Carrie watched as she stomped off, veering toward the far side of the street. There, two men were lying in a growing puddle of blood. A third had his hands tied behind his back with zip ties. He muttered and cursed. Two armed men stood over him, their pistols out as they scanned the street for threats.

Less than a minute later, she was back at their side. "We've got more officers on the way. In the meantime, I want you all back at the condo."

Carrie looked at her sisters. Andrea had her eyes closed, her lips moving. Was she praying? Impossible to tell, but that's what it looked like. Sarah was sitting on the ground, leaning against the car. Her eyes stared off into space, expression not that different from the way she'd looked in the hospital those weeks after she was injured and Ray killed.

Alexandra was saying something urgently to Dylan, her eyes boring into him.

"No," he said. "I won't. I did exactly what needed to be done."

"You could have been killed."

"I could have been killed anyway, Alex. I could have been run over on the way here. I could have been killed in Afghanistan. It's my job to protect you, and that's what I'm going to do."

Her response had an edge of hysteria. "Even if I end up a widow like Carrie?"

Carrie took a step back from the two of them, feeling as if she'd been punched in the gut. A hard, ruthless punch, delivered cold and with precision by someone who loved her.

Dylan's expression said much the same thing. But Carrie didn't wait around to find out what his response was. She turned to her youngest sisters, Andrea and Sarah, and said, "Come on."

She knew they followed her. Because that's what happened when Carrie gave orders. And because seconds later, she heard Sarah's voice, in a hiss. "That was a shitty thing to say, Alex."

Armed escort at their flanks with pistols out, Carrie led her family back toward the condominium.

3. George-Phillip. April 29

It was 11:54 pm, but a low buzz still filled the card room of White's on St. James' Street in London.

White's was a gentlemen's club. Not the modern definition of the word, with women swinging on poles, though George-Phillip had been given to understand that a similarly named *White's Gentlemen's Club* in London was exactly that. This White's, however, was considerably more reserved. Founded in 1693, it was an extremely exclusive club. For more than three centuries it had been men only, a private reserve for the extremely powerful and wealthy. One did not just request membership in the club: White's was invitation only, and often the only way onto its membership roles was proximity to royalty.

George-Phillip, at last count 46th in line for the throne, was still close enough to rate membership in the club. George-Phillip had been sponsored for club membership by the Prince of Wales in

1983. That sponsorship was a result of his father's death in a car accident when George-Phillip was seventeen, leaving him the Duke of Kent at far too young an age.

Sadly, it was an issue of membership that was on everyone's lips right now. In 2008 the Prime Minister had publicly resigned from the club. Others had actually turned down their offers of membership. All because of the fact that White's—a gentlemen's club, after all—did not count women among its members.

George-Phillip, egalitarian though he was about most issues, saw no difficulty with a men's only club. Nor would he have concerns with a women's only club. Sometimes one needed a place to be undisturbed by members of the opposite sex.

"The problem is the liberal newspapers," said Rory Wheeler, the *gentleman* currently sitting across the table from George-Phillip. "They print these libelous stories about the club and it generates hostility. I shouldn't be surprised if it were sponsored by foreign spies, George-Phillip. You really should have your MI-6 people look into it."

George-Phillip didn't bother to correct that his agency was no longer known as MI-6. He also never discussed his work as head of the Secret Intelligence Service with anyone, especially newspaper owners such as Rory. He felt a moment of pain as profound as midnight. Anne, his wife, would have appreciated this story. He and Anne had never been passionate—that was reserved for George-Phillip's first love—but they'd been partners. They had enjoyed each other's company, they had loved, and they had laughed. She would have spent an unreasonable amount of time chuckling over Rory Wheeler's bizarre opinions.

It was a blessing, really. Jane was only 13 months old when Anne passed away on Christmas Eve of 2008 after a very short, painful battle with pancreatic cancer. Jane had no memory of her mother.

He shook his head to clear it. Intrusive memories. Lovely memories, but now was not the time.

"Rory, I'm sure you know my agency is primarily concerned with disrupting terrorists and nuclear proliferation. We don't monitor what is happening with the newspapers."

Rory took a sip of his whiskey, then whispered, "Come now, Georgie."

George-Phillip winced at the overfamiliarity.

The old gasbag continued, his face seeming to expand from the alcohol fumes. "Think about it, George. It's Labour at the center of it. First they'll let women in the club, and next thing you know one of them will be leading the country."

"Like Mrs. Thatcher?" George-Phillip asked.

Wheeler waved a hand dismissively. "An aberration."

A nervous looking steward entered the room. He stood on his tiptoes and waved at George-Phillip.

George-Phillip raised his eyebrows and waved the man over. "Yes?"

"Your Grace, I'm very sorry, but there is a man here to see you. A Mr. O'Leary." He leaned close. "If you'd prefer, I can get rid of him."

O'Leary was *here?* That was unusual in the extreme. A phone call, certainly. But he could only remember two occasions when O'Leary had sought him out here at the club, and the last time had been at the behest of the Prime Minister.

"I'll see him, of course. Actually, O'Leary should be on the pre-cleared list."

George-Phillip knew he was blowing smoke. None of the staff ever paid attention to the standing pre-cleared list unless the visitors were royalty—in which case they were likely a member of the club in the first place.

He quickly moved out into the hall, saying, "Please make one of the private rooms available immediately. I'll retrieve Mr. O'Leary."

He checked his watch as he strode to the front door of the club. 12:34 am. Unusual indeed.

The steward had, of course, left O'Leary on the front step of the club in the slight drizzle and fog. George-Phillip quickly invited him in and led him down the hall to a small sitting room. Inside, he moved to the small bar and poured a drink for himself and one for O'Leary. The table was mahogany, sumptuous, excessive. It had likely sat in this room for two hundred years. This wasn't the first time he'd sat here: George-Phillip had met with the Prince of Wales here in 1984, at this very table. Even then, one leg was too short, and the table rocked just slightly, disturbing both of their drinks. But tradition said the table was not to be replaced—or, apparently, repaired—because one did not meddle with tradition. Not in a club like White's.

"I presume this is urgent?"

"Yes, sir," O'Leary said.

"Tell me."

"Charlie Frazer, sir. He was shot in Washington."

"Dear God. Who?"

"We don't have a positive ID yet."

"Details, please."

"Frazer and Linden were trailing the Thompson sisters, sir. They're in Bethesda, outside Washington, DC."

George-Phillip felt unreasonably irritated by this. "I know where Bethesda is, O'Leary."

"Of course, sir. Several of the sisters were walking to a local restaurant, accompanied by Diplomatic Security agents."

"All right."

"Frazer reported that he felt there were others watching them, but we don't know who."

"Saudis, maybe. Or CIA," George-Phillip mused.

"Regardless, sir, there was an altercation, and Frazer was shot. He's being treated at a local hospital, his prognosis is good."

"Any other injuries? The Thompson sisters?"

"They're fine, sir. No injuries."

George-Phillip closed his eyes, a sense of relief flooding him.

"How are the local police treating it?"

"Mugging. Frazer and Linden both had diplomatic ID. But Frazer's cover is likely blown."

"We'll recall him from Washington, I think. Switch to a different team. And O'Leary..."

"Yes, sir?"

"Have an armed covering team. I want contingency plans. Including one to evacuate the sisters."

O'Leary's overactive eyebrows bunched together. "Sir?"

George-Phillip leaned close. "Get me options, O'Leary. Right now that bastard Thompson holds all the cards. We need to get control of this situation."

"Yes, sir," O'Leary said.

George-Phillip stood. It was long past midnight now, and long past time to get home.

4. Andrea. April 29. 6:18 pm

That *was a shitty thing to say, Alex.*

Sarah's words echoed in Andrea's head as they hurried back to the condo at a near-run, Diplomatic Security agents clearing the way through the crowd on the sidewalk. Her words. The sound of gunshots. The sight of Dylan, face red, mouth open as he yelled a screaming challenge, running directly at an armed man.

A pool of blood spreading on the sidewalk.

She came to a sudden stop behind Carrie, police blocking the sidewalk. She heard the word *witnesses* and someone said *can't leave the scene* but then Leah Simpson was waving her badge and ordering the local police back. Then they were moving again, into the building, up the elevator, and she felt lightheaded and confused.

Why was any of this happening? None of it made any sense. Shock upon shock had been piled on her, starting with the call from Carrie only a few days ago, the flight to the United States and her sudden kidnapping *yesterday*, then this? As they stumbled down the hall, escorted by Leah Simpson and the other two agents, she found herself shaking, hard.

She didn't even really look as they entered the condo. Carrie immediately rushed to the back room to check on Rachel, while Sarah sank into the couch, haphazardly throwing her combat-boot encased feet onto the coffee table with a loud thump that caused both Dylan and Alexandra to jump.

Andrea stood there shaking for just a moment as Alexandra said, "You could have been *killed*."

"Alex, just let it go." Dylan's reply was sharp. He kept walking toward the sliding glass doors as he spoke.

"*No*, I'm not letting it go. You can't just put yourself in danger like that."

Dylan's response was swift. He spun around and pointed a finger at her face, anger written across his features like a map with driving directions to hell. "That's enough."

He turned, slid the door open, and then walked out, slamming it shut behind him.

Alexandra sagged a little, watching him light a cigarette and lean against the wall.

Sarah said, offhand, "Why don't you just cut his balls off?"

Andrea's eyes widened as Alexandra gasped.

"What did you just say?"

Sarah began methodically untying the laces of her boots. "I said, why don't you just cut his balls off? Isn't that your purpose here?"

"Shut up, Sarah. You don't know what you're talking about."

"I know your man there just acted to try to save our lives. That makes him a hero in my book. You should lay off him, maybe hug him or something instead of trying to emasculate him. And just in case you missed the message, what you said to Carrie was unforgivable."

"Can you all just stop fighting?" Andrea asked. "Things are bad enough."

Alexandra sank into the chair across from Sarah. "I'm sorry," she said, her voice shaking.

Sarah nodded her head toward Dylan, who stood, pensive, smoking on the porch, looking out at the darkening sky. "Not me you need to apologize to."

"I'm just so worried, Sarah. He's not been himself since Ray died."

"Who has been?" The question came from Carrie, who stood in the doorway to the hall. "Everything's been upside down since then."

Sarah shook her head. "Not just since then. Since…always."

Andrea sighed and slid into a chair. She looked at her sisters and whispered, "I don't get it. I don't get *any* of this."

Carrie nodded. "That's it. There's…things we don't know. A *lot* we don't know."

Andrea looked at her older sister. "Does Mom?"

Carrie looked thoughtful for a moment. Then she said, "I think so."

"Then we have to find her. And talk with her."

CHAPTER TWELVE
It's not personal

1. Sarah. April 30. 8:54 am

"**Y**ou're going to be fine," Sarah said. "And Carrie would be here too, if she could."

Andrea shrugged. "I know I'll be fine…it's just… I don't know how to explain it…"

Sarah reached up to put a hand on her shoulder. "You're afraid. Not because of the donor match, but…"

Andrea nodded. "Look at us. You're practically a midget compared to me. We don't look at all alike."

"You look a lot like Mom. At least your eyes."

"Right. But who is my father?"

Sarah thought: probably not that son of a bitch Richard Thompson (*her* father, she was sure), who was so busy *preparing for his confirmation hearings* that he couldn't be bothered with his sixteen-year-old daughter. That was for sure.

But if her father wasn't Andrea's father—what did that mean? How did it happen? And Andrea and Carrie looked like twins.

None of it made any sense at all! She tried to remind herself that, first of all, it had only been two days now since Andrea came home. Not even two full days. If it hadn't been urgent for Rachel's sake, Sarah would have thrown a fit. Andrea needed more time. But according to Rachel's doctors, the longer they went before a bone marrow transplant, the more transfusions she would need, and the more damage her body would sustain.

Andrea shook her head. "It doesn't matter. I'm sorry. Even if he is my father, he isn't."

Sarah winced.

Andrea looked her in the eye. "Tell me I'm wrong."

Sarah's mouth curled up in a half grimace. "I can't."

"Can we take this inside?" asked one of the Diplomatic Security agents. Terry Segal, his name was. Mid-to-late twenties and buff. Andrea had the feeling he was armed to the teeth, and that was kind of hot. On the other hand, every time he gave her his toothy grin, she noticed the bottom row of his teeth were stained badly. Chewing tobacco, she suspected, which was quite possibly the grossest thing in the world.

"Sure," Sarah said. She took Andrea's arm and they began walking in step toward the clinic. The Children's National Medical Center was an ultramodern glass structure with windows jutting out at odd angles, trees and grass surrounding a lake. It all seemed silent, pristine, calm and professional. It all seemed designed to calm. It all seemed incredibly fake.

"Where exactly is Carrie?" Andrea asked just before they reached the entry doors.

Sarah shook her head. "She said she had an appointment. Her nanny's coming at ten. I think she said she'd be back early afternoon."

Alexandra had stayed at the condo. That morning she had mumbled a barely coherent apology to Carrie. Predictably, Carrie forgave her on the spot and hugged her.

Sarah had her doubts. Because *no one* was that good and strong. No one kept their shit together under that much pressure. No one was that kind. But being the caretaker was Carrie's identity, and she wasn't going to give that up for anything. Sarah thought one day Carrie would explode from her own self-imposed sainthood.

Segal, the diplomatic security guard, jumped ahead of them and opened the door. Andrea led, with Sarah right behind.

"This way," Segal said. "We already have security in the lab suite, and they're expecting you upstairs."

Andrea's eyes were round. "That's...reassuring."

Sarah knew it wasn't reassuring at all. What sixteen-year-old wants a battalion of security guards accompanying her to get blood tests? But there was no going back. Since the shooting in Bethesda last night, the security presence had dramatically increased. Their guards were in uniform now, with visible sidearms and driving escort vehicles. She couldn't even imagine what all this was costing.

Her father had retired from the Foreign Service when she was still young, and the family's last overseas posting to Moscow she'd been very young indeed. So she'd never experienced this kind of intense security.

She didn't like it. It made her want to get on Eddie's Harley and just ride out of town as fast and as far as she could go.

Speaking of Eddie. She'd received several urgent texts from him already this morning asking for updates.

Everything is fine, she sent back.

As they stepped on the elevator, Andrea said, "You've been texting a lot. Boyfriend?"

"Sort of," Sarah replied.

The elevator door closed. The two DSS agents stood near the doors, their backs to the sisters. Sarah continued. "Eddie's a med student. He was part of the ambulance crew that...he pulled me out of the accident last summer."

"Oh my God," Andrea said. "That's so sweet! And he's your boyfriend now?"

"Not exactly." In fact they'd only been on four dates. She remembered her mother's red face and caustic words vividly when Eddie had shown up at their place.

Not until my daughter is eighteen.

The rules were set. Eddie could visit at the condo. He ate dinner with them every fourth Sunday. But until her eighteenth birthday, she was never once in a room alone with him.

The early months, that had been fine with her. Her leg had been swollen and ripped open like an overcooked sausage, and the pain was indescribable. There were days when she'd done nothing but scream, Carrie had done nothing more than weep, and Adelina, their mother, had done little more than stare at them in hollow-eyed shock as she tried to care for her daughters.

She knew Julia and Carrie would never trust their mother. She knew Andrea had left home and wanted nothing to do with her.

But Sarah would never in her life forget the nights when the morphine just wasn't enough, the nights when she'd whimpered and wept in the most awful, unimaginable hell. And it was her mother's arms around her that brought her through those nights. It was Adelina's voice in her ear, whispering, "You can do this, Sarah. Only another hour, then we can get another shot. You can make it. You're strong enough. All my daughters are strong enough."

Sarah knew her mother was crazy. She knew her mother had some fucked up past, though she didn't have a clue what it was all about. But she knew that when push came to shove, that woman dropped everything, left her home and lived with her and Carrie through the worst months of their lives.

By December, the pain was mostly dull aches, and she was dealing with the pangs of coming off the painkillers. But from what she'd seen during her twin sister Jessica's rendition of "grace" during Christmas dinner, that was an even bigger issue for her twin. As a result, their mother had gone home after Christmas, returning to San Francisco with Sarah's twin sister Jessica—exchanging places with their prick of a father, who promptly decided the condo was too small and found his own place.

That was fine. Sarah stayed and took care of Carrie. They took care of each other.

Oddly enough though—those months of her mother whispering soothing words in her ear—they changed something. Even when her mother was gone, she waited, and didn't go out with Eddie, until her eighteen birthday, just a few weeks ago on April 1st.

Her first date with Eddie was her present to herself. And it was a doozy. The hulking Puerto Rican medical student took her to a play at the Kennedy Center, followed by a late dinner at the Roof Terrace, overlooking the National Mall on one side and Arlington National Cemetery on the other.

As they rode up the elevator, Sarah found herself telling Andrea a little about Eddie. He came from a wealthy family, but for reasons he'd refused to explain, his father had disowned him during his third year of pre-med at George Washington University. Eddie kept going, getting a job as an EMT to help pay some of the bills and praying to cover the rest.

"Are you dating anyone?" Sarah asked Andrea as they reached the third floor.

"Javier," Andrea said. "But he just wants to have sex. I keep him distracted, but he's no boyfriend."

Sarah laughed. "I bet you run circles around him."

Andrea smiled mysteriously.

"This way, ladies," said Segal, their security guard. He was the only one now—the other one stayed at the elevator doors as they followed Segal down the hall. Another guard was barring the door to the lab.

Segal stopped at the door to the lab, spoke with the guard at the door, and opened the door.

Sarah and Andrea stepped into the lab.

Andrea walked up to the reception counter. "Miss Thompson?" asked a lab tech, a woman in her mid-thirties.

"Yes, ma'am."

"We've had the lab closed until you're finished. Please come this way and we'll get you taken care of."

Andrea nodded and followed. Sarah followed.

Sarah overheard one of the other hospital staffers mutter, "And then maybe we can get back to business..." She froze and gave a cold look to the woman, then sneered and kept going.

Two minutes later, a rubber band was wrapped around Andrea's arm and the lab tech had inserted a needle.

"How long will it take before we know the results?" Andrea asked.

The lab tech shrugged and responded in a brusque tone. "Normally I'd say two or three days, though rush transplant matches sometimes are the same day. I'm certain they'll rush yours, what with all the attention."

Sarah glanced back toward the door, and said, "It's not her fault she was kidnapped, you know."

The lab tech froze and blushed. "Of course."

"So maybe we can get on with this? So your coworkers aren't *inconvenienced* any more?"

"Sarah..." Andrea said. "It's okay..."

Sarah took a deep breath. "Sorry," she whispered. "Let's just finish this up and get out of here." What she wanted to say was: it didn't matter what the blood test was for. They were sisters no matter what. The blood test was to find out if Andrea was a donor match. Not to determine her parentage.

Somehow it felt like they'd both lost sight of that.

2. Mitch Filner. April 30. 9:15 am

Mitch Filner said into the phone. "Just in case you forgot, we lost one of our guys last night because of your stupid orders."

As he said the words, Mitch scanned the balcony of the high-rise directly across the street through his binoculars. The former soldier—Dylan Paris—was pacing on the balcony, smoking a cigarette. Mitch would have loved to have put a bullet right between his fucking eyes for interfering the night before. Now, Joe Paretski was in the custody of federal agents, and if they didn't find him soon, this whole operation could come crashing down.

Not that it wasn't all bullshit to begin with. Leslie Collins thought he could drop a few hundred thousand here and a few hundred thousand there and contain a major disaster, but it didn't work that way. Mitch knew that much, and he was working as fast as he could to make his own insurance, even as he followed Collins' orders.

Kidnapping a teenager? Seriously? That was bullshit. They weren't in some Third World shithole, nor was Andrea Thompson some anonymous girl who could be snatched off the street without anyone noticing. She was the daughter of the fucking *Secretary of*

Defense. Yeah, asshole hadn't bothered to tell him that until after it was international headlines.

That was okay. Mitch had been recording his conversations with Collins. Because one thing was for sure, Leslie Collins wasn't acting within the bounds of any approved intelligence op. No matter how much he thought he was in charge, no matter how often he had fucking cocktails at the White House, there was no way in hell the President had authorized the kidnapping of the daughter of a cabinet member. Collins was playing his own fucking game. Mitch didn't know what it was, but he was putting away plenty of information to put Leslie Collins away in prison forever.

Right now the family was split all over the place. Mitch had agents tailing the oldest daughter, Julia Wilson, spoiled rich girl husband of a fucking rock star, out in Los Angeles. He had two more tracking Carrie Thompson, the next oldest sister, currently en route to the Pentagon to have lunch with her father. That ought to be a barrel of fucking laughs. The two youngest, including the bitch who had killed two of his contractors, were at Children's Hospital. Getting blood tests, which Collins had ordered him to procure and destroy.

He ought to just put a bullet through her head rather than steal her blood tests.

Collins spoke, his voice a slow clip. "I didn't ask your opinion, Filner. I gave you instructions."

"Collins, you're losing your grip."

"Just get the blood tests and do it quietly. Switch them out with somebody's. I don't care what you do."

Filner rolled his eyes. Fine. He'd follow instructions. But it was a waste of time. They'd just get another blood test.

He eyed the former soldier on the balcony again.

Earlier that morning he'd run into a familiar face. Jackie Prince. Or at least that was the name she'd gone by when they met four years ago. Jackie had been lounging with a paperback at the Starbucks, a hundred yards away from the condo.

Filner had slipped into the seat across from her.

"Well, hullo there, Mitch," Jackie said. Her clipped London accent was as annoying as always.

"Jackie," Filner had responded. He raised an eyebrow. "Doing a little vacation reading? A little tourism here?"

"Well, of course," Jackie replied. "What else would I be doing in the United States?"

"Not a little bit of spying? Interesting place you chose here."

Jackie had smiled and leaned close to him, her nose inches from his. "I'm no more involved in intelligence operations than you are, Mitch."

Filner wiggled his eyebrows up and down; an expression he'd come to believe was somehow seductive. "You should come join me, then," he said.

She smiled. "Perhaps you should come join me," she had replied. "I've got a friend, his name's George? He's looking for some American employees."

Mitch snorted. "It's hard to beat self-employment."

She smiled and leaned close. Then she whispered, "Security's worth a lot, Mitch. Think about it. It would be a shame if you got involved in something that was going to be trouble. And just between you and me? There's trouble coming. Big trouble."

She slid a card across the table at him. He stared at the card in surprise. It listed the name and address of a comic book shop in London.

"Comics?" he had asked.

"I've got a weakness for superheroes," she had replied.

Mitch memorized the number. Then he had gotten up and walked away, leaving the card behind.

Now, with Leslie Collins droning on in his ear over the phone, all Mitch could think about was the relative security if he took her up on her offer. He knew SIS would be good for it: he had enough information to bring down Richard Thompson *and* Leslie Collins.

"Filner? Did you fucking hear me?"

Filner sighed. He thought about the operations of the last five days. Installing bombs in houses. Kidnapping teenagers. He didn't want to do this crap any more. He wanted to sit in a lounge chair on the beach in France or Spain or some place and fucking retire from this crap.

"I heard you, Collins. Let me make sure I'm hearing you. You want me to steal her blood tests."

"Yes!"

"And then?"

"We're going to contain this thing, Filner. I want contingency plans. To wipe out all of them. Am I clear?"

That was it.

"You're perfectly clear." He hung up the phone. Then he checked to make sure it had been recorded properly. *Yes.*

He stood up. He was done. Done with this bullshit. Done. Done. Done. He dialed Jackie's comic book shop from memory.

"James Street Comics," said a male voice.

"I'd like to speak with Jackie. My name's Filner."

A pause. Then a voice said, "Jackie's not in. But I'm authorized to speak on her behalf. She told me that you might be calling. Is this about the job opening?"

"Yeah. Um...you guys offering any relocation assistance?"

His phone started beeping. An incoming call. Probably Collins.

"That's doable provided we get the right employee. With the right...skills."

"All right...see, the thing is, I don't feel really secure in my current job."

"Security, we can offer, sir. But it's not a one-way street."

"I need to move right away."

A pause. Mitch felt his heart beating faster. He waited for almost three full minutes. Then someone came back on the line. "Sir? One of our recruiters would like to meet you. I understand you're in Bethesda right now? Can you get to the metro and meet our man at DuPont Circle?"

"Yeah. How will I know him?"

"He'll know you."

Mitch nodded, then hung up the phone, just in time for it to ring again. Leslie Collins. He ignored the call and quickly tossed a few things in his pockets, then walked to the door and yanked it open.

Then he stepped back in shock, a hand at his midsection, covering the sudden sharp pain. He felt hot liquid begin to pour out onto his hand and he gasped.

Danny McMillan was standing in the doorway. "Sorry, Mitch. It's not personal. Collins heard you were looking for another job."

"Fuck, Danny." *What the fuck? Was Danny here as a backup all along?*

"Yeah...that's the breaks, man." Then he reached out and with a swift jab, stabbed Mitch again, this time between ribs. Mitch gasped and fell to his knees, his vision wavering.

"I'll take that," Danny said the words as he pulled Mitch's phone out of his hands.

Mitch fell to the floor.

Danny said, "Sorry about this, buddy."

Then Mitch felt a cold line against his throat. A second later, everything went black.

CHAPTER THIRTEEN

Secret wars

1. Bear. April 30. 9:45 am

By the time Bear made it to the Russell Senate Office Building on Wednesday morning, he was exhausted. And with good reason. Following the shooting in Bethesda, a jurisdictional battle took place between the Montgomery County Police, Diplomatic Security, and the FBI.

Montgomery County had a good case. The shooter had no identification and was refusing to talk. From their perspective, he'd shot a British citizen who was in town on a tourist visa and had no diplomatic connections. But when the shooter was booked, his fingerprints hit on the National Crime Information System database. Ronald Sanderson. 32 years old. Army veteran, former Airborne, former Special forces. He'd been thrown out of the Army with a medical discharge for a personality disorder. In Bear's experience, that usually meant improperly diagnosed post traumatic stress. Sanderson had disappeared for three years after his discharge, but attracted the FBI's attention in a bank fraud investigation. No one, however, could find him. Until yesterday.

Diplomatic Security wanted him, of course, because of the connection to the Andrea Thompson kidnapping. Unfortunately, for now at least, Sanderson was in the Montgomery County jail while the different jurisdictional arguments got worked out.

It was well after midnight before Bear had dealt with the custody issue, then beefed up security assignments for the Thompson family. At 1:30 in the morning he'd stumbled back into his studio apartment near DuPont Circle and crawled into the bed.

He was up early, and at 5:30 walked into the Starbucks around the corner from his apartment to sit, read the rest of the Thompson file, and wake up.

Bear was intrigued still by the complete lack of information in the file about Thompson's postings to Spain and Pakistan in the early 80s. No performance evaluations, no official reports, no photographs. *Nothing.* It was as if the assignments simply hadn't existed. In January 1984 Thompson was reassigned to the State Department in Washington, DC for what appeared to be a normal three-year assignment. The next three years in his file were perfectly normal. Official reports. Commendations letters, including one signed by Ronald Reagan.

The commendations were very vague, however. *For exemplary service during the period of June 1985 to July 1985.* With no specifics or description of what the assignment was.

Again...everything in his file was slightly off.

A photograph from early 1984. Bear recognized the condo currently occupied by Carrie Thompson-Sherman. In the photo, Richard Thompson sat at the large dining table with his wife Adelina and several other people. A quasi-official dinner party. On the back of the photo, someone had labeled the names in now faded, uneven type.

Richard and Adelina Thompson
Prince Roshan and Myriam al-Saud

Leslie Collins
Prince George-Phillip, Duke of Kent
LTC Chuck Rainsley and Brianna Rainsley

Bear stared at the photograph in shock. Then he took a sip of his coffee, wishing he had some whiskey to top it off.

Roshan al Saud, a member of the royal house of Saudi Arabia, was now the director general of al Mukhabarat Al A'amah...the Saudi Arabian intelligence agency.

Leslie Collins was the Director of Operations—the second-highest level executive—of the Central Intelligence Agency. In the photograph, he sat with his arm on Richard Thompson's shoulder, a sly grin on his face as he stared at the camera.

George-Phillip Windsor was a cousin of Queen Elizabeth and currently the head of the Secret Intelligence Service of the United Kingdom. He looked no older than twenty in the photo, but was clearly recognizable with his dark features and long aquiline nose.

Chuck Rainsley—then a Marine Lieutenant Colonel—was now the senior senator from Texas and head of the Senate Armed Services Committee. He wore his uniform in the photo, medals looking resplendent as he stood behind the others at the table. Bear remembered that Rainsley, an exceptionally tall man, had been one of the commanders of the Marine task force that had been so devastated by the truck bomb in Beirut that killed more than two hundred Marines.

Bear didn't understand what this was all about. But he knew that something was seriously wrong. In this photograph, they looked young, Thompson and Collins and Prince Roshan all in their early thirties, Prince George-Phillip not even twenty-five. But now, these men were some of the most powerful in the world.

And now he was on his way to face one of them. After looking at the photo, Bear had returned to his apartment, where he'd reviewed all the biographical information he could find on Senator Chuck Rainsley.

Rainsley was a conservative and one of the most powerful men in the Senate. Bear's recollection had been correct. A Vietnam veteran, Rainsley was a senior commander of the peacekeeping force deployed by President Reagan to Lebanon. In October 1983 suicide bombers attacked the Marine barracks with truck bombs, killing 241 US service members. Bear reviewed the reports—they were brutal. Unusually restrictive rules of engagement prevented sentries from responding effectively to the attack, and a political and intelligence rift in the White House and between the Pentagon and State Department prevented an effective response. In the photograph, early in 1984, Rainsley was still in uniform. But Bear knew that by March 1984, Rainsley had resigned his commission and announced he was running for Congress.

Bear felt a little better prepared, then, as he walked into the Russell Building. He didn't know the connection between Senator Rainsley and Richard Thompson, but he knew that at least as far back as 1984, the two men knew each other. He knew that on at least one occasion, Senator Rainsley sat in the same room as Thompson and the future heads or deputy heads of intelligence of three different nations.

There was no longer any question in Bear's mind that Richard Thompson had been CIA.

What did the new Secretary of State, Perry, have to do with all of this? He'd also been on the Armed Services and Foreign Relations committees in the Senate, and was known to be a good friend of Rainsley's, despite the fact they sat on opposite sides of the political aisle. Perry was a Democrat and had served in the Senate from Massachusetts for twenty years. Rainsley was a Republican from Texas. But the two of them had worked together for decades. So what would Rainsley have to say that Perry couldn't tell him?

Bear was annoyed he had to turn in his weapons at the entrance to the building. But he needed to get upstairs. He made his way down the gleaming white hallway toward the stairs, watching as men and women, legislators, aides, lobbyists, and tourists wandered the halls.

It was quieter on the third floor—only those people who had actual business came here. His shoes echoed off the marble floor as he walked down the hall, and he felt an urge to whisper.

Halfway down the quarter mile long hallway, he found the seal of the state of Texas: a lone star, circled by olive and oak branches. The door itself was thick polished wood and had gleaming brass handles. Bear reached out and opened the door.

Inside, it took his eyes a moment to adjust from the bright white marble hallway to the dark wood paneling inside the office. A receptionist sat at a desk—young, pretty and earnest. She smiled at him and said, "May I help you?"

"Jim Wyden, Diplomatic Security. I have an appointment with Senator Rainsley."

"Yes, sir. If you can wait right here, Senator Rainsley will be right with you."

It wasn't a long wait. Less than a minute later, Senator Chuck Rainsley appeared in the doorway of the anteroom. Bear's first impression: Rainsley would make a good candidate for the father of Carrie and Andrea Thompson. At six foot six, he towered over Bear. A good looking affable man with an easy smile and a broad hand, he clasped Bear's hand and said, "Mr. Wyden, it's a pleasure to meet you. Secretary Perry told me to expect you. Please come in."

Bear followed Rainsley into the office, his thoughts racing. *Could* Rainsley be the father? He'd have to look at dates. He muttered a curse at himself. He should have checked their birth dates. But it didn't make any sense, really. It didn't explain why Andrea Thompson was kidnapped. It didn't explain anything really.

"Have a seat," Rainsley said, gesturing toward a leather chair in front of a huge, highly polished desk. Bear's shoes sank into the thick carpeting of the office as he walked to the chair and sat down.

Rainsley's office was spacious. Memorabilia and photographs covered the walls. Rainsley in his Marine Corps uniform, as a young Lieutenant in Vietnam, on an aircraft carrier, at an Embassy, in Lebanon. Later photos of him in the Washington uniform, a dark suit and tie, or on the campaign trail in Texas. On the wall, a mix of items. A Bronze Star medal. A plaque from the city of Dallas. A photograph, black and white, of a twenty-year-old Chuck Rainsley in a basketball uniform with the letters USNA. Naval Academy.

Rainsley slid into the seat across from Bear. Even seated he was an imposing, impressive man.

"What can I do for you, Mr. Wyden?"

"Bear, sir."

"Right. Bear. What can I do for you?"

"Sir, you're probably aware that the night before last, the daughter of the Secretary of Defense was kidnapped at BWI airport. A foreign national with known intelligence ties was involved in the kidnapping."

Rainsley nodded. "I've been following the story. Please don't take this as nitpicking, but just a reminder, Thompson's confirmation hearings aren't until next week. He isn't the Secretary of Defense yet."

Bear nodded. "I stand corrected, Senator. I'm running the investigation into Andrea Thompson's kidnapping. And—to put it bluntly—I've got some unanswered questions that don't make sense, and Secretary Thompson is being less than cooperative."

Rainsley grimaced. "That's no surprise."

"Sir, what can you tell me about Richard Thompson?"

Rainsley grimaced. "First of all, I want to make it clear, this is not on the record."

"Fine, Senator."

"All right, then. Richard Thompson is a snake and a liar. He's one of the most dangerous men in government, and if the President thinks Thompson's nomination as Secretary of Defense is going to fly he is out of his mind."

Well, that was clear enough, Bear thought. "Can you be, um…a little more specific, Senator?"

"All right. First of all—you know Thompson's not really State Department, right? He's CIA, through and through."

"You're certain of that?"

"We held closed hearings in 2001 when he became ambassador to Russia. His CIA assignments were the reason for the closed hearings."

"I see. I understand you were responsible for the delay in that appointment?"

Rainsley grimaced. "I tried to stop it entirely. We held the nomination up for two years, and it cost me a lot of political capital."

"Tell me why."

Rainsley leaned across the desk. He held up one finger. "First… early 80s, when Thompson was in Afghanistan, he got up to some very shady stuff. *Criminal* stuff. And then he did everything he could to prevent any oversight or control from Congress."

"He was officially assigned to Pakistan, I believe."

Rainsley sneered. "So was half the Central Intelligence Agency. The Russians were in Afghanistan, and we had a lot of operatives in there. Secret little wars. Crazy stuff."

"Okay. What else?"

"All right. Second... and this you can't quote me on. But Thompson had a cruel streak. Power games in his personal and professional life."

"What sort of...power games?"

Rainsley looked disgusted. "Let's just say I feel sorry for Adelina Thompson."

"You know her." It wasn't a question.

Rainsley gave a vague answer. "We've met a few times. She's a lot younger than Richard Thompson."

"They've been married since...1981?"

"That's right."

"I thought it was unusual. His assignment to Spain was only a few months."

Rainsley leaned close. "The agency ordered him to marry her to prevent an international incident."

That didn't make any sense. Unless..."Was she raped?"

The Senator shrugged. "I don't know all the details. But they married them off and got him the hell out of there."

Bear sighed. "Sir, this is all interesting, but it doesn't really tell me anything. Did you know...there's a photograph of you with Thompson? And his wife?"

"I'm not surprised."

"The picture also has some interesting people in it. Prince Roshan from Saudi Arabia. Leslie Collins. Prince George-Phillip."

Senator Rainsley nodded. "That's right."

"All three of them ended up very high in their intelligence establishments."

"What does that tell you?"

"That I've got unanswered questions. That none of this makes sense."

Rainsley smiled. "That's all I'm going to say for now."

"Senator, one last question."

"Yes?"

"Who is Carrie and Andrea Thompson's real father?"

Rainsley raised his eyebrows. Then he said, "That's not a question for me to answer. Have a good afternoon, Mr. Wyden."

2. Carrie. April 30. Noon

The Army Sergeant who led Carrie down the hallway wore dress blues like Ray had worn to their wedding. He'd been in the Army a *lot* longer than Ray had, though. Three strips on top, three on the bottom, a dozen diagonal yellow hash marks on his sleeve and dozens upon dozens of ribbons. She recognized the Combat Infantryman's badge. Of all Ray's decorations, that one had been the most important to him.

"In here, ma'am," the Sergeant said.

The door opened into a small anteroom. A woman in her forties sat behind a desk. Two younger sergeants sat in chairs across from the woman. One read on a Kindle, while the other played a handheld video game. She wondered what they were doing. At a second desk, an Army Colonel sat. He stood up as Carrie entered the room and said, "Miss Thompson-Sherman? I'm Colonel Billingsgate, your father's aide-de-camp. He'll be available in just a few moments, ma'am."

"Thank you," Carrie said.

The secretary, still behind her desk, said, "Can I get you a drink? Coffee?"

"No, thanks."

"Please feel free to have a seat."

Carrie sat down. She was uncomfortable. Beyond uncomfortable. Her father was a lifelong diplomat, and while his appointment as the new Secretary of Defense might make sense in some political sense she didn't know about, what she did know was that her experience with the Army as an institution was not good. Not good at all. Ray had been practically persecuted, called back up by the military on a pretext because of a crime someone else had committed. He'd been put on trial, dragged through the mud, and then murdered.

She'd just as soon not spend a day here, in the Pentagon, where her husband's death had effectively been engineered.

So while she waited, she played solitaire on her phone and tried to calm her nerves. Carrie was protective of her daughter—obsessively so. And leaving her in the hands of the nanny, even for a few hours, was excruciating. She'd had to do that several times in the last couple of days.

The main door to the office opened. She looked up. Her father stood in the doorway, a politician's smile on his face. Something was wrong. Her father had always been distant. He'd always been... baffling. A little cold. But his recent behavior had been almost bizarre. She didn't understand it, and it seemed to have started right around the time they figured out that Rachel was sick.

"Carrie, darling. Please, come in."

Her father put his hand on her arm as he led her into the office. "Have a seat. Lunch will be served in just a moment."

She walked to the indicated seat, a small table not far from the desk. White tablecloth and lunch settings. Was he kidding? She'd asked to meet her *father* for lunch. Instead, she was getting the *Secretary of Defense*.

A steward—an Army sergeant—in a white uniform entered the room and filled the water glasses at the table.

"Something to drink, ma'am?"

"Thanks, just water, please."

"And you, Mr. Secretary?"

"I'll have a vodka-tonic, please. Light."

The steward disappeared.

"How are Andrea and baby Rachel?"

Carrie winced a little. Something was really wrong here. She'd never been close to her father—but of all of his daughters, she'd been the closest. But right now she didn't feel close at all. His question seemed as superficial as possible. *How are Andrea and baby Rachel?*

She blinked at her father and said, "Andrea is terrified. She was kidnapped at the airport, and neither one of her parents could be bothered to be there for her."

"Carrie, surely you're aware that my confirmation hearings begin next week."

She leaned forward and said, "Father. What in God's name is *wrong* with you? How could you treat her like this?"

"You don't understand how—"

Her father's mouth closed suddenly when the side door to the office opened. The steward returned, with two enlisted men behind him. One carried a tray with two covered dishes, and the other brought drinks. Quickly, lunch and drinks were arrayed on the table in front of them. Carrie sat uncomfortably as the soldiers bustled around arranging the table.

Lunch was roast lamb.

As the stewards left, her father coughed into his napkin. "Carrie...there are things you don't understand."

"Right," she said. "I don't understand how you can be so cold to your own daughter."

He closed his eyes, visibly trying to contain his patience.

"Please relay to your sister my love, and let her know that the moment my confirmation hearings are complete, I'll be available."

God, she missed Ray. The grief that ran through her at that thought was overpowering, almost as if she'd been run over. "Do you know what she thinks?"

Her father leaned forward, spreading his napkin across his lap. Then, with careful motions, he cut a piece of lamb and speared it on his fork, bringing it to his mouth. Only after he'd chewed and swallowed did he say, "What does she think?"

Carrie felt a tightening in her chest, knowing that once she said it, she wouldn't be able to recall the words. Knowing—believing—for the first time, that Andrea's suspicion might be true. Believing that everything she'd ever been told by her own father was a lie.

"Andrea believes that she and I are sisters. But that you aren't our father."

He raised his eyebrows then wiped his napkin across his lips. "She does?"

Carrie nodded once.

He sighed. His face looked closed off. No emotion. No...nothing. He looked like someone about to walk into court, not her father.

Carrie pressed forward. "Is that why she's spent most of her life in Spain?"

"You'll have to discuss that with your mother," he said. His tone of voice was irritated, clipped.

"Why did Andrea get sent off and not me?"

"Again, you'll have to speak to your mother about that."

She shook her head. "Is it true?"

He didn't answer. *He didn't answer.* Something in her was cut adrift. She'd lost her husband already. Now she had to lose her father too?

Her voice ragged, Carrie asked, "Who...who is my father, then?"

Her father—no, Richard Thompson—closed his eyes. Then he shrugged, as if to say it was of little importance to him. His tone of voice was disgusted when he spoke. "Unfortunately, your birth father is Senator Chuck Rainsley."

CHAPTER FOURTEEN
The best I could

1. Carrie. April 30

Unfortunately, *your birth father is Senator Chuck Rainsley.* The sentence rolled around in her head, a wildfire destroying everything in its path, a flood of sludge and lies clogging her ears and thoughts. Thirty years of memories. She thought of holidays in San Francisco, of birthdays, of her father's isolation in his work, of the gifts he gave her over the years. All of them lies.

Senator Chuck Rainsley.

She thought about what she knew about the man—the man Richard Thompson claimed was her actual father. Nothing really. Senator from Texas. She was under the impression he was married. He'd been the primary opposition on the Senate Foreign Relations committee to her father's nomination as Ambassador to Russia. She vaguely remembered the news, hearings, and Rainsley banging his fist on a table on television. She remembered Julia's suicidal depression, and learning years later that her parents blamed *Julia* for the stalled nomination.

Rage gripped her. *Was it true?* Had Rainsley blocked the nomination out of spite? Had he somehow used Julia to hit back at her... not her father.

"I don't even know what to call you," she said.

"I'm still your father, Carrie."

"A father is the person who gave you life. *Or* it's the person who gave you love. Or both. But you gave neither."

He winced under the onslaught of words. "Carrie, darling, that's not true."

She slowly stood up. "But it is. You may have showered me with gifts and cash...but..." She shook her head. "What kind of man are you? What kind of woman is..."

"I did the best I could. I didn't even know until..."

"You didn't know until when?"

"You were five."

"How did you find out?"

He gave a grim smile. "Your blood type is A positive. Your mother's is O positive. Therefore, your biological father can't be type B. I am. Simple really."

He leaned back in his chair, rubbing his hand across the bridge of his nose. "Your mother and I had a lot of trouble. A *lot*. But I was never unfaithful. Unfortunately, your mother was. But even so, I forgave her. She was young, and I'd spent so much of our married life away. Virtually all of it. She was a young mother alone with her daughter while I was off on assignments. I forgave her."

He nodded at her as he spoke, his expression grave. "Truly that would have been the end of it. And you can't tell me I treated you any differently than your sisters. I'm not the warmest parent in the world. But I've done my best."

Carrie stared back. "You found out in, what...1990? And you still had Alexandra that year."

"I told you I forgave her."

"What about Andrea?" she hissed.

"What about her?"

"What about her? How can you ask that, Dad? I was *twelve* when she was born! And we have the same father? How did that happen? How did the twins and Alexandra...I don't *get* it."

"I began to suspect while she was still pregnant with Andrea. And blood tests at birth confirmed it. Rainsley was briefly in China in 1996 on a political junket. I presume that's what happened."

Carrie shook her head. Trying to figure out the timeline. Julia was a freshman in high school in 1996. The year she'd struggled with an abusive, much older boyfriend. The year her mother had done nothing to help her. Carrie remembered when Julia had confronted her mother about it, years later. Winter of 2002? 2003?

"That was the year Julia..." she whispered. But she froze. Julia had accused her mother of having an affair with someone named *George Lansing*. Not Senator Rainsley. Why did she say that? It didn't make any sense. *None of this* made any sense. She *almost* interrupted and asked her fath—

She didn't know how to think of him.

Thompson leaned forward and said, "Carrie...I'm sorry. But... there's something seriously wrong with your mother psychologically. She loves you in her own way. But I don't believe she can help herself."

"I don't see how you stayed married to her," Carrie said. "She betrayed you. *Twice.*"

He sighed and shook his head. "We don't touch each other. Ever. But...you don't blame someone who has cancer, do you? She's sick. So I do what I can to take care of her." He leaned his forehead on his hand. "In truth, it's why I was so opposed to your marriage, and Alexandra's. It's not that I didn't like Ray—he was a man to be proud of. But I've spent my life married to someone who was mentally ill. I was worried about the trauma from the war—"

"Stop." Carrie said the word before she consciously thought about it.

"I'm just trying to explain—"

"Just *stop*," she said. "Don't you dare compare Ray to...all of... *that*." She couldn't say the words. Not out loud. She couldn't bear to have his name mentioned in the same breath as her mother. All her mother's lies, and spitefulness and infidelity.

Rage swept over her when she realized she was starting to cry. She stood up. "I have to go."

"Darling..."

"Stay away from me."

"Carrie, it's not my..."

"You lied to me. You lied to all of us. You've lied to me for thirty years."

She reached in her purse for a tissue and blew her nose, loud. "Seriously. I have to go. I've got a daughter to take care of."

She backed away from the table, and her father stood, taking a step around the table, closer to her. Involuntarily, she stepped away from him. His eyes narrowed, and he said, "Look, you need to calm down a little, Carrie."

"You've just told me you aren't actually my father, and you want me to calm down?"

"It appears to me that you came here expecting that answer."

"And what am I supposed to do with this information?"

"Nothing, Carrie. You keep raising your daughter. You keep doing what you've always done. Nothing changes."

She sighed. "Everything's changing. Dad...*what* happened with Andrea?"

"I told you. Your mother knows the answer to that."

"You didn't send me away. Why did you send her?"

He shook his head, muttered, "Jesus," and turned away from her. His back to her, he said, "Can you imagine what it's like *knowing* you've been betrayed? Lied to? The only thing I ever asked of Adelina was loyalty. So when I knew at birth that Andrea belonged to another man I just..." His head bowed toward the floor.

Bile flooded Carrie's throat.

"What about *me?*"

He raised an eyebrow. "You were five before I knew. We'd already...bonded."

Carrie swayed. *They'd already bonded?* In other words, if he'd known, he would have turned her away too? Sent her off to live in a foreign country with the in-laws he never saw? Abandoned her like he'd done to her sister.

"I hate you," she whispered. "I've spent my life cleaning up your and mother's messes. Loving your daughters because you couldn't. As far as I'm concerned you and mother can both go to hell."

She turned to march away from him.

He grabbed her arm. "Carrie."

"Don't *touch me.*" She jerked her arm away from him.

She backed away and he stared at her, his face red with chagrin. "Carrie, please don't react this way. I'm your father."

She shook her head. "No. No, you're not."

Back out of the office, and through the anteroom, and then into the wide, confusing hallway of the Pentagon. She made it about fifty feet before one of the young soldiers from her father's office caught up with her.

"Mrs. Thompson-Sherman, let me escort you, please."

"Just Sherman, please," she replied. She'd use a name she could still be proud of.

"Yes, ma'am," the soldier said, neither understanding nor caring.

As she walked, she thought back over a million interactions with her father. He'd always been free with cash. No problem paying for college. Buying her a car. Giving her a ridiculous trust fund, with an allowance in the tens of thousands a year while she was still in college.

But he didn't touch. He didn't embrace his children, or kiss them. Especially her and Andrea. He was a father only in name, preferring the isolation of his office, the intrigue of diplomacy, the draw of politics and power. Family life evaded her father as if it were an ancient foreign language with no Rosetta stone, the complicated rituals of a mystery religion to the uninitiated.

Which left Carrie and her sisters at the mercy of Adelina Thompson. Erratic. Anxious. Vicious sometimes. Her mother was *literally* crazy, and Carrie and Julia had absorbed the worst of that crazy over the years. And their father did nothing to protect them. Nothing to help. He just...went to work. And left them to fend for themselves when the most powerful person in their lives was a disaster.

She thought about the holidays last year. What it was like to walk into Thanksgiving dinner with Ray's death still a raw, bleeding wound. The holiday dinner had been even more stilted and silent than usual, if that were even possible. Alexandra and Dylan were in Atlanta. Sarah only lasted half the meal before she had to be wheeled back to bed, her leg swollen and red from the effort of being upright for longer than thirty minutes. Carrie sat there, staring into space, mechanically going through the motions, barely noticing as her father mechanically presided over a catered meal.

He never asked her how she was doing. He flew into town from San Francisco with Jessica in tow—Jessica, grey skinned, eyes confused and lost. He should have been taking care of her, but Carrie guessed he'd not come out of his office in months except for basic functions like eating and sleeping. Jessica was on her own, and from the looks of it, she was suffering.

At the time, Carrie had no strength or bandwidth to think of it. And so she just—didn't. She moved on, didn't think about it, and didn't give a second's thought to how distant her father was.

Because that was *normal*.

Because he wasn't actually her father.

Christmas had been worse, if that was even possible. Her father had asked Jessica to say grace, because she was the youngest, by five minutes. Jessica hadn't hesitated.

Lord, thank you for this food, given to us by minimum wage caterers, Jessica had started. Mother had gasped, and Dylan started almost out of his chair. Then she continued, *Lord, we thank you for giving us this cold family, with a psychotic mother and an icebox of a father.*

The family Christmas meal came to an early end.

Of course he was an icebox. Of course. It all made sense now.

Carrie didn't realize she was crying. Maybe that's because she'd done so much crying in the last year. Maybe it was because the nerves in her face, the nerves that would normally feel the wet slide of a tear down her cheek—those nerves were dead. Numb. Too much sensation, too much grief, too much pain. But even though she couldn't *feel* it, her body responded.

The Army Sergeant who escorted her back to the main Pentagon entrance and the vast surrounding parking lots tactfully ignored the tears that streamed down her face. Others in the hallway did much the same. The Pentagon, with its thirty thousand daily inhabitants, was a small city, complete with its own police force. Like many large cities, it turned a blind eye to the pain of transients. Carrie and her tears received little more than curious looks as she finally made her way to the exit.

There, her escort broke his professionalism. He spoke in hesitant tones. "I...I hope everything's okay, ma'am."

She gave him an ungainly smile. Fuck Richard Thompson. And fuck Chuck Rainsley, her birth father who had never done a damn thing for her or her sisters. Right now, she had one focus. Getting help for her daughter. And nobody was getting in the way of that.

"Thank you, Sergeant. It's not okay now, but it will be."

2. Andrea. April 30

"**A**nd that was it. I got home as quickly as I could."

As Carrie spoke, she sat back in her cushioned chair, the one that didn't match any of the other furniture in the room, nursing Rachel. Andrea shook her head. The revelations had come hard and fast. They weren't surprises. Not really. That Richard Thompson wasn't her father. That he wasn't even related to her.

But that just raised the question.

Where the fuck was her mother?

Andrea couldn't bring herself to resent Carrie. Unlike Carrie, she'd never had any expectations that her parents loved her or cared about her. Or at least she hadn't in a long time. This revelation might be a surprise, but it wasn't devastating. It wasn't a loss. You can't lose what you never had in the first place. So on the one hand, Carrie had the love her father for a while. Whatever that was worth. But that also meant she was hurting now in a way Andrea had long since moved on from.

So she reached out, leaning toward Carrie, and put a hand on her knee.

"We need to know more," she said.

Carrie shook her head. Her eyes were wide, confused. "What else is there to know? Our parents are liars. Our *parent*. The other one is just some guy."

"For one thing, we need to know if Senator Rainsley...our father...is a donor match. Just in case I'm not."

Carrie froze. Then she took a breath, and said, "You're right. I'm going to call his office right now. Let me just put Rachel down."

Sarah, who sat across the room from them, paperback novel open in front of her, said, "Are you sure—"

"Yes," Carrie interrupted.

Rachel was asleep, latched on. Carrie shifted the baby's position, very careful, never moving her eyes from Rachel. From her daughter. Andrea watched her...watched that fierce look of love she gave her daughter. Andrea swallowed. The emotion was too powerful.

A few moments later Carrie put the baby down in her room then slowly returned to the living room.

"Shall we?" she said, then picked up her phone and dialed directory information. "Hello? Yes. Washington, DC. United States Senate...um...I'm not sure...is there a main operator? Yes, that will work."

A fifteen second wait, then Carrie spoke into the phone again. "Senator Rainsley's office, please."

Another wait, as the main switchboard transferred her to the Texas Senator's office. Then she spoke again. "Hello. Yes, this is Doctor Carrie Sherman. I'm calling to request an appointment for tomorrow afternoon with Senator Rainsley?"

Another wait. Then she said, "Yes, I'm well aware of that. You can tell his Chief of Staff that this is a personal matter, that it involves the Secretary of Defense and Adelina Thompson, and that the Senator will know *exactly* what it's about. And...please tell the

Chief of Staff that if I don't have an answer by 4 pm, my next phone call will be to the press."

Damn, Andrea thought. She doesn't kid around. Of course, for Carrie this wasn't an academic exercise. It wasn't about reconnecting with their long lost father. It was about getting a blood test. It was about her daughter's health.

After another wait, this one much longer, Carrie sat up. "Hello? Yes, this is Carrie Sherman. You're the Senator's Chief of Staff? Oh...yes...no, I don't think the Senator would thank you if I were to tell you what it was about. It has to do with Adelina Thompson, my mother, and it's a potential scandal, and I think the Senator will want to hear from me, and that's all I'm going to say..." She smiled, then said, "Yes. I'll be happy to."

Another long wait. Then, Carrie was giving them her phone number.

"Do you think they'll actually call back?" Sarah asked.

"It all depends on whether or not the staffers took me seriously enough to mention it to the Senator. If they do, he'll make sure we get a meeting. I'm certain of that."

"In the meantime, I've got a lot of questions," Andrea said.

"Me too," Carrie said. "And I think the only people who can answer them are the Senator...and our mother."

"Try her again?"

"Yeah," Carrie replied. She began dialing her cell phone again. She put it on speaker, and the three of them heard the ringing... two, three, four, then five rings. Finally, their mother's voice, unusually calm. "This is Adelina Thompson. Please leave a message."

"Mother, this is Andrea, Sarah and Carrie. We're calling...because Dad told us about Senator Rainsley. And...we...just...please call."

She disconnected the phone.

"When did you talk with her last?" Andrea asked.

"A few days ago. The thing is...you know she stayed with us, after..." Carrie looked at the floor. "After the accident. And honestly, it was...so strange. Mother's never been...I don't know. Close? Touchy? She's always been distant. A little crazy."

"Not always," Sarah said.

"True. Not always. She was there for me after the accident." Carrie's voice came out rough. "Anyway...after the accident last year, she stayed here through the fall. Dad went home to San Francisco with Jessica, so she could finish her senior year of high school."

"I got to home school," Sarah said.

"Right. Screaming and bitching all the way," Carrie said. The words had sting, but the loving tone of voice smoothed out the rough edges. "Anyway...when Dad and Jessica got here for Christmas, it was obvious something was wrong. Jessica was...a mess."

Sarah leaned forward and said, "She was all strung out. Drunk, drugs, I don't know what."

"*Madre de dios,*" Andrea said. "Drugs?"

Sarah nodded, but it was Carrie who continued the story. "Yes. Mom was pissed at Dad...really pissed. It was the first time I ever heard her really launch into him. So right before New Year's, Mom came and talked to me. She said..." Carrie swallowed, hard.

Sarah continued the story. "She said something like, we were strong enough to pick up from here, and that Jessica needed her more now."

"Right," Carrie said. "And so she went back to San Francisco with Jessica. Dad moved back east a few weeks later, when the administration started talking about asking him to come out of retirement."

Andrea shrugged. This was all interesting, but it didn't really answer anything. "So where is she *now?*"

Carrie said, "I don't know. But... I'm worried."

CHAPTER FIFTEEN
Want a beer?

1. Dylan. Last fall.

In any kind of a decent world, you would only lose your best friend once.

But Dylan Paris had known for a long time that decent was a relative thing. Some days he woke up and stared at the ceiling and saw dead bodies. The bodies of his friends, the bodies of the people they killed. Because he lost two best friends. The first, Roberts, shredded by a bomb buried in dirt road. Roberts had probably lobbed a hundred thousand prayers in his lifetime, but they weren't enough to save him. Eighteen months later, when Dylan had finally healed, Ray was murdered by a fellow soldier.

Most of the time he was afraid to admit it to Alex, or even to himself. But—occasionally, in times of stress, in times of emotional upheaval, he saw other dead bodies. Of the people he *wanted* to hurt, but wouldn't. Because when Dylan Paris thought about Roberts being blown up in Afghanistan, when he thought of Kowalski's death saving a life in Dega Payan, when he thought of the closest friend he'd ever known, Ray Sherman, being run down by a fellow soldier, it filled Dylan with unspeakable rage. The kind of rage that can spontaneously combust. The kind of rage that could take a soul and twist it, turn it black and brittle, the kind of rage that could destroy a life.

The worst part was that Dylan couldn't tell anyone. He couldn't talk about it. He couldn't look his wife in the eyes and say, "Remember how I dealt with all that stuff and moved on? Just kidding." He didn't know where to turn. Once upon a time he would have turned to Ray. Ray was his sergeant, his leader, his best friend. Ray was his hero. Ray was the man who had inspired Dylan to heal.

Ray was gone.

After the funeral, Dylan moved on, because he had to. He cried in Alex's arms. But he didn't reveal the rage. He didn't tell her, because giving voice to that anger meant he might act on it. Giving voice to that anger meant he'd failed. A week after Ray's death, Dylan was back in classes at Columbia, buried in his schoolwork even as Ray had been buried under the ground. He went from class to class, physically healed from his injures in the Army, but internally isolated.

He knew other students talked about it. Even the other veterans. Sometimes he would hear whispers when he limped into class and slid into his seat in the back of the room. A buddy approached from the Milvets group on campus, and Dylan told him to leave him alone.

The hard part was, he knew his behavior and his isolation was hurting Alex. They'd only been married a couple of months when Ray was killed, and nothing had been right since. Every week she looked a little more haggard, a little more frustrated.

The third week in September, they took the train to DC, catching the 2 pm train out of Penn Station on Friday afternoon, both of them skipping their final class of the day. They leaned on each other the entire ride down. Sarah had been scheduled to go home that Friday, but a staph infection prevented that.

When asked how serious it was, Carrie didn't mince words. "It's serious. Very serious."

Dylan remembered the train ride down. Alex had been a mess of worry. Dylan stayed wrapped up tight, his arms around her but his emotions a million miles away. They'd taken this same nightmare train ride down just a few weeks prior, a trip that ended with his best friend's funeral.

"She'll be okay," he'd whispered to her, over and over again, as Alex fell apart. Inside, Dylan felt increasingly claustrophobic and angry. At one point he closed his eyes and imagined that he had somehow found Sergeant Hicks right before he pressed the gas pedal, right before he launched his jeep into a murderous downhill drive that ended with broken glass and dreams on a street in Washington, DC. He imagined that he reached over with a knife and cut Hicks's throat, the blood spattering everywhere.

Even that vision did nothing to ease his anger. It felt cold, almost clinical.

Nothing could bring Ray back. Nothing could change anything.

They spent that weekend in Washington, holding hands with Carrie, talking with Sarah, who lay desperately in an isolation room in the intensive care unit, harboring an antibiotic-resistant infection that could easily kill her.

Alex cried the whole way home, and Dylan held her. But his heart wasn't in it. At one point, she whispered into his neck, "You feel like you're a million miles away, Dylan."

Not quite a million. Kabul, Afghanistan was seven thousand miles from New York. Seven thousand miles of heartbreak. Seven thousand miles of loss.

Sarah pulled through. Dylan spent untold hours on the phone with her. After all, he'd been nearly crippled when his leg was severely injured in a bomb blast. As she began to struggle to recover and finally got out of bed, beginning physical therapy, Dylan stayed in touch on the phone almost every day. Encouraging her, because the fact was, recovery from that kind of injury was a bitter, awful process.

Finally, just before Columbus Day, Sarah went home. Not back to San Francisco, where she'd grown up, but to Carrie's condo in downtown Bethesda, Maryland.

That weekend, Dylan and Alex returned to Bethesda. They'd settled into a new equilibrium. Not distant, but not as close as they'd once been. Dylan loved Alex. He'd do anything for her, up to and including stopping a bullet if that's what it took.

But he couldn't tell her the truth. Because, by October, Dylan had a secret.

It happened almost by accident. On a Friday night at the end of September, he'd dropped in at a friend's dorm after class to go over an assignment.

"Want a beer?"

The question was casual, unintentionally deadly. Conrad Barstow had no clue Dylan had struggled with drugs as a teenager. He had no clue Dylan's dad was an alcoholic. So when he handed Dylan that beer, it was completely unexpected. Dylan popped the tab and took a long drink.

He had sighed. Relief flooded through his bones. Dylan had been subsisting on rage for weeks. The drink didn't fix that. It didn't get him drunk. But it took the edge of the rage off in a way that made Dylan close his eyes and nearly weep. "Thanks, man," he'd said.

It was that simple.

Dylan didn't run out and become a raging alcoholic. For one thing he was newly married, and he loved his wife. For Dylan, control mattered more than anything. Control over his life. Control over himself. Control over the alcohol. Because no matter what, he was never going to hurt her. He was never going to do what his father had done.

No matter what.

Alex knew something was wrong, but she didn't know what.

His mother, on the other hand, saw right through him. In November they flew to Atlanta to spend Thanksgiving with Dylan's mom. She met them just outside the security gate at Hartsfield Atlanta Airport, running forward and crying at the sight of her son. Dylan staggered under her weight as she caromed into him.

Linda Carlin was 42 years old. An active alcoholic until well into her thirties, her already greying hair and sagging skin made her look older. Her face was the contradictory tale of a gambler who was born again, a lifelong sinner who found God. In Linda's case, she hit bottom when she woke up lying beside a dumpster behind one of the city of Atlanta's many bars, her dress pushed up around her ears, sore all over her body and with no recollection of what had happened to her. Her alcoholic husband was nowhere to be found, and her twelve-year-old son was at home alone. That night she went to her first AA meeting.

Dylan only knew the barest outline of her story. But he knew that when she told others about it, her face glowed. She'd overcome the terror of that night, the shame of her drinking, the horror of its consequences. She'd learned to take care of herself, to lean on her God, and finally, in halting, difficult steps, to become the mother Dylan needed.

"Welcome home," she said to him. Then she turned to embrace her daughter in law. Alex clutched her as if she were a life preserver.

As they walked out of the terminal, Dylan lit a cigarette. His mother said, "We won't go until you finish—I finally quit, I don't really want the smoke in the car."

"You quit?" Dylan asked.

"Two months ago."

"Jesus. Congratulations, I had no idea."

She gave him a compassionate look. "You've had a lot on your mind."

What was that supposed to mean? Dylan thought. Did she somehow guess he was drinking again? He didn't know how to gauge her reactions, because he knew she was watching him very closely. Linda Carlin knew her alcohol and she knew her alcoholics. And, while Dylan never counted himself as a fullblown alcoholic like his parents, he knew it was in his blood. He knew that it wouldn't take much to push him over that edge, and he'd sworn he'd never go there.

But that didn't mean he couldn't drink at all. That didn't mean he had to completely restrict his life. Complete abstinence made sense for someone like his mom, who had completely wrecked her life. That's not who Dylan was.

So he rode in the backseat of her late 80s Ford Escort station wagon, complete with cracked dashboard, fuzzy dice on the rearview mirror and a One Day at a Time bumper sticker. Dylan stared off into space in silence as his mother drove them back to her place. Alex sat up front, making awkward conversation.

His mother and his wife couldn't have more disparity in their backgrounds. Alex came from the wealthy Thompson family. Daughter to an Ambassador. She'd lived in Belgium and China and Russia and spoke flawless French. Like all of her sisters, she'd trained on a classical instrument (the violin) from a young age and was an accomplished musician, yet she didn't judge his amateurish, self-taught guitar playing. Alex was so far out of Dylan's league that some days he was still astonished he'd won her over.

Linda Carlin—she'd gone back to her maiden name after giving Dylan's father the boot—was from a dirt-poor north Georgia family. Her father occasionally found work as a short-order cook, but usually couldn't hold a job long. Her mother was killed by a drunk driver who ran across the lane on a winding two-lane blacktop in the North Georgia mountains in 1988, Linda's junior year in high school. His mom didn't graduate high school—Jimmy Paris—the charmer with a lopsided grin, broad shoulders and too-quick fists—got her pregnant the summer before her senior year.

Despite the dramatic differences in their backgrounds, Alex and Linda got along amazingly well. They had little in common besides their love for Dylan, but that was enough to create a powerful common bond. So as they chatted on the way to her apartment in Stone Mountain, Dylan just stared out the window at the passing cars. In the front seat, Alex and his mom talked about school, about their tiny studio apartment on 102nd Street in Manhattan, and finally about the events that had rocked their lives: Ray Sherman's death.

That caught Dylan's attention, his eyes darting back up to the front of the car. He didn't say anything. Just listened. But that strategy wasn't going to work, because his mom asked him directly, "How are you holding up, Dylan?"

He shrugged. "I'm good."

"That sounds like a crock of shit to me, Dylan."

Dylan winced. Not that his language was any better. But Alex came from a much more refined background. "Mom, come on…"

"Don't you 'Mom' me, Dylan. I was worried about you before, and now even more so."

"I'm doing all right."

"You talking to your therapist?"

Christ on a crutch. He *had* been, right up until July. When Dylan had arrived in New York in the fall of 2012, he didn't kid around. Focused on healing from his injuries, he'd spent five mornings a week at the VA hospital in Manhattan. Three days for physical therapy, two for post-traumatic stress. His psychologist was a fully qualified mental health practitioner, but more important for Dylan, he was also a combat veteran with two tours in Iraq under his belt. When Dylan talked about digging entire families out of the snow, when he talked about people being blown to bits by grenades, his therapist knew *exactly* what he was talking about.

Until July, right before Sherman was killed. Then, his doctor was replaced by a twenty-three-year-old intern, Heather Katz. Heather was cute, perky, and clueless. Dylan missed two appointments, then two more, and pretty soon he was only going to his now weekly physical therapy appointments. He'd leave the apartment early in the morning, take the subway downtown, then sit on a park bench reading. It was calming and peaceful, but he didn't like that he found himself telling more and more lies to Alex.

He finally answered his mother. "Yeah, I'm talking to my therapist. It's just grief, Mom. Everybody goes through it."

"I'm worried about you," she said, eyeing him in the rearview mirror.

"Mom, leave it alone, will you?"

The rest of the awkward ride continued. Finally, they pulled up to his mom's house. A one-story, two-bedroom ranch house with brick facing on the front and 70s style wood paneling throughout the interior. The last time he and Alex had been there was midsummer, two weeks after their wedding. His mom had done a considerable amount of landscaping in the months since, planting fall perennials.

When she parked, Dylan lagged behind and got the bags out while his mom unlocked the door. Alex hung back, leaned close, and said, "Why are you being so rude to your mom?"

His eyes widened. "What?"

"You're being mean, Dylan."

"Shit. Sorry. I'm just grumpy today."

She sighed then touched his arm. "You're always grumpy, lately."

Dylan swallowed, then said, "Sorry, sweetheart. I'll try." He turned and picked up the bags and began to carry them toward the house.

Inside, Dylan's mother's house had made progress. Growing up, he'd lived in whatever shitty apartment his parents could afford. A couple of times—when he was younger—that meant fairly nice apartment complexes. But by the time he was a preteen, they mostly lived in weekly rooms and tiny roach-infested apartments. But after six years clean, during Dylan's senior year in high school, his mother had announced a surprise. She was buying a house. It was tiny, in a depressed area well outside the city of Atlanta. But it was hers. During the months after he got out of Walter Reed and before leaving for Columbia, Dylan had stayed here. Every day she'd kept herself busy: painting, refinishing floors, and patching walls. What had been a crappy, terrible house was now a showpiece on the inside.

Along the mantelpiece were photographs. The display and the silver frames were all new, part of his mother's ongoing rehabilitation of both her living quarters and her life. Alex approached the photos eagerly when they entered the house. Dylan was a little more wary.

"This is new," Alex said, smiling.

His mom gave Alex a proud look. "I bought the frames at an estate sale for a dollar each."

"They're beautiful," Alex replied.

The frames were, indeed beautiful—silver filigreed with costume gems. The photos were something else entirely. His grandparents, before his grandmother died in the accident. His mother's older brother, crouched on the front slope of an Abrams tank in Iraq in 1991. Jay Carlin was an Army Master Sergeant now, and he'd encouraged Dylan to think about the military. The largest photo made Alex and Dylan gasp. In the center, Alex was in her white wedding dress, Dylan's arm around her waist. They were flanked by their unnaturally tall best man and maid of honor—Carrie and Ray Sherman, who had secretly married the day before. Ray looked sharp in his dress blues.

Dylan felt his eyes go wet, and he sniffed.

"I love that picture." Alex slid a hand up his arm.

"I miss him," Dylan whispered.

"Me too," she replied.

He tried to shake it off. "Come on," he said. "Let's get this stuff put away."

When Dylan awoke on Thanksgiving morning, he was disoriented. His neck hurt and his back was sore, and he was curled up on his side on the edge of a none-too-comfortable mattress in his mother's house.

In the kitchen, his mother bustled about, preparing a Thanksgiving meal as she and Alex talked. Dylan could easily hear them from the room—his mother's house was tiny, after all. So he lay there on the bed, his eyes closed. He wanted a cigarette and a cup of coffee, as soon as possible. But for the moment, he lay on his side listening.

They were talking about *him*.

"I don't know," Alex said. "He's been through an awful lot."

"Dylan's stronger than you may think," his mother said. "Even before he went into the Army, he'd lived more than a lot of adults twice his age."

"I know. But the one person who doesn't believe in him is himself. Ray used to be able to shake him out of his moods. But I don't know how to."

He heard his mother sigh. "It's a tough road. He loved Ray."

"I loved him too," Alex replied. "But I'm not dropping out of life. I'm worried about him, Linda."

His mother said something, he couldn't tell what, and Alex replied, "I don't know how to help him."

Fuck.

He rolled out of bed and threw clothes on. He didn't care what. He needed to get a cigarette and a cup of coffee. He stumbled out of the room, and both of them went quiet. Alex looked guilty. He murmured, "Morning," as he walked by, then poured himself a cup of coffee. In silence, he prepared his coffee with his back to Alex and his mom, then went and sat outside on the porch.

He lit a cigarette and stared up at the sky, grateful that it wasn't gray or raining.

Four hours later the first guest arrived—his mother's sponsor in AA. Mary Lou Sorensen was a conservatively dressed sixty-five-year-old woman, so tiny and frail Dylan was afraid a stiff breeze might carry her away. As Mary Lou got out of her car and headed slowly up the walk, she teetered a little on her heels. She wore a red and white suit, with a long string of pearls around her neck and bracelets at her wrist. Her hair was teased and poufed in a style that was probably popular in the decade before Dylan was born.

"Is that little Dylan? Well, I'll be…I haven't seen you since you was in high school."

"Hey, Mary Lou, happy Thanksgiving."

As she approached, he saw the signs of age. More wrinkles underneath the makeup around her eyes, her hair now fully grey. Dylan took her arm and led her toward the house.

"How is Columbia, Dylan?"

"It's going well," he said. "I love the classes. How about you? You still teaching at the pen?"

"I am," she replied, smiling. Mary Lou spent most of the 1970s as an *inmate* in the Atlanta Women's Prison, following her 1972 conviction for murder. While there, she'd gotten sober, found God, and begun a new life. Now she went back to the Metro State Prison, a women's maximum security prison, three times a week to lead AA meetings and teach classes.

Dylan opened the door and led her in. Alex met them as she came out of the kitchen.

"Alex, this is Miss Mary Lou. May Lou, this is my wife, Alexandra."

"Oh, Lordy," Mary Lou said, her face flushing red. "I'm so excited to meet you, Alexandra. What a beautiful name."

"I mostly just go by Alex."

"Some names shouldn't be shortened," Mary Lou replied. "And yours is one of them. That's a name that says royalty. I love it. Come sit and talk to me, dear."

Just like that, Mary Lou had Alex by the arm and was leading her off to the living room. Dylan chuckled a little as he walked into the kitchen.

His mother was still bustling around.

"Hey, Mom, Mary Lou is here."

His mother said, "Oh, can you keep her company—"

"Don't worry." He cut her off. "She and Alex are chatting."

His mother smiled. "Well, then, that's good. Maybe you and I could talk for a minute then?"

She didn't wait for an answer. Instead, she turned back into the kitchen, expecting him to follow.

He did, of course, automatically reaching to help as she stooped to pull a huge turkey out of the oven.

His mother didn't pussyfoot around. "Your wife is worried about you, Dylan. So am I."

Shit, he thought. "Mom, you gotta give it a rest—"

"No. Listen to me. I know you've had a rough couple of years. I know it's been much harder than you ever expected. You just have to stop trying to do it all on your own. You've got a lovely woman there who wants to help you."

"Ma, I'm all right—"

"You're drinking again, aren't you?"

He froze. She nodded her head. "I thought so. How much?"

"Not much. Just every once in a while. Mom, I'm not like you and Dad, I don't fall apart every time I have a drink, okay? That was your issue, not mine."

She shook her head. "You're fooling yourself. You're not out drinking at parties or social occasions."

"No, just one every once in a while to take the edge off."

"If you're drinking to *take the edge off*, you're going to turn into a drunk, Dylan. That's the way it works."

He shook his head. "Not everybody's like you, Mom."

"No. But you are. You're my son, and I'm worried about you. You haven't told her, have you?"

"No," he replied. "And I don't want you to. I'll talk to her when it's time."

"Oh, Dylan. I can't promise you that. It's not just about you."

"I don't know what that's supposed to mean."

She shook her head. "She's your wife. You need to talk with her. You need to ask her for help."

Dylan stared at his mother. "Are you seriously going to do this? You ruined my entire childhood, and now you're going to ruin my marriage?"

His mother gave him a long, sad look. "Dylan, you're making your own choices. You need to get help."

2. Alexandra. Last fall.

Alexandra Thompson was probably the least experienced and least cynical of the Thompson sisters. But that didn't make her an idiot. She'd been through heartache. She'd been through sexual assault. Step by step, she'd helped the man she loved rebuild his life. And then she'd gone through the heartache of seeing Dylan's best friend, her sister's husband, killed.

What Alexandra learned in the weeks following Ray's death were lessons she wished she'd never had to think about. She'd never minimize or underestimate the incredible pain Carrie went through with the loss of her husband. The two of them had been passionate lovers, and Ray's loss was a staggering blow to Carrie.

But Alexandra also saw what it did to Dylan. Because he had walked into that hospital room last August to say goodbye, and he shambled out a dead man. Cold. Isolated. His eyes a thousand miles away. He didn't speak. He didn't cry. He walked to the waiting room chairs and slumped into his seat, staring straight ahead, eyes unfocused. He broke Alexandra's heart, because she knew right then that the grief he felt was going to take a long time to deal with. She knew right then that Dylan Paris wasn't going to be healed in an hour or a day or a week or a year—this was going to be a lifetime effort.

She struggled the first few days. In the past, faced with such an emotional gut punch, she would have instinctively called her big sister Carrie. Carrie, who had taken care of all of them. Carrie who'd been a shoulder for Julia to cry on, a protective shield for Alexandra and the younger girls. Carrie, who had been stripped of everything that mattered. She *couldn't* go to Carrie and burden her with even more problems, especially problems rooted in the same loss she'd suffered. One night she found herself picking up her phone not long after dinner. She dialed Julia without really paying attention.

Julia had just left a lunch meeting in Canberra. Alexandra didn't kid around, quickly briefing her.

"Do you think he's drinking again?" Julia had asked.

The question haunted Alexandra. Less because of any inherent concern about alcohol—she'd never known or had to live with a practicing alcoholic—but more because of the implication that Dylan might be keeping secrets from her. Because if he was hiding that from her, then she had no idea what he might be doing.

So she kept an eye out. She paid attention. When he came home late from class, she watched him. She surreptitiously smelled his breath, and sometimes her eyes fell on a receipt in the trash that she wouldn't have noticed or paid any attention to. Without being consciously aware of it, she'd slipped into the role of the suspicious or concerned wife. And she hated that. She hated even the idea of that role. For her entire life she'd seen her mother and father manipulate each other to the point where it was impossible to know what was truth and what was a lie.

Sometimes, even though she loved Dylan with all her heart, she asked herself if she'd really screwed up by marrying someone with an admitted drinking problem, someone with post-traumatic stress, someone who was the child of alcoholics. She loved Dylan. But sometimes, when he was sitting and looking out the window a million miles away from her, she was scared of him.

The one thing she never did was ask him directly if he was drinking. She wanted him to come clean on his own. She wanted him to ask for help. She wanted him to finally do what he needed to take care of himself and of her. So she didn't put him in a position where he'd lie. And, at this point, she knew if she pressed him on it, he would lie to her.

So they went to Atlanta for Thanksgiving to see his mother, and she let things slide. One night in early December he stumbled home. Not drunk, but not sober either. And his breath smelled of fresh mouthwash.

She let it go. She held him, even when he pushed away. She loved him.

But it was hard.

On December 23rd they took the train from Penn Station to Washington, DC for their third trip to the city after Ray's death. This time they'd be crowded in—the entire Thompson clan would be in town, with the exception of Andrea.

"Why isn't Andrea coming?" she'd asked Julia.

Julia just sighed. "I tried to persuade her. But can you blame her? She doesn't believe Mom and Dad want her."

Alexandra had difficulty fathoming that. She knew her father was cold and her mother difficult, but so were a million other parents. She never quite understood the level of drama Julia brought to the table when it came to their mother, even though she did remember some horrible confrontations between the two when she was younger. *Of course* Mom and Dad wanted Andrea.

Except...did they?

One day in the summer of 2002 Carrie had sat down with her. They'd taken the trolley to the waterfront and walked along the beach next to the Hyde Street Pier, both of them licking ice cream.

You know I'm leaving for college in a few weeks, Carrie had said.

Of course I do, Alexandra replied.

"I've always kind of tried to be...sort of a big sister to you and the twins and Andrea. Almost like a mom when I could. You know, for when Mom's all crazy."

Alexandra shrugged.

"The thing is," Carrie said. "Me and Julia, we made a pact. That we'd always watch out for you guys. That we'd always watch out for each other. Sisters."

The words were intense, dripping with heavy meaning that Alexandra didn't completely get. Finally she said, "What about Mom?"

"She's...not always the best mom she could be. You know? I'm just saying...with me gone...it's up to you, Alexandra. To watch out for the twins and Andrea. Just to make sure they're okay, you know?"

Alexandra nodded. "Of course, I'll watch out for them."

Carrie had stopped and looked her in the eye.

"Promise me," she said.

"I promise."

The thing was, you can't keep promises like that. You can try, you can do everything you can, but Alexandra was only thirteen years old when Carrie left for college.

Thirteen year olds can try to keep promises, but they can't keep their younger sisters from being sent away.

She did everything she could. But in the end, it wasn't enough. Andrea *did* go away, first for a few weeks, then a summer, then eventually for the school year. By the time she was a pre-teen, Andrea only came home for the holidays.

This year, not even that.

Nobody said anything to her. Julia and Carrie didn't look her in the eye and say, *You failed her.* They didn't say out loud that they blamed her for not protecting Andrea. But she knew. She'd heard about their promise to each other, to the family, for years. That's *all* she'd heard about was their sacred fucking promise.

The promise she couldn't keep. Julia and Carrie had cared for each other, and they'd cared for her. But Alexandra couldn't manage to watch out for her sisters. She'd left behind a rebellious punk rocker, a pill popping preppie and the sister who went away and wouldn't even return her phone calls.

Alex's legacy was failure, but she didn't intend to keep it that way. She wasn't going to fail Dylan. No matter what.

So she kept him close. She talked to him every day. She *tried*.

When they arrived in Bethesda for Christmas, the family was already in an uproar. Dylan followed Alex into the condo, where they immediately heard Adelina's voice from a back room. She was shouting. Alex gave Dylan a worried look as they walked in. The first person they saw was Sarah, sitting in her wheelchair near the couch, a book open in front of her. She looked up at them over the top of the book. Her face was shiny with sweat.

"Hey, Alexandra," Sarah had said.

"Sarah!" Alex rushed over to Sarah, who said she was fine, just running a bit of a fever.

The next four days were chaos. Jessica spent the bulk of her time in her room, because every appearance resulted in another outburst of argument between Richard and Adelina.

"You were supposed to be taking care of our daughter!" Adelina would shout.

"I'm fine, Mom!" Jessica replied.

"Have you seen her report card?" Adelina called out.

Richard, as always, retreated. He hadn't regularly occupied the office in the Bethesda condo in more than ten years—it was Carrie's office now—but that didn't stop him from disappearing into the office and locking the door behind him.

The sisters were torn on how to react. Julia was staying with Crank at the Hyatt Regency a block away. She said, "Mom's making a crisis out of nothing, as always."

Carrie was more reserved. "I'm concerned. Dad probably stayed locked in his office the entire fall. God only knows what Jessica's been up to."

Alexandra, who had done more than her share of drinking in college, backed her mother.

Sarah, fighting another infection, mostly stayed in bed or parked in her wheelchair near the couch, glassy eyed from painkillers.

It was an incredibly uncomfortable, tense couple of days. Dylan spent a fair amount of it standing out on the balcony, freezing his ass off, smoking.

This time, he didn't have Crank to keep him company. "Trying to quit, man," Crank said. "I'm not getting any younger."

Dylan gave Crank a wry look. "You're not exactly an old man yet. What are you, thirty?"

"Thirty-three. But that's not the point. Point is, you gotta grow up some time."

"Yeah," Dylan said. "True enough."

The fussing and yelling between Adelina, Richard and Jessica continued right up until the morning after Christmas. It was a little after 11:30 in the morning, and all of the sisters (except Andrea) were seated around the table with their parents, Crank and Dylan. The family only rarely used the formal dining room in the condo, but with this many people, they were seated around the large table. Platters were piled high with bacon and eggs, pancakes and French toast, all of it carefully laid out by caterers from the Hyatt.

"You're staying in Washington," Adelina announced just after breakfast, glowering at Richard. "I will return to San Francisco with Jessica."

He raised his eyebrows, then took his napkin from his lap, carefully wiped his mouth, and tossed the napkin on the table.

"I think that's a good idea," he said. "It appears I need to move back to Washington, anyway, I've been asked by the President to come out of retirement."

With that, he stood and walked out of the room, leaving a stunned silence in his wake.

CHAPTER SIXTEEN
It started in the womb

1. Jessica. April 30

Jessica Thompson leaned against the wall, her eyes drooping, shivering a little.

"Do you need a break?" The question came from Sister Kiara Langley, her therapist. Sister Kiara was a web of contradictions. An African-American from Los Angeles. A Roman Catholic nun with a PhD in psychology. For the last ten days, she'd been in Jessica's room three times a day to probe and ask questions. Questions Jessica wasn't prepared to answer.

For the first several days she'd said as little as possible. A few times she screamed until Kiara left. But by the end of the fifth day, she felt nothing but exhaustion. Her skin and her soul were numb. Everything was numb.

"No," Jessica said. "I'm just...still tired. So tired." She closed her eyes.

"Jessica, I need you to stay awake for a while. I told you, you're going to feel tired for quite a while, and probably depressed. It's a common side effect."

"Yeah, I know," Jessica said. Depressed was an understatement. She couldn't laugh. She just felt dead inside. The night before, a dozen or so of the residents of the retreat had gathered to watch a movie: a romantic comedy. Her mother had laughed, a lot. So had a lot of the others there. But Jessica just sat there, staring. It wasn't funny.

"Why couldn't I laugh?" she asked.

Kiara said, "Well, it's complicated. You know what dopamine is? In your brain? Basically, that's what gives you pleasure. The meth makes it so you can't produce as much of it. And on top of having less of it, the dopamine receptors are...basically burned. There's less of them functioning. And it's going to be a long, long time before those function normally again."

"And in the meantime?"

"In the meantime you stay clean. When you go home, you'll be in therapy. You'll go to a long-term treatment program. But it's mostly up to you. You're eighteen years old. I can't keep you here, and your mother can't keep you here. It's up to you now."

Jessica didn't want it to be up to her. She wanted to just curl up and let someone else take care of her.

"I want to stay clean," Jessica said.

"So what do you need to do, Jessica?"

She nodded, slowly. "Talk."

"Right."

She crossed her arms across her chest. "Can we turn up the heat in here? It's freezing."

"Sure," Sister Kiara said. The nun walked to the door and adjusted the thermostat, then returned to her seat. "Tell me a little about when all this started."

"The meth? Or the other stuff."

"All of it."

Jessica took a deep breath. "It started in the womb, really. My twin got all the personality and smarts and...everything, really."

"What's her name?"

"Sarah. She won't tell you, but Sarah means *Princess*, and that's just what she is. She likes to dress all shocking—combat boots and black clothes and makeup, but even when we were little girls, it was always Sarah who had the attention. Sarah made friends. Sarah smiled, and—she had it all."

Jessica shook her head. "Don't get me wrong. I'm not blaming her for all of this. That was just the way it was. Sarah smiled and everyone came running. Sarah got in trouble, said something funny, and everyone laughed. For me it was just—always a little harder. I stayed quiet and in the background and just...did my thing."

Sister Kiara smiled at her and said, "How did that make you feel?"

Jessica looked away. Then she turned back to Kiara and said, "Sometimes I felt really alone. My oldest sisters were all gone. I used to get along great with Andrea—she's my youngest sister—but she moved away to Spain to live with our grandmother. I did make some friends at school, and...I dated a girl for a while. But she broke up with me."

Jessica looked away again. Up until now, Kiara had mostly just asked questions, but she was certain the admission that she was attracted to girls would prompt condemnation from her. After all, Kiara may have a PhD, she might have been dressed in jeans and a button down shirt, but she was a nun.

Kiara, though, only said, "Talk to me about your relationship with your sisters."

She rolled her eyes. "I have almost no relationship with my sisters. I'm the good one. The quiet one. Besides, can you even *imagine* the pressure I'm under? Julia went to Harvard and runs a multi-million dollar business she built herself. Carrie went to Columbia and Rice and is a scientist at the NIH for Chrissake. Even

Alexandra, she's at Columbia in pre-law and had *perfect* grades and the *perfect* boyfriend and then the *perfect* wedding. Everything's so *perfect* for all of them I could just puke."

Sister Kiara leaned back in her seat and murmured, "Now we're getting somewhere. Do you really feel like their lives are perfect?"

"No," Jessica replied in an empty voice. "Carrie's a widow. She just had a baby."

Kiara looked startled. Somehow her briefings from Jessica's mother hadn't included this bit of information. "Tell me more."

Jessica said, "Car accident last summer. I was in the car too. Sarah was hurt really bad, and Ray—that's Carrie's husband—was killed."

"Drunk driver?"

"No. Murder. Or...murder-suicide, I guess."

"I see," Kiara said, her eyes wide. "Were you hurt?"

"Just some glass fragments. Scratches."

"So what is home life like now? Is Sarah in school? Do you two get in much conflict since the accident?"

Jessica shook her head. "I don't really see her. She stayed with Carrie and my mom in Washington after the accident. I came home with Dad."

Sister Kiara looked troubled. "Are you and your father close?"

Jessica snorted. "Are you kidding me?"

2. Adelina. April 30

The dream always started the same.

It was 1981. She was in what should have been her normal seat, violin at her chin, eyes fixed on Antoni Ros-Marba, principal conductor of the Orquesta Nacional de Espana *in Madrid. Eyebrows arched over his rounded glasses, his hair swept back on his head, he held his conductor's baton high in the air. A broad smile on his face as his eyes met her. She knew that he knew she had talent that would one day land her in the first chair. They all did. She held her breath, and the audience stirred in anticipation.*

Ros-Marba's arms fell, signaling the music to begin, but she froze. Her stomach twisted in pain. Richard was there, in the audience. Thirty-one years old to her sixteen. Handsome. His dark hair fell down over his forehead, his lips curled up in a cruel grin. He stood, but no one else in the audience noticed as he made his way down the aisle. She couldn't breathe. She couldn't think. Richard reached Ros-Marba and shoved him out of the way effortlessly, and the other members of the orchestra turned away.

Adelina dropped her precious violin. The instrument cracked, fragments of wood flying everywhere. Her right hand uncurled and the bow fell to the floor with a crash.

Richard finally reached her. Almost gently, he reached out a hand and wrapped it around her throat.

"What are you doing up here, Adelina? You know better."

The room was dark and smelled of ammonia and sweat. In the first row of the audience, her mother and brothers slowly turned their backs.

She woke up choking.

A blanket was stuffed in her mouth, balled up in her fist, keeping the pain inside, where it belonged. She lay on her side, curled up, knees drawn up to her chest, the chest pains familiar. She slowly pulled the blanket away from her mouth, once she was sure the accumulated regret and terror wouldn't force its way out in the form of sound.

She was drenched in sweat. It was nearly six o'clock, and the day wasn't going to get started on its own. Out of habit, she rolled over and picked up her phone. No messages. No signal still. Ironic, she thought. For years she'd done everything she could to make sure she was never out of cell phone range. Checking for messages, checking for *that* phone call, was second nature. But when she'd arrived at Saint Mary's ten days ago with Jessica, she'd noticed there was no signal and just shrugged it off. It had been sixteen years. If the call was going to come, it would come. Jessica came first. Richard had the number for the retreat center if there was an emergency.

Not that her children wanted her around anyway.

She slid out of the bed and padded her way to the shower. The rooms here were simple, but more than adequate for her needs. This retreat had been to save her daughter. But she was beginning to wonder if—just maybe—there was hope for her too.

The dreams had been troubling her increasingly in the last few months. Except for a few days at Thanksgiving and Christmas, she'd not slept in the same bed—or even the same city—as Richard. Not since last August. She would have thought the nightmares would get better. She would have thought the anxiety would get better. But it hadn't. In fact, it had been worse, sometimes so bad that she lay paralyzed in bed, unable to function at all.

It didn't make any sense. It was like she was a prisoner, just out of jail, just looking for an opportunity to go back. To go back to safety. To go back behind locked doors.

Ironic, because for thirty years she'd believed that when her children were grown, she was going to leave him at the first opportunity. Instead, her reprieve would soon be over. Jessica would graduate from high school in June (probably) and she would no longer have a legitimate excuse to avoid her husband. She would go back to Washington, the city she hated most of any in the world, and smile and be the diplomatic wife to the new Secretary of Defense and one day she would give up, walk into her bathroom and bleed out because there was no longer any point.

But for now, at least, Jessica needed her. This was their last day at Saint Mary's Retreat. The retreat center was situated on the edge of the Sequoia National Forest, and had provided the most peaceful ten days Adelina had experienced since her childhood. She didn't want to leave.

The days had a structure here. Each morning she awoke and joined one of the three meals served in the common area, sitting next to Jessica, her sullen, resentful daughter. The first three days Jessica didn't eat at all, but since then, she'd begun to astonish everyone in the center, putting away two or three meals at a sitting and sleeping almost all the rest of the time. She'd gained weight, a lot of it, in the last few days. It wasn't enough—even after the weight gain, she was only approaching 90 pounds, and looked dangerously unhealthy.

Their next stop, had this not worked, would have been a psychiatric institution.

After the morning meal, Jessica typically slept most of the morning, then met with Sister Kiara, the no-nonsense nun and therapist who had so impressed Adelina.

Adelina herself walked every morning on the well-marked path through the forest. The sequoias were staggering in their beauty. She found herself stopping for long periods of time. Sometimes to sit. Sometimes to pray. Sometimes to weep. For years she'd held herself aloof, but here, it was impossible to deny the immensity of God. Here, she felt Him just in reach, in the deep shade below the

trees, in the glades and the deep foliage, in the flowers that unfolded in the windows of sunlight that shone down to the forest floor.

After her walks, she often returned to the retreat center in a
state of tears. Nobody commented on it, except for Jessica. On the
third day of her withdrawals, she'd seen her mother crying, and
said, "What the fuck is wrong with *you*?"

In the afternoons, she met with Father Ross, one of the spiritual
directors.

Ross generally dressed casually in blue jeans and thick flannel
shirts, except on the days he performed Mass. All the same, he
challenged Adelina.

"Everybody gets forgiveness, Adelina. Even you. That's what
grace is."

She just shook her head. They argued. He gave her verses in
scripture to read. Some of them helped. Some of them decided-
ly didn't. But all of them made her think. All of them made her
question. She was deeply concerned with both the spiritual and the
temporal questions. She couldn't solve the temporal ones...not today, anyway. But her soul, and the souls of her children...that was
something else.

But she knew she didn't rate forgiveness.

"Jesus didn't talk about grace," she said.

Ross sighed when she said things like that. "He talked about
forgiveness, Adelina."

"He talked about law. He said adultery was forbidden. That
even *thinking* about adultery was forbidden. He said that *wanting*
to murder was the same as murder."

"You haven't committed murder, Adelina."

But she wanted to.

Ross took her hands. "Adelina, listen to me. We are all sinners.
But you, me, all of us, can be forgiven."

She knew better. But she still prayed.

Her discussions with Father Ross were challenging on a host of levels. Intellectually and spiritually. It was apparent that he genuinely cared about her welfare. It was equally evident that he was hopelessly naive and didn't have the first clue what she was talking about. He lived in a retreat center amidst the sequoias, where God was apparent right outside his front door. She didn't get to live in that world. She lived in a world where charming diplomats turned out to be liars. She lived in a world defined by anxiety and fear. She'd lived in that world for thirty-three years.

Thirty-three years she'd protected her daughters from that bastard. Thirty-three years she'd suffered, alone.

For Adelina Thompson, it was time to leave that world. No matter what it took.

CHAPTER SEVENTEEN
It seems I found one

1. Adelina. February 23, 1981

Adelina Ramos felt her cheeks heat up. The American diplomat, Richard Thompson, had stopped in the shop for the third time in a week. He wore a dark double breasted pinstriped suit with a narrow black tie, and his hair, too long for Spanish tastes, was swept back on his forehead. He had a broad face, blue eyes and a strong chin. She guessed he was somewhere in his late twenties, and by the look of the suit, he was quite rich. Whenever he was there, she stammered and acted like a fool.

Adelina wore an ankle-length white linen dress with embroidered flowers, hand sewn by her grandmother.

The previous week, he'd come into her father's flower shop, three blocks from the *El Palacio del Congreso de los Diputados,* the lower house of the Spanish parliament. He'd come in to place an order of flowers. Dozens of flowers in multiple arrangements to be delivered to the US Embassy, then on from there to the *Cortes.*

Her father, Manuel Ramos, a dour and serious man, took the order. Always polite, but never charming, her father made halting conversation with the diplomat. Richard Thompson, from San

Francisco, California. Thompson had a ready smile, startling blue eyes and charming manners.

Three days later Thompson was back to take the initial delivery. This time he wore jeans and a plain black t-shirt, which highlighted a lean but muscular frame. Her father, unfortunately, was out at the time, leaving Adelina to mind the store. She helped him load the flowers into the back of a boxy looking yellow SEAT Bocenegra. The back seat was folded down, so there was just room for the flowers.

"What sort of function are the flowers for, Señor?" she had asked. In Spanish. Most of their rare American customers spoke no Spanish, but Thompson spoke functional, if not perfect Spanish.

"We plan to deliver them to your *Cortes* as a goodwill gesture," he replied.

A week passed after his second visit before he returned again.

"Señorita Ramos," Thompson said when he stepped into the shop.

"Señor Thompson," she replied. "Can I help you with something?"

He smiled, a crooked, wolfish grin. "I came here looking for a flower. It seems I found one."

Her eyes dived for the floor. "You're too kind, Señor."

"Señorita Ramos. In all seriousness, I'm here to see you. I have tickets to the theater for Friday evening. I would be grateful if you would attend with me."

She shifted uncomfortably. "Sir, I'm sixteen."

His eyes widened. "I hadn't realized, Señorita."

Her tone prim, she said, "Even if I wasn't, I have an audition for the National Orchestra on Friday. I'm sure I'll be too busy for you."

"Well, then. Another time."

With that, he whisked out of the shop, and at that moment, she assumed out of her life.

Forty minutes later, the phone rang. She knew who it was. At fifteen minutes before six, it could only be her father, calling to tell her to lock up at six o'clock. That happened once or twice a week, usually when he got caught up having one too many glasses of fino with his friends and cousins.

It was fine. She'd grown used to it. Every day she went directly from school to the shop, where she would do homework at the counter until closing time, often while eating a snack. Her father worked hard. Born the Marquis of Cerverales, he'd lost everything during the Franco dictatorship because of his support of the left-ists. He started over in the early 1970s with nothing but a flower cart, but by the time Franco was gone and King Juan Carlos began to implement democratic reforms, he'd built a new life.

He'd lost his title—and nearly his life—but her father still had his bragging rights. He often drank too much at the cafe down the street from the *Cortez*, where he talked of old political battles long since won and lost. During the spring, summer and fall, the cafe spilled out onto the sidewalk. Since November, though, it had been buttoned up tight. It pained Adelina to see her father when he was lost in nostalgia. But she also felt pride for him. Her parents were separated—her mother had returned to live in Calella with two-year-old Luis—but her mother still taught her to take pride in her father.

In the year since her parents had separated, Adelina had stayed with her father. Divorce, though technically legal in Spain for the first time as of that year, was still largely unheard of.

Adelina was in her second year playing violin for the National Youth Orchestra, and her father spent a substantial portion of his meager earnings on her continued lessons. Her hours sitting behind the counter—often with little business—were all she could offer in return.

At five minutes after six she locked the door and rolled the steel shutters down over the front door, then tightened her scarf and tugged on tight leather gloves to ward off the icy wind. It was dark already, and she felt a shiver as she slid the padlock in place to secure the shutters.

She stepped back, startled, as a large truck barreled the wrong way up Calle los Madrazo. The truck spit out black smoke, and she saw soldiers sitting in the truck as it sped away.

Adelina turned in the other direction to head home, just in time to see Richard Thompson approaching. She let out a startled gasp, suddenly very aware of the fact that most of the shops were closed and it was dark and very cold.

"Señorita," he called out. Commanded.

She tucked her head down and began to walk, her shoes clicking on the sidewalk. He followed. "Señorita," he said, his voice louder.

"Please leave me alone." Adelina's voice shook as she said the words. Then she staggered at the sound of a loud explosion.

Thompson stopped in his tracks. Another truck had pulled up to the end of the street, and soldiers poured out of it. They had their weapons at the ready and one of them shouted.

That's when she heard the cracking, high-pitched sound of a machine gun. One, two, a dozen shots, then more. Adelina screamed and backed against the side of the lane as soldiers ran up the street.

Thompson backed up against the wall next to her.

"Señorita, we must get under cover. I'm afraid it's Basque terrorists. Or a coup."

More shots. A lot of them.

Her eyes rolled as she desperately sought an avenue of escape. "Come! Now!" Thompson shouted. He reached out and grabbed her gloved hand. Even though the shots were in the distance, the proximity of the shouting soldiers and the gunshots terrified her. She gripped Thompson's hand harder and ran behind him.

He came to a stop in front of her father's shop. "Unlock it," he ordered. His voice was unnaturally calm, as if he were used to hearing gunfire. "We'll stay in there until the trouble has cleared."

Her hands shook so hard she dropped her keys. He grabbed them and unlocked the padlock, slid the shutters up only halfway, then pulled her inside.

1. Julia. April 30. 1:15 PM Pacific.

Julia Wilson felt disoriented as the driver took the exit off I-105 onto Crenshaw Boulevard. Hawthorne Municipal Airport was a single-runway public airport south of Los Angeles. Julia had called ahead to ensure their charter was ready to fly, including the extra passengers.

Flying a charter aircraft could be expensive. But as often as they traveled during the touring season, it actually worked out cheaper to charter a plane for three or six months out of the year. Operating expenses worked out to about a thousand dollars for every hour they were in the air, but that was *still* cheaper than other forms of travel for a dozen or more people at a time. Several years before Julia had run the numbers on buying a private aircraft and just hiring a full time crew, but the charters worked out to be a lot cheaper.

Her confusion was due to what her sister Carrie had just told her on the phone. "I can't believe that," she said.

"I know," Carrie replied. "He's been lying our entire lives. *They've* been lying our entire lives."

"It doesn't make any sense," Julia said. "It wasn't even Senator Rainsley she had the affair with. It was George Lansing." Her eyes darted to Crank, sitting next to her, and Anthony, who sat in the front passenger seat. Anthony's eyes were wide.

She mouthed, "That is *off* the record. Mouth. Shut."

Anthony mimed turning a key at his mouth.

"I remember you telling me about that...who was George Lansing?"

Julia shrugged. "I didn't really know him exactly—he worked in consular affairs. I just remember Mom spending a lot of time with him in the fall of '96. I stayed as far away as I could. I was busy with school and all that stuff too, I don't really remember that much."

"But Mom told you for sure about him?" Carrie sounded almost desperate.

"Not exactly. No. Now that I think about it, *she* never said she had an affair with him. But she didn't argue when I accused her, either."

"Whatever," Carrie said. "I can't believe she was such a fucking liar."

Julia sighed. "Listen, let me call you back. We're just getting to the airport."

"All right. If she's home...just...I..." Carrie trailed off. Somehow her inarticulateness captured how they both felt.

Julia hung up the phone.

"Everything kosher?" Crank asked.

She nodded. "Yeah, just...you're...wow."

Crank's eyes widened. "Jesus, baby, what's wrong?"

"I'm *fine*."

"Babe..."

Julia let out a loud groan. "All right, fine. But he has to swear this is all off the record."

Anthony, in the front seat, said, "Of course."

The car came to a stop. Julia huffed and had the door open before the driver could put it in park. Within seconds she was marching across the tarmac, with Anthony and Crank trying to keep up. The jet, operated by a Boston-based charter company, sat on the runway, engines already warming up.

She led the way up the stairs, both of the men following behind her.

Inside the plane, the pilot said, "Ma'am. We're just about ready, once your baggage is stowed."

"Thank you," Julia responded.

The pilot disappeared back into the cockpit. Julia took a seat in one of the luxurious leather chairs. As Crank and Anthony got themselves situated, the flight attendant offered drinks. Julia promptly ordered a vodka tonic.

As the attendant turned away, Julia said, "Make it a double, please."

Crank's mouth dropped open. "All right, Julia. Spill. If he can't hear it, I'll kick him off the plane."

Anthony held his hands up, palms facing her. "With God as my witness. Whatever you tell me is off the record."

Julia rolled her eyes. Then she said, "Fuck it. I don't need to protect him. Turns out, Carrie and Andrea have a different father than the rest of us."

"Wait...what?" Crank said.

Anthony's eyes widened. "You know I suspected as much when I saw the pictures from the wedding last summer. The two of them stand out, a lot."

Julia leaned her head forward. "And *where* did you see the wedding pictures?"

He shrugged. "It's my job to research things. A friend of your sister—"

"Which sister?"

He shook his head. "Alexandra."

"You've been working on this for a while, haven't you? This is all some bullshit smokescreen."

"Yes, and no."

The pilot interrupted, speaking over the cabin speakers. "Flight attendants, please prepare the cabin for takeoff."

"Explain yourself," Julia said.

Anthony sighed. "I followed the court-martial last summer with a great deal of interest. War crimes interest me. Plus, I thought it was an interesting coincidence that it took place in the same province as Wakhan."

"I don't know what that is. Wakhan?"

"Ancient history. Soviet war crimes. Some awful stuff went down in Afghanistan in the early 80s."

Julia shook her head. "That makes no sense...what does it have to do with us?"

"Nothing," Anthony said. "Point is...yeah I'm interested in the foreign policy angle. I'm interested in your history, and your dad's history. Who wouldn't be?"

"Well. I can't give you permission to write about this. You'll have to talk with Carrie about it first, because it affects her first."

"All right," he said.

"Jesus," Crank said. "Whatever. He agreed to keep it under wraps. What the fuck? Who is their dad?"

"Senator Chuck Rainsley."

Anthony pursed his lips. "Senator Rainsley?"

Julia nodded. "That's what Dad reports."

"Jesus Christ," Crank said. "I can't fucking believe it."

"I believe it," Julia said. "You know my mom's fucking crazy."

Crank shrugged. "Well, yeah, but...that's a big deal. And there were three daughters in between. Who does that?"

Julia rolled her eyes. "My mother, obviously."

Anthony said, "Tell me about your mother."

2. Adelina. February 23, 1981

The battery powered radio crackled with confused and conflicting announcements. The new Prime Minister, Leopoldo Sotelo, was dead, murdered by the revolutionaries. No, he wasn't dead, he was held prisoner. The members of the lower house of Parliament were all dead. No, they were held prisoner. The rebels were led by Basque terrorists. Or the Guardia Civil. King Juan Carlos had been killed. Or he was allied with the rebels. The leader of the rebels was Lieutenant Colonel Antonio Tejero, who had already served prison time for involvement in an attempted coup in 1978. None of it made any sense to Adelina. She knew politics from listening to her father—that was unavoidable. But the seizure of Parliament by the Army? It was frightening. What would come of her family? Her father? For that matter, when would she would be able to go home?

For two hours, she'd peered out the slats of the metal shutters while listening to the radio. The phone wasn't working. She didn't know where her father was. And the Guardia Civil patrols outside still blocked the street, the soldiers marching up and down, machine guns slung over their shoulder, their breath billowing out in great clouds of frost in the cold air.

Above all, Richard was starting to scare her.

Inside the shop, it was freezing cold, and they had no light except a candle casting weak light through the room. Along with the phone lines, there was no electricity—cut by the rebels, according to Richard. He paced like a caged animal. Angry muscles, sometimes vibrating with tension. Twelve steps, from one end of the shop. Stop. Turn. Twelve steps back.

At one point he spun toward her and grabbed her wrists. "I've got to report in. Stay here."

Then he spun away, pulled the front door open and ducked under the halfway rolled up shutter.

Immediately she heard shouts. "*¡alto! ¡no te muevas!*" Stop! Do not move!

Richard froze, only his feet and legs visible to her. She stopped breathing.

"Who are you? What are you doing here?" The questions were demanding, harsh.

Richard stumbled over his words, answering in halting Spanish, as if he were a tourist who had learned the language from a phrase book. "I—I was the flower shop. Please no shoot."

The soldier, or soldiers—she couldn't really tell how many there were—demanded his papers.

A few moments later, he slipped back in, then closed and locked the door. He closed his eyes. "It appears I'm not going anywhere," he said.

She shivered. His eyes were glassy as he looked at her.

"Don't worry," he said. "I'll take care of you."

"I just want to go home," she said.

"You're a very pretty girl," he replied.

She took a deep breath, her eyes dropping to the floor. Where was her father? Why hadn't he come to her? Soldiers or not, her father would come to her. Wouldn't he?

The radio was going on. Mindlessly. They knew nothing. The radio announcer said that the rebels had tanks on the street in Valencia, and that the army had gone over to the rebels.

Where was her father?

Richard moved by her. He put his hands on her shoulders and ducked his head to meet her eyes. "Do not be afraid, Adelina." His tongue brushed his lips as he said the words. He stood close to her. Close enough she could smell his acrid sweat.

"Please, Mr. Thompson..."

"Call me Richard."

"Richard, stop."

"Adelina," he whispered as if he could taste her name on his lips.

"Stop."

He brought his lips to hers. She didn't respond, but her body shook, frail. In response, he gripped her arms harder, and his lips forced hers open.

"I need you, Adelina." His voice was hungry. He didn't *need* anything. This was desire. It was lust. It was hideous.

She jerked in fear at the sound of a gunshot outside, her heart pounding. That served only to inflame him more. He pressed her against the wall, pawing at her breasts. She could feel his fingertips, gripping as tight as if they were metal, pressing into her skin. Terror flooded through her as she realized that she had no way to stop him. She began to struggle, throwing her arms out and hitting at him.

"*Stop!*" she cried out, tears threatening to spill over.

"Stop fighting me, damn it!" he muttered. Shoving her against a wall. "And what happens if we die tonight? The Army is out there overthrowing your government. If they realize who I am, they'll kill me."

He was crazy. Richard's face was flushed, his breathing rapid, excited. He leaned close and whispered in her ear, "You're going to love it." Then his hands were all over her. Aggressive. Urgent. He began to pull at her dress.

Adelina screamed.

CHAPTER EIGHTEEN
Feliz compleanos

1. Adelina. March 21, 1981

Feliz *compleanos, Adelina. Happy birthday.* Seventeen years old, and her life was already ruined. As she whispered the words to herself, she thought, bitterly, *I'm so sorry, Papa.*

Her father couldn't hear her, of course. She stood, head bowed, in her black dress, the same black dress she'd worn for days. Manuel Ramos had finally returned to his home in Calella, dead at sixty-one years old. And she missed him, terribly.

Her father's death was sudden, but his worry for her had gone on for weeks. She'd wept after the night of the failed coup. She remembered crying as she heard King Juan Carlos give his speech ordering the Army home. She cried for days afterward, and her father asked her over and over again what was wrong.

She never told. Because she believed Richard when he said he would kill her father, kill her little brother, if she ever told. He was a cruel man, who enjoyed lies and pain. He was *evil.* She believed him because of his smell. She believed him because of the ice cold look in his eyes. She believed him because of the way he hurt her.

In the days after, she'd wept. She'd prayed. But she'd kept Richard's secret. Even after he came back and hurt her again and again.

It was agonizing. Agonizing to see the condition her father was in. Agonizing to know she was responsible for his pain. She had begun to waver. Until finally one day, she said, "Papa, I need to talk to you. It's important."

He smiled. Then he said, "As soon as I get back to the shop, Adelina. I promise. I'll only be gone twenty minutes."

Her father never returned. Twenty minutes later he was dead, run over by a truck on Calle Santa Catalina.

"I'm afraid, Papa," she whispered the words. Then she kneeled. The ground was cold and moist, and soaked through her dress to her knees. She whispered, "I'm afraid he'll kill me, or Luis, like he did you. I'm...I'm afraid. I'm so afraid."

She leaned forward, nearly prostrate in front of the grave. "Papa, I'm so sorry. Please tell me what to do. Tell me what to do, Papa."

Her shoulders began to shake in great sobs. Her father was gone, her life was over, and she was going to have a baby.

I should never have let you stay in the city with your father.

The words echoed through her mind. Words that she couldn't erase. Words that crushed her soul.

I didn't raise my daughter to be a slut, Adelina.

The pain was overwhelming. The shame was overwhelming.

Who is he, Adelina?

The questions. The demands. Four days after her father was laid to rest in the tiny churchyard of the parish church of Santa Maria in Calella, her mother dragged her in to the priest, demanding she go to confession. On her knees in the church, in between the Parish priest and her mother, she confessed her sins.

In a sober, cold voice, the priest said the words she'd been afraid of.

"Adelina, I would gladly grant you absolution. But I'm sure you know, I cannot do so if you are not truly in a state of contrition."

She stammered. She begged. She cried. But the priest's words were final. "Adelina. In order to return to a state of grace, you must be truly contrite. You must remove the sin, and regularize your situation."

Fear staggered her. She knew what he meant. She had to marry him. If she didn't—if she told the truth—he would surely hurt Luis just as he'd hurt her father.

She broke down.

"What is his name?" the priest thundered.

"Who was it?" her mother screamed.

Finally, she'd broken down. Out of fear for Luis, she didn't say the worst. She didn't say how it happened. All she said was the name.

Richard Thompson.

2. Julia. April 30.

Julia leaned back in her chair. Furiously, she wiped a tear from her eyes.

"That's it. I know it's ridiculous. I mean, I'm thirty-two years old. But I still—I still resent her. I like to think I could forgive. I don't want to be the kind of person who can't. But when I needed her, she wasn't there."

Anthony flipped back two pages in his notebook. "Okay, let me make sure I've got it straight. You were pregnant. At fourteen."

Julia nodded.

"And your mother?"

"She was—too preoccupied with her affair. Or whatever. I don't know what was going on with her. But I needed her."

"Do you regret the abortion?"

"Asshole." Julia's response left little doubt of her opinion of Anthony's question, but it communicated little in the way of an answer.

"Sorry," he replied.

"Yes, I regret it," she said.

Crank sat up. "You do?"

A tear ran down her face. "Of course I do. If she—or he, I guess—were still alive, she'd be sixteen now, same as Andrea."

Anthony leaned forward and said, "Look, I'm sorry. That was a shitty question to ask. Just...tell me this—"

"Stop."

Anthony stopped. But then he said, "Stop what?"

"Stop probing. You want to write about the album, fine. You want to write a puff profile piece on me and Crank? Go for it. But this is—"

Anthony sat forward. "This is bigger than that. This is bigger than you've ever realized, isn't it? Your father's going to be the Secretary of Defense, and suddenly you're finding out you don't even know who he is."

"Stop." Her tone was stiff, but he kept going.

"Not to mention, one of your sisters was kidnapped. And you don't know who was responsible."

"You can't seriously believe my father—"

"I don't know what I believe, Julia. I think you need to let me pursue this where it leads."

Crank leaned forward. "Anthony. Shut the fuck up."

"Excuse me?"

Julia held a hand up. "Please, Crank. Just—stop a second. I don't know what it is you expect to find."

"I don't either," Anthony replied. "Just bear with me."

She sagged into her seat. "All right," she said.

"Okay..." He shuffled through his notes for a moment, then said, "All right. Your mom was pretty young when they got married, right?"

"Eighteen."

"And she moved to the United States then?"

"Right. I was about three months old when they moved to the U.S."

"Washington, DC?"

"San Francisco...I think. I was a baby."

"Your dad's official bio says he was posted to Pakistan from '82 to '84."

"I guess he was then. At that age I wouldn't have known the difference between Pakistan or Disneyland."

"And your earliest memories?"

"In Washington. I think. I remember when Carrie was born, vaguely."

He checked his notes. "January '85."

"Yes."

"Were your parents close then?"

Julia raised her eyebrows and shrugged. "Not so I could see. I was really young. I don't have a lot of memories from then. Mom used to spend a lot of time in her room alone and Dad was always at work."

"Who took care of you?"

Julia smiled, but it wasn't a warm smile. "Miss Reyes. I remember her. She sang to me a lot. I do remember we'd have breakfast together sometimes on the weekend. Mom would let me sit in her lap. That was before things got really awful."

Crank said, "It's hard to imagine your mother singing."

"She was an accomplished musician, Crank. Why do you think she made all of us learn an instrument? When she was a teenager, she played for the national youth orchestra in Spain."

"What happened?" Crank asked.

Julia smiled and held a hand out to her husband. "She fell in love. It happens, you know."

Crank took her hand. "It does, doesn't it?"

3. Adelina. January 1984.

"**J**ulia, come."

Adelina Thompson took her daughter's hand in hers. In her other hand she held a leather suitcase. She was exhausted, frazzled. Her flight had been delayed, then diverted around a storm cell, finally landing almost three hours late.

The delays were welcome. Except for a few days here and there when he'd gotten leave, Richard hadn't been home since April two years before. Two years she'd had to learn English, to raise her daughter.

Two years to regain her sense of self.

She'd prayed about it. Sometimes she was ashamed, because she knew that despite his lies, Richard's assignment took him to places that were not safe. And more than once, she'd prayed he would meet an accident. That he would leave her with an insurance policy and their house in San Francisco and her daughter, little Julia.

Julia, who was innocent.

Julia, who reminded her every day of how it felt to be used.

He hadn't met an accident, and unexpectedly, he was home a year early. Promoted. His letter and subsequent phone call said nothing of the reasons why. They merely gave instructions, as if she were in the military, to pack their things and fly to Washington on January 28th. It didn't matter that she'd made friends in San Francisco. It didn't matter that she'd found a home in the church there, that she'd tried to reconstruct her life. She didn't belong to herself. Not anymore.

Not as long as he was in a position to hurt her. To hurt her daughter, or her little brother.

The terrifying part was, no one would ever believe her. Richard was charming. He smiled and shook hands and spoke reasonably. He was eloquent, soft-spoken, and generous. He wore beautifully tailored suits and had perfect teeth and in a hundred subtle ways reminded everyone they encountered that she was young, delicate, incompetent.

She was trapped.

As she stepped off the plane and into the jetway, she straightened her dress, then kneeled in front of her daughter.

"Let's get you cleaned up," she said, quickly wiping Julia's face with a napkin.

"Go potty," Julia said.

"In a few moments, Julia. We've got to go see father, first." Her stomach twisted a little in fear at the words. She knew he was only a hundred feet away at the end of the jetway. She straightened Julia's dress.

There was no point in putting it off any longer. She stood up and took Julia's hand and the two of them walked down the jetway.

She spied Richard in the terminal. It had been six months since she'd seen him—he hadn't come home for Christmas, leaving her and Julia to celebrate alone for the second year in a row. His skin was dark from exposure to too much sun, his skin roughened.

She felt a little woozy as she walked toward him. The combination of first-class tickets and a two-year-old daughter meant they didn't check her age on the plane, and she'd had enough drinks to boost her courage and damage her judgment.

"Adelina," he said. He leaned close, pulling her into a not-too-close embrace, and murmured the words under his breath, "It's lovely to see you dear. You've been eating well, I see."

Bastard. "You look well," she replied.

He knelt in front of Julia. "Hello, Julia. Do you remember me?"

"Poppa?" Julia asked.

He put his arms around their daughter. Adelina felt her gorge rise, and she closed her eyes and whispered a prayer to Mary. When she opened them, Richard stood again. He smiled at her in a way which probably appeared endearing to people who walked by them, but which served only to frighten her.

"Come, then," he said. "I'm anxious to show you where we'll be living."

That was simple. He'd purchased the house in San Francisco without consulting her and done the same here. She didn't actually know *where* they were going this morning, which was typical of her whole life. Richard took her suitcase, and she followed, hand clamped around Julia's.

Twenty minutes later they were getting in the car. It was unseasonably warm for Washington, DC in January, which meant the temperature was close to that of San Francisco. The sky was steel grey, threatening rain. Richard had been irritated about Julia needing to use the restroom, as if there was any way Adelina could have controlled that.

"How was your flight?" he asked. "It took long enough."

Adelina shrugged as she buckled Julia into the back seat. "The flight was fine. It took forever. We need to get a car seat," she said.

"A what?"

"My friend Linda has one. It's to protect her."

"She's two years old. I don't think that's—"

"She needs one."

Richard blinked. He wasn't used to her being assertive about anything. "Fine," he said. "Anything else?"

"Yes." She said the word as she got in the front passenger seat of the car.

He raised his eyebrows. And waited, hands on the wheel.

Her heart thumped wildly as she said the words: "I want to go to college."

He shrugged. "And?"

She kept going, so terrified she couldn't stop talking, the words coming out faster and faster. "I know we didn't start off the best—whatever. I'm nineteen. I didn't get to finish high school. I lost everything. I want to go to school. I want to—"

"Fine."

"What?" she asked, her voice raising to a squeal.

"Go. Whatever. But I expect you to host dinners, I've got a lot of important people I need to cultivate for my career."

"Sure. Of course," she said.

He started the car, and as they drove out of the airport, he said, "I don't know why you were so anxious about this discussion. I love you, Adelina. I want the best for you."

Her eyes widened at the words *I love you.*

Despite her fear, Richard kept his word, not interfering when she made arrangements to register at Montgomery County Community College. The home he'd purchased was a surprise. Unlike the old Victorian townhouse in San Francisco, he'd bought an expensive condo in Bethesda. With five bedrooms, it was larger than they could possibly ever need, though she took his injunction to be ready to host *important people* seriously. It was only a few days later that Richard announced in a peremptory fashion, "We're having guests over next Saturday."

"Oh? Who? How many?"

"Let's see—Colonel Chuck Rainsley and his wife. He's retiring in a few weeks and planning to run for the Senate from Texas, and I'm guessing he's going to win. We need to cultivate him. Leslie Collins—he works for some accounting firm in Virginia, but he's a friend of Prince Roshan, who will be here with his wife. George-Phillip, the Duke of Kent, who is playing at diplomacy, he's assigned to the British Embassy."

She swallowed. "Prince Roshan—Saudi Arabia? Will there be any dietary restrictions?"

"That's right. You've been paying attention, I see."

Irritated, she said, "My father was a Marquis, Richard. I've dealt with dinner parties before."

"*Was.* Your father was a near penniless shopkeeper who lost his title and position long before you were born."

She felt her fists clenched involuntarily. She might be stuck with Richard Thompson, but she would *never* let him get under her skin. She *knew* better.

She spat out the words. "Your dinner party will be flawless." Then she turned her back, stomping to the room she'd converted into her own study. It had nothing of Richard in it, and she intended to keep it that way.

CHAPTER NINETEEN
Loved?
Past tense?

1. Jessica. April 30.

The picture on the wall, an Ansel Adams print of a waterfall or a river or a cloud was almost a stereotype. But Jessica let her eyes bore into it, almost as if she would discover real answers buried somewhere in the image. At Sister Kiara's suggestion, she'd tried to run through her catalogue of memories of her father.

They were few. He was always calm. Always collected. Always locked away in his office, or sternly presiding over dinners at which Jessica and Sarah were expected to stay silent. She remembered holidays, around the big dining table. She vaguely and distantly remembered trips to the zoo and Golden Gate Park. Was her father along for those? Her mother? All she could remember for sure was Carrie.

Sister Kiara leaned forward and said, "Do you need a break? I'm reluctant to quit now that you're finally talking." Her smile was easy as she said the words, but Jessica knew she had a point. In her ten days at the retreat center, Jessica had barely spoken a civil word to anyone.

"You're afraid I'll clam up again?"

Kiara raised her eyebrows. Then she nodded, slowly. "Yes. Yes, I am."

"Um...would you mind if I walked down and got some coffee? And we can talk on the way?"

"Yeah," Kiara said. As if reluctant to break the spell, she stood, and the two of them left the office.

Outside, in the cool mountain air, Jessica stopped and looked up at the sky. "Okay, so here's what happened."

With no further transition, she began to tell Sister Kiara her story.

In Jessica's mind, it all went back to the first week of junior year. For ten years, she and her twin had shared everything. Birthdays. Bedrooms. Their crazy-ass mother still bought them matching clothing, and everyone expected them to like the same things.

But they didn't. Sarah liked punk rock, leather and boys. Jessica liked pop, pink and girls.

She still remembered the first time she realized that she wasn't like other girls. Alexandra, Sarah and Jessica were at the beach, five, maybe six years before. It was a beautiful day, unseasonably warm, the sun shining down on them. They were still close then.

At one point, a crowd of high school boys marched along the beach in front of them. Sarah had leaned close and whispered something, blushing.

Jessica didn't feel whatever it was Sarah did. But two months later, she was invited to a party at Liese Hamilton's house. Six girls attended the party, and Jessica stayed over. They sat up talking half the night, and at one point she found herself focusing on Liese's eyes. Pretty eyes. They were sitting close to each other, really close, and Jessica wanted to kiss her very badly.

Jessica didn't think about it again for a long time.

It was funny, really. It's not like being a lesbian was anything that horrible. She lived in *San Francisco*, after all. This was the twenty-first century.

At the same time, in recent years, she'd spent more and more time in church with her mother. She'd hear the words spoken at school, at church, in her life. It wasn't the big things. *Everybody* knew the Catholic church didn't approve of homosexuality. *Everybody* knew that only certain states allowed gay marriage. Those things mattered, but only in an abstract way.

What mattered to Jessica were the small things. Her mother would give friendly advice. *When you find the man you love, don't let anything get in the way, Jessica.* Because, to her mother, it could be nothing but a man. After all, Adelina Thompson's life had revolved around her husband's for more than thirty years. Jessica's friends would say *Oh, that was gay.* In a thousand small and large ways, they'd express their disdain of all things gay and lesbian.

Freshman and sophomore year in high school, she began to feel more and more isolated. More and more unsure of herself. More and more afraid to tell anyone who she was.

And then it happened. One evening during the summer before junior year of high school, Jessica was standing in line for tea at the Purple Kow when she saw a willowy, blonde girl in a blue dress that matched hers. Her hair was flowing, shoulder length and a deep shade of indigo. And her intense blue eyes tracked Jessica as she got in line.

"I'm Jessica Thompson."

"Chrysanthemum Allen."

Seriously? Jessica thought.

They both ordered German Lite Cheese Cake and iced milk tea, and Jessica laughed at the coincidence. They sat down at the bus stop and began to talk as the cars drove by.

Chrys was seventeen and was starting her senior year. She wore contrast as armor. Indigo hair and conservative dresses. Beautiful lace ruffled tops with pajama bottoms. When she talked about music and math her eyes glowed. Spoken word poetry excited her. The written word not so much—she'd barely passed English her junior year.

A week later, they climbed out Jessica's window and lay on the roof of the back porch, looking up at the stars.

"Sometimes when I look at the stars," Chrys said, "I think everything's actually going to be okay."

"What do you mean?" Jessica had asked.

Chrys clammed up. She always did. She was sexy and alluring. She was maddening. She rarely revealed weakness or concern, and then when she did, it was indirect.

"I know I'm not good at talking about myself," she said, more than once. "But I love you."

And she did. Jessica loved Chrys, Chrys loved Jessica, and that was okay. But sometimes it was so frustrating. Chrys was so *needy* sometimes.

Two days before Thanksgiving, Chrys showed up at her door. Tears were running down her face, and she said, "I was going to text you, but I couldn't do it."

"What?"

Chrys looked pale and sad as she said, "Break up with you."

Jessica backed into the front door of her house, stunned. "What? Why?"

"I love you, Jessica. But I can't."

"I don't understand…"

"You don't have to." Chrys leaned forward and kissed her on the lips, then ran.

Jessica texted her, over and over again. Finally, Sarah shouted, "What is *wrong* with you?" and Jessica screamed, "Leave me alone!"

The next two days were excruciating. Alexandra and Carrie came home for Thanksgiving, then Crank and Julia, and on Thanksgiving night Dylan Paris showed up by surprise and proposed to Alexandra.

It was a giant, chaotic mess. The whole family hugging each other, Alexandra bursting into tears, her mother crying and her father acting as if he cared. The dinner, after the chaos was over, had a slightly frantic air; as if the gossamer threads of joy and love were so fleeting that it would take nothing but a slight wind to blow them away.

After everyone settled down again, Jessica's mom, the insensitive witch, said to her, "You know, one day you'll meet a man who loves you like Dylan loves Alexandra."

For the first time in her life, Jessica cursed at her mother. "Go to hell," she said, bursting into tears, then she ran upstairs and locked her room. She sent the first of what would be dozens of text messages to Chrys then, asking her how she could be so heartless.

A week later, Chrys had shown back up on her doorstep, begging forgiveness.

Telling Sister Kiara about it now was like the wind coming in off the bay blowing the fog away. "The thing is, I really loved her," Jessica said. "I really loved her."

Sister Kiara leaned back in her chair. They were sitting in the small common dining area of the retreat, and Kiara had a steaming cup of coffee in front of her. "Loved? Past tense?"

Jessica's face twisted in pain. Then she whispered, "I'll always love her. But she's dead."

2. Adelina. February 11, 1984

The dining room was set with eight places. Fine china, set off with crystal wine glasses and candlesticks. A sumptuous white tablecloth, and a four course meal centered on roast duck in plum sauce. Adelina Thompson hated her husband. But she would play his game. She had children to protect. She had a little brother to protect.

Julia was down for the night, in the room furthest from the dining room and accompanied by her nanny. Two hired cooks assisted in the kitchen, and two servers helped in the dining room. But this was Adelina's production.

At five minutes before seven, Richard walked into the dining room. His eyes scanned the perfectly set table.

"Where is the wine?"

The server brought him the bottle, a 1976 Cos Pithos Cerasuolo di Vittoria. A very dry wine, detailed, with a brace of acidity, it was perfect for roast duck.

His eyes darted to hers, eyebrows raised. "You chose this?"

Adelina nodded, giving nothing in her expression.

"I approve." No smile accompanied the bare accolade.

She didn't allow herself to feel any pleasure or pride from his approval. She despised him.

A knock on the door. "That will be our first guests," he said.

She felt a brush of contempt for him. Why he felt the need to state the obvious she didn't understand. But something was different about him. In the three weeks since he'd returned from Pakistan, it was clear that he was different. Just an edge of worry. Something had happened there, something that frightened him, and shook his confidence. He'd spent long nights in his study, virtually ignoring her—a relief from his constant physical demands the first months of their *marriage*.

She turned and walked out of the dining room. She had no desire to speak with him. He followed her all the same, and when she opened the door, he put a hand at the small of her back, making her skin crawl. She smiled at him. After all, they were a happy couple.

At the door stood a remarkably tall man with pale blue eyes in the dress blue uniform of the Marine Corps. At his side, a woman perhaps ten years his junior.

"Come in, come in," Richard said, a patently false smile on his face. "Colonel Rainsley, this is my wife, Adelina."

Rainsley took her hand in his. Warm, but not sweaty. No brute force. His eyes met hers directly and she felt a shiver. "Adelina. It's a pleasure to meet you. I'm Chuck Rainsley, and this is my wife Brianna."

"It's lovely to meet you, sir," Adelina said. Her English had improved dramatically, thanks to a year of lessons in San Francisco. "Can I get you a drink?"

Brianna preferred white wine, and Colonel Rainsley asked for a bourbon and Coke. Adelina walked to the kitchen and issued the instructions, then returned to the living room. Colonel Rainsley and his wife were seated already. Adelina said, "Your drinks will be up in just a moment."

Rainsley said, "Adelina, Richard tells me you met when he was posted in Madrid?"

Adelina plastered a smile on her face, hiding the thumping she felt in her chest. "That's right. He stopped in one day at my father's shop—Papa was a florist—and one thing led to another."

"You're quite the catch," Rainsley said.

Adelina felt her face heat up.

"The moment I saw Adelina the first time, I knew I wanted to marry her."

She wanted to scream when she heard Richard's words. Misery competed with rage as she kept a smile clamped on her face. Her chest hurt and she wanted to turn her eyes to the Marine Colonel and say, *rescue me*.

But there would be no rescue. How could there be? Instead, she turned her attention to the Colonel and his wife.

"And where did you two meet?"

Rainsley looked at his wife, adoration clearly on his features. "Ahh, well, the Marine Corps sent me to graduate school at Fletcher in '75."

Adelina raised an eyebrow. Richard had gone to the Fletcher School, though a different year.

"Anyway, we met there. Brianna was majoring in music at Tufts."

Adelina flushed with pleasure. "Music major? What was your focus?"

"Viola," Brianna said. "I've taught elementary school music."

"I played with the National Youth Orchestra in Madrid," Adelina said.

Brianna's eyes widened. "Oh, that must have been amazing."

The two women began to chat about music. For the first time in nearly three years, Adelina found herself discussing something with animation and excitement.

"Tell me more about the Youth Orchestra?"

With pleasure, Adelina began to describe the nearly daily rehearsals in Madrid. The performances at the Auditorio Nacional de Música, and her preparations to audition for the National Orchestra.

Wistfully, she said, "If I'd made it to the audition, I'd have been the youngest violinist in Spanish history to make it into the National Orchestra.

"Really?" Brianna said. "How old were you?"

"Sixteen."

"You must have been *really* good, why didn't you go through the auditions?"

Adelina froze, her heart suddenly pounding. Richard's eyes had darted to her, for just a second, then back to the Colonel. He was listening. And he'd warned her. More than once. She had a carefully reconstructed history, which started with an earlier birthdate.

"Oh," she said, trying to cover with a lie. "My father passed away, and my um, mom, wanted me to come back to Calella..."

She trailed off, and Brianna said, "Oh, I'm so sorry about your father. I—weren't you working at your father's shop when you met Richard?"

A knock on the door startled Adelina. "Excuse me," she said, standing up and walking quickly to the door.

Two men stood there. The first—short, balding, with a ruddy, freckled complexion, wore a rumpled suit. Next to him stood a much taller and younger man with dark hair and green eyes. The tall man wore an impeccably tailored suit.

"Welcome..." Adelina said, trailing off.

Richard came up behind her, gripping her upper arm in his hand. Tightly. Too tightly, it hurt.

"Good evening, gentlemen. Come in." He released the pressure on her arm quickly. It had merely been a reminder. To watch herself.

Thompson presented the two men. "Adelina, Colonel and Mrs. Rainsley, may I present Prince George-Phillip, the Duke of Kent. Prince George-Phillip is with the British Foreign Service. And also this is Leslie Collins. He's a good friend of mine who did some accounting work for the US Embassy in Islamabad when I was there."

Colonel Rainsley and his wife stood.

"Pleasure to meet you, sir," the Colonel said, shaking George-Phillip's hand. Adelina watched as the two of them shook hands, each taking the measure of the other and liking what they saw. George-Phillip was clearly young, in his early twenties, but he had the confidence and bearing of a much older man.

George-Phillip turned to Adelina, his eyes widening a bit. He took her hand and bent over it with a quick kiss. "A pleasure, madam." Colonel Rainsley frowned at the gesture, then frowned even more when George-Phillip turned toward Brianna Rainsley and did the same.

Before they were able to ask for drinks or anyone returned to their seat, the doorbell rang. A moment later, the final guests were admitted. Richard introduced them.

"May I present Prince Roshan al Saud? And his wife Myriam?"

Prince Roshan was in his early thirties. He wore a conservative grey suit with a muted green tie. His wife, Myriam, wore a smart looking red dress.

"If you would like, we can all move to the dining room," Adelina said.

Five minutes later, the assembled company had taken their seats. Richard sat at the head of the table, of course, and Adelina at the foot. To Richard's right, Prince Roshan. Prince George-Phillip was to Adelina's right. Roshan had been seated in the place of honor by Richard primarily by virtue of his proximity to the throne of his country: Roshan was the Saudi Arabian king's son. George-Phillip was a cousin—and a fairly distant one at that—to England's Queen Elizabeth.

To Adelina's left sat Colonel Rainsley, and Leslie Collins was to Richard's left. The two wives, Myriam and Brianna, were in the middle of the table.

Moments after they were seated, a server poured wine around the table.

"Prince Roshan," Adelina said, "would you prefer water or soda in respect to your faith?"

"Wine, please, madam. I am, of course, devout to Mohammed's teachings, but I also live in the modern world." He paused for a moment, and said, "Water for Myriam, though."

"Of course," Adelina replied as smoothly as possible. Roshan was a pig just like her husband. The drinks were poured as Collins, Roshan and Richard began to discuss political developments in Soviet occupied Afghanistan.

"I'm afraid I'm somewhat at a loss with regards to the minutiae of Afghanistan," Prince George-Phillip said in an aside to Adelina.

"You're very young for a Foreign Service officer," she replied. "And a Duke at that."

George-Phillip shrugged, a self-deprecating motion. "I achieved my seat through no skills of my own, of course—my father was killed in a car accident when I was seventeen."

"My condolences," Colonel Rainsley said. "Do you plan to continue his work?"

George-Phillip scoffed. "As head of his private club? Hardly. I have two more years to my Foreign Service commitment, then it's Sandhurst for me." Sandhurst was the Royal Military College.

Rainsley said, "Are you considering the military as a career?"

"I am, Colonel."

"You could do worse."

"I believe you're correct. Plus—let me be frank—my father did nothing to bring honor to our family or country. I feel it's my role to do my part."

At the other end of the table, the three men, Richard, Collins and Prince Roshan, were speaking in low voices. Collins said something that caused the other two men to chuckle.

Adelina turned to Rainsley. "Richard tells me you are considering a run for the Senate, Colonel?"

"Not considering, ma'am. I've made the decision."

"Please, call me Adelina."

"With pleasure. I'm Chuck." He smiled at her. Across the table and in the middle, Brianna Rainsley frowned at her husband.

"What are you plans for the Senate?" George-Phillip asked.

"I'll tell you. I watched my men get butchered in Beirut six months ago, and there was nothing I could do about it, because of bullheaded, incompetent orders engineered directly out of the White House. I plan to make that my first priority."

As he spoke the words, Rainsley's eyes were bright. He was a man on a mission.

Adelina said, "I think that's admirable."

"Not admirable, Adelina, just my duty as an officer to take care of my men."

George-Phillip leaned forward and said, "Would that all officers felt the same, Colonel." Then he did something odd. At the opposite end of the table, Leslie Collins said in a low tone the name of a place—Wakan or Wack Hand or something like that, his voice at a low drone. George-Phillip stiffened just a little at the word, and his eyes narrowed slightly.

Adelina tilted her head. Something was going on there, but she didn't know what. She wondered if it was something she could use against her husband.

3. Jessica. April 30

"The thing was, Chrysanthemum was a basket case. We would date a month, and she'd break it off. No explanation. She'd make crazy demands. I had to show my love by skipping a class. Or kissing her in front of the Cathedral. Or...just... crazy stuff. She needed help."

Sister Kiara said, "Why do you think that was?"

Jessica shrugged. "Drugs. She was abused. Broken home. Who the hell knows?"

Kiara shook her head. "How did she die, Jessica?"

"Last June and July she'd gone off the edge. Really crazy stuff, and in July I broke up with her. I just couldn't take it any more, you know? I loved her, but...love can only go so far. Love can't make someone not crazy." Jessica sighed and leaned forward, resting her head on her hands.

"It was my fault," she said.

"No, Jessica. Chrys's mental health—whatever was going on with her isn't your fault. She made choices. We all do."

Jessica shook her head. "Yeah, but if I'd been there for her. I don't know. I wasn't. And in August, I went to stay with Carrie and Ray in Washington, along with Sarah. And...we got in the accident. Sarah was in the hospital, Ray died. I was out there for a long time."

She sniffed. "Chrys left me a message. Saying she was afraid she was going to hurt herself. She begged me to call her back. And...I didn't get the message. For days. When I got back to San Francisco she was dead."

Kiara closed her eyes. Then she whispered, "What happened to her?"

"Overdose," Jessica said. "It was intentional. She took a whole bottle of pills and drank it down with a bottle of vodka."

Kiara shook her head. "I'm so sorry."

Jessica remembered the blinding pain. She'd come home from Chrys's house that night, her first night back in San Francisco. Her father had left her a note. He'd be out, probably all night, and there was forty dollars to order a pizza or whatever.

She paid a homeless man ten dollars to buy her a bottle of vodka and took it back to her room, where she drank herself to insensibility.

The next weeks were the darkest she could remember in her life. Her father was never home, or when he was, he locked himself in his office. They ate three meals together in as many weeks. She went to school, barely, but racked up an impressive number of detentions, stopping just short of what might result in a phone call to her father.

The house was deadly empty. They'd lived in San Francisco full time since she was six years old, when her father retired from the Foreign Service. The house had always been full of people—her father and mother, Carrie, Alexandra, Sarah, Andrea. But slowly they'd faded away. Carrie went away to college. Andrea went to live in Spain. Then Alexandra left for Columbia. For two years it had been just the twins and their parents, and that seemed awfully quiet.

But it was nothing like the tomb the house had become now. Sarah was in Bethesda, Maryland, staying with Carrie as they both recovered from the mental and physical injuries of the accident that had killed Carrie's husband. Her mother had stayed on the east coast, leaving it to Richard Thompson to watch out for Jessica.

What could happen, after all? Jessica had it together. She was the goody-two-shoes. She had perfect grades. She watched in derision as her sister Sarah got in scrape after scrape. She was better than that.

Jessica came and went to and from that tomb of a house every day. She called her mother twice a week to let her know she was doing fine, even though it was a lie. She went to school when she had to, she ate when she had to, and she sank into a dull but terrifying depression, her only company the sound of echoes as she walked through the house.

The week after Thanksgiving, she went out for the first time since Chrysanthemum's death. A party. Mick Babcock was hosting it, which meant it would be a drunken bash, but she was on the hunt for something more. She wanted to be held. She wanted to be touched. Chrysanthemum's death had left her disastrously lonely. Jessica Thompson wandered into that party a disaster waiting to happen.

Forty minutes after her arrival, she found herself sitting on a couch next to Rob Searle, another senior. Rob had shoulder length hair, long in the front and swept back with gel like a pop star, and a ridiculous peach fuzz mustache. She'd drunk three glasses of vodka-laced punch and smoked a joint, and was feeling almost giddy. That's when he said, "I think we've got something, babe," and grabbed her, bringing his lips down on hers.

Jessica wriggled her arms and legs in shock for just a moment. Then her hand closed on an irregularly shaped object on the table. A *fork*.

In a swift motion, she clenched the fork in her fist and swung it, stabbing Rob in the back.

He screamed, jerking back from her, his eyes wide.

"The fuck! Did you just fucking stab me?"

She stood up, her whole body swaying, and said, "Keep your hands to yourself."

"Jesus Christ, and I thought we had something. Agggh, that hurts!" He bent, reaching over his shoulder, trying to remove the fork from his back. It had penetrated his shirt, driven right through, and opened up a wound in his shoulder that was going to hurt a lot worse when he sobered up.

"Dude, what the fuck happened to you?" It was their host, Mick.

"Bitch stabbed me," Rob said. Then he burst out laughing. Mick let out a loud belly laugh, then reached around and grabbed the fork. A little bit of blood spattered when he pulled it out, and Jessica stood and backed away.

"Fucker," she muttered. Rob just laughed more. She rolled her eyes and walked away. As she headed for the door, Marion Chen blocked her way.

Marion was a pretty girl. Or used to be. She'd have been a senior in high school if she hadn't dropped out in September. Now she worked waiting tables at the Fisherman's Wharf and was saving money to take her GED and start college. Jessica knew her. Or knew *of* her rather—they hadn't moved in the same circles when Marion was still in school, except the last couple of months of junior year.

Marion didn't look so good now. She'd always been pretty, but slightly overweight, at least by unrealistic American magazine standards. Now, the Korean-American girl's face had leaned out, her cheeks slightly concave. Dark circles bordered the bottom of her hollow eyes.

"Jessica." Marion crossed her arms over her chest like a couple of drumsticks.

"Hey, Marion. You doing okay?"

Marion's eyes narrowed. "What the fuck are you asking that for?"

"Just curiosity," Jessica said. "Hadn't seen you in a while." *Not to mention, you look like a fucking concentration camp victim.*

"Yeah, I'm doing fine."

"I'm glad," Jessica said. She started to steer around Marion.

"Hey," Marion said. "I gotta ask you something."

Jessica sighed. This party was a bust. She should just go home. "What?"

"Chrysanthemum told me she kept trying to call you, and you wouldn't answer. She was all fucking broken up about it. That was right before she offed herself. Is it true?"

Jessica closed her eyes. And she couldn't control it, even though she wanted to. A tear ran down her face. "Yeah, it's true. I was in a bad car accident, and my brother-in-law died, and my twin was in the hospital for months, and I didn't return her call for a couple days. Fucking sue me."

Marion winced. "Jesus. That's the fucking breaks. Sorry."

"Shit," Jessica said. "Just...whatever. Anything else?"

Marion shook her head. "You want to blow this place? Let's go get high."

Jessica blinked. Was Marion serious? She looked at Marion's full lips, at her pretty, high cheekbones, and said, "Yeah, let's go."

CHAPTER TWENTY
He's really a
fucking spy

1. Adelina. May 8, 1984

"Something's** different about you."

Adelina froze. She was in the process of putting away groceries, and had unconsciously been humming Tina Turner's new hit, *What's Love Got to Do With It?* For two days, she'd been trying to shut out her news. Not think about it. The implications were terrifying.

She stood up straight. Richard was leaning on the doorframe. His face was openly curious and distrustful.

"What do you mean?" she asked. She set the can of peas down on the counter next to her hand.

He narrowed his eyes. "You've been very cheerful lately. It's nice to see."

Bastard. She was cheerful because for the first time in her life she had some vague idea of what it felt like to be loved. To be valued. Cherished. But now—here—she had to deal with *him*. Her rapist. Her captor. Her husband. She felt a cold chill in her gut, as she always did when he looked at her like this. With lust in his eyes. Richard was rarely gentle, never loving, always contemptuous. Until March, she'd never imagined that making love could be something enjoyable. Something amazing.

He'll kill me if he finds out. Or he'll kill my daughter.

That's crazy, he had responded. *Just leave him.*

You don't know him. He murdered my father.

You don't know that for sure.

I do.

Adelina swallowed. She felt a pit of fear in her stomach, as she often did with Richard. Because she had missed her period. And— it wasn't possible that Richard Thompson was the father. She was trapped. She couldn't leave him because he'd take Julia. Or hurt her. But she couldn't go on like this. Because she was dying inside.

"Seriously," Richard said. "What's going on with you?"

She couldn't meet his eyes. "My class. I'm just really enjoying it. I've made friends." *I'm in love and dying because I can't leave you.* She closed her eyes, trying to force back tears. She had too much pride to let him see her cry.

"Tell me about your friends," he said, his voice cool.

Change the subject. "You tell me about yours. You've been out with Leslie Collins a lot. Is he really an accountant?"

"No," he said, his voice contemptuous. "He's really a fucking spy."

Asshole. "He just doesn't seem your type," she replied, ignoring his caustic response. Ever since the night he'd huddled with Prince Roshan and Leslie Collins, she'd realized something was wrong there. Richard Thompson wasn't the type to ignore genuine British royalty in favor of a jumped up nobody from Saudi Arabia whose only claim to *royalty* was the recent discovery of oil. She knew him well enough to know that if he paid more attention to Roshan than to George-Phillip, something was suspicious.

Unfortunately, she'd had little luck figuring out what it was. Richard was, as always, secretive.

"Leslie isn't the point. The point is your newfound cheerfulness. I want to know what the fuck is going on."

His eyes had narrowed, and she felt the temperature in the room plummet from the ice in his eyes.

Be careful, Adelina. Piss him off, but not too much. She whispered a quick prayer to Mary. Then she shrugged a little. "I turned twenty last month. I guess I realized it's time to make the best of our situation." Swallowing back vomit, she continued with the words she'd rehearsed. "I guess I've been a bit spoiled. I should be more grateful."

"You *should* be more grateful," he said. "I take care of you, don't I? Do you ever have to worry about food? About anything at all?"

Just my freedom, you fucking bastard. "No," she said. "I just never planned to have children."

"What the fuck do you mean?" His tone had a hard edge to it. For a second, she wished the nanny were here, instead of at the park with Julia. He was never violent when other people were there.

She swallowed. "Sorry. I didn't mean to upset you."

"I'm not fucking upset."

She knew the next words would set him off. They *always* did. "Richard, calm down..."

"Don't tell me to fucking calm down. If you hadn't gotten pregnant, I wouldn't have had to deal with an international fucking incident. The agency *made* me marry you."

"Well, my mother made me marry *you*." She knew the next words were going to hurt her. Or rather, *he* was going to hurt her in response to what she was about to say. But right now, she needed him to. Because otherwise, she was going to have no way to explain the pregnancy. So she said the words, quiet, her tone vicious, calculated. "Do you *really* think I'd ever marry my rapist voluntarily?"

Richard's eyes bugged, and he reached out and grabbed her by the throat. Silent, his face controlled, the only sign of his anger those bulging eyes and his hand gripping her.

For just a second, she started to panic. Had she miscalculated? He was always so controlled. She couldn't *breathe*. But then relief swept over when he let go of her throat and muttered in a guttural voice, "You fucking whore."

Then he started to tear at her clothes.

Adelina didn't cry. She didn't weep. A tear slid down her face, a desperate, lonely tear, but she wiped it away before he could see it, and inside she closed her heart, she disassociated, she left her body behind and turned her mind and her heart to a prayer to God to deliver her and protect her daughter. Richard Thompson might have her body, but he could never have her soul.

2. Bear. April 30

Jesus, *Joseph and Mary,* Bear Wyden thought as he got out of the cab on Pennsylvania Avenue. He was frazzled. To say the least.

After his unsatisfactory meeting with Senator Chuck Rainsley that morning, he'd regrouped his team at Diplomatic Security with new instructions. Priority number one was to dig into Richard Thompson's past, but he couldn't tell anyone that.

However, as a matter of *routine investigation*, he'd detailed investigators to pull every detail they possibly could, not only of Richard Thompson's private life, but that of every member of his family. Credit reports, FBI files, even college applications. A search of the National Crime Information System database turned up a hit in San Francisco in February 1990, but the file wasn't actually in the system. Worse, the file, which was on paper with the San Francisco Police Department, was a secured file. He'd had to personally call the chief of police to request a copy, which he'd been told should be faxed to him some time that night.

It was probably some drug addict with the same name. But Bear knew that in February 1990, the Thompsons were in San Francisco on compassionate leave when Richard Thompson's mother was dying.

He felt like he was just getting his teeth sunk into the investigation when Secretary Perry called. It was a short call.

"Meet me at the White House at 3 pm."

It was 2:45, and Bear was being patted down by the Secret Service agents at the Pennsylvania Avenue entrance. He didn't know why he was here. Other than the Secretary of State he didn't know who he was meeting. But he knew the fucking White House was so far above his pay grade that he'd gladly go back to Whogivesafuckistan if it meant he didn't have to deal with this bullshit. Bear was a security agent. A cop. Not a politician. He wanted to retire from the Foreign Service and go look at pretty girls on the beach in Florida—not get retired early because of some stupid-ass political shootout.

But then he thought about that sixteen-year-old girl, Andrea Thompson, taking out two hardened terrorist fuckheads with her bare hands while her father dicked around behind his desk at the Pentagon. That girl deserved some justice, whatever form it was going to take.

Forty minutes later, Bear was still sitting in a waiting room in the West Wing, sending instructions to his investigators via text message and email.

That's when he saw the email from one of his senior investigators.

Mitch Filner was a former CIA operative and had been placed with the US Embassy in Singapore in the late 90s. After a rape charge in Singapore, he was dropped by the agency, but had done some freelance work in Iraq and Afghanistan over the last decade.

Mitch Filner had turned up dead of multiple stab wounds in a dumpster in Northern Virginia. Normally a local crime wouldn't come to anyone's attention, except that a real estate agent had walked into a condo in Bethesda that morning, expecting it to be empty. Instead, the carpet was flooded with blood stains.

The blood was a match for Filner. And the condo had a naked eye view of the Thompson's condo in Bethesda.

What the hell did it mean? Why was a former CIA operative watching the Thompson daughters? At the scene of a shooting from the night before. Something stank to high heaven.

At 3:25, the Secretary of State finally walked into the waiting room. Bear jumped to his feet.

James Perry looked put together and well rested, which was more than Bear could say after digging through Richard Thompson's file all night.

"Bear. Come this way. We don't have time for a briefing."

Bear followed as Perry headed down the hall. A secret service agent walked along with them and opened a door just ahead. For a panicky moment Bear thought they were walking into the Oval Office. But instead, he recognized the figure behind the desk the moment they walked in. Former Senator Ben Olin, now the National Security Advisor to the President.

Olin stood up. Also in the room, unfortunately, was acting-Secretary of Defense Richard Thompson, along with his military aide-de-camp, an Army Colonel. To his left, Max Levin, the Director of the Central Intelligence Agency, flanked by another man with a ruddy, freckled face. In moments, that unfamiliarity was addressed. The freckled guy was Leslie Collins, the Director of Operations at CIA.

Bear stared openly at Thompson and Collins. Thompson was CIA and had been for thirty years or more. There was no doubt about it. There was no way they didn't know each other.

Did Thompson know *Mitch Filner?* How fucking tied up was he with the people who had kidnapped his daughter?

The National Security Advisor leaned forward and said, "Secretary Perry, I've just received the most interesting briefing from the Secretary of Defense and the Director of the CIA. I understand your department is conducting the investigation into Andrea Thompson's kidnapping. Why?"

Perry answered off the cuff and without reference to any notes. "The kidnapping involved foreign nationals who may have been engaged in espionage. One of them we are certain was hired in the past by the Defense Department and CIA for intelligence related activities."

Bear coughed. "Two, sir."

Perry turned towards him.

"Two?"

"I just got the news, sir. A former CIA employee turned up dead this morning. His blood was found all over an apartment which overlooked the Thompson condo in Bethesda."

Richard Thompson visibly started. "What?" Then he turned, purposefully, toward Collins.

Bear thought *that* was fucking interesting.

The National Security Advisor asked, "What do you have to say about that, Max?"

Max Levin was unruffled. Prior to his tenure at CIA, he'd been a Marine Corps General, then head of the National Security

Agency. He'd seen his share of crises. "First I've heard of it. What's this guy's name?"

Bear answered, "Mitch Filner."

Leslie Collins shook his head and scoffed. "We fired Filner ten years ago. He raped some girl in Singapore."

Olin, the National Security advisor, closed his eyes and muttered, "Dear God." He appeared to count to twenty. Bear watched as he did it. Finally, Olin said, "All right. For now, State keeps the investigation. The rest of you, turn over whatever they need. We don't need any political liabilities. Is this going to be a liability?"

As he asked the question, he looked at each of the men in the room. His meaning was clear. It was an order. Make this problem go away, before it became a problem for the President.

3. Leslie Collins. April 30

Leslie Collins sat in the back of the Lincoln Town Car. He looked at his watch. He was going to be late for dinner. *Again.*

He shook his head. Then he picked up his secured phone. "Yeah, Danny? It's Collins. I need a status."

Danny McMillan wasn't just an employee. He was a trusted friend, who had served his time in some nasty places—some of them, side by side with Collins.

"Yeah. Here's what I have. First thing—Carrie and Andrea Thompson called Senator Rainsley's office. They have an appointment tomorrow evening."

"Shit," Collins said. "All right, what else? What are their plans tonight?"

"As I understand it, some of them are going out, but Andrea Thompson is planning to stay in. Our guy on the security team thinks she's burnt out."

"All right. What about the mother?"

"No sign yet. No cell phone signal, no credit cards."

"And the oldest sister?"

"She's on a charter flight to San Francisco right now with her husband and a reporter."

Collins was silent for a moment. "A reporter? Does he have a name?"

"Uh...Anthony Walker. He's an entertainment reporter with the *Post*, apparently."

Collins closed his eyes and set the phone down on the seat beside him. He counted to ten, and then counted to ten again for good measure. Then he picked up his phone. "Are you fucking kidding me?"

"What, sir?"

"Anthony Walker isn't a fucking entertainment reporter, he won a fucking Pulitzer for his international affairs coverage. Walker did a whole feature on Wakhan three years ago when the UN dug up the bodies."

Now it was Danny's turn to be silent at the other end of the line. Finally he came back and said, "What do we do?"

"Take it down. I want everyone who can possibly blow the lid on this thing to be completely discredited. Or dead. How long will it take to execute?"

"Most of it, twenty-four hours or less. GP might take a bit longer, and he's the wildcard."

"All right, pull the trigger. All of them. We don't know who knows what, and I don't see how we're going to contain this thing."

"Done, sir."

Collins hung up the phone. Then he dialed his wife.

"Dear, I'm going to be a few minutes late, traffic coming from the White House."

Part Three

CHAPTER TWENTY-ONE
I'd never
hate you

1. Carrie. April 30. 5:17 pm

"**Okay,**" Leah Simpson said. "We'll have the car brought around at six."

"Thank you," Carrie said. She rocked Rachel in her arms unconsciously as she spoke.

Leah paused as she started to walk away and said, "Listen. I promise we'll take good care of you and Rachel and your sisters, all right? My job is to make sure you're safe."

Carrie gave a half smile. She hadn't felt safe since the day a jeep plowed into her car, killing her husband and upending her life. But saying that sort of thing makes people uncomfortable, so she merely answered, "Thanks."

As if she sensed Carrie's skepticism, Leah touched her arm for just a moment, then stepped away.

Sarah walked into the room, her boots thumping on the floor. She looked strangely subdued in a plain black dress and combat boots. "I'm ready whenever you guys are. I swear to God if I don't get out of this house I'm going to explode."

Carrie touched her sister's shoulder. "Pretty soon you won't be so stir crazy, you'll be off to college."

Sarah snorted. "Yeah, I guess. I just never imagined I'd be home schooling my senior year in high school."

"This year wasn't what any of us expected."

Sarah looked stricken. "Sorry, Carrie, that's not what I meant."

Carrie pulled her sister close. "It's okay. You get to grieve for what you lost too, Sarah. Don't think I don't know how hard it's been for you this year."

"Sorry. I'm gonna listen to some music, just let me know when you guys are ready?"

"Sure," Carrie responded as Sarah broke away. "The car's coming around at six."

Sarah wandered out of the kitchen. Carrie stood and walked Rachel, now fully asleep, back to her crib. Very carefully, so as to not disturb the baby, she laid her on the bed and tucked her in. She stayed momentarily, looking down at her daughter. When Rachel slept, it was with abandon you didn't see in adults. Her arms were splayed out, hands clenched in tiny fists as she breathed in and out.

Sometimes it was breathtaking when Carrie realized how much her daughter looked like Ray. In her smile, and the tiny dimples that formed in the corner of her mouth. She leaned close, closed her eyes and smelled Rachel.

Eyes closed, she felt a rare sense of inner peace. Everything was shifting underneath her. Andrea (and possibly all of them) was in danger, her father wasn't who she thought he was; everything in her life was in question. But she knew that somewhere, Ray was thinking about her. She knew her daughter was right here with her, and that she would do *anything* to protect Rachel. Anything at all.

In the end, that was what mattered. This baby, sleeping right here.

Gently, she kissed Rachel on the forehead and stepped out of the room.

As she walked back down the hallway, she heard Dylan's voice. He sounded tense, aggravated.

"Do we have to discuss this now? Look, I just want to relax, okay? You go out with Carrie."

Alexandra answered him, sounding sad. "Dylan, I don't understand what's wrong."

Carrie paused, not wanting to eavesdrop, but saddened by Dylan's tone of voice when he responded. "I'm just exhausted, Alex. I miss Ray and I'm tired and sick and just...please. Go without me tonight, okay? I'll be fine."

Carrie sighed and kept walking. The tension between Alexandra and Dylan was too much to bear. It reminded her so much of the awful pain and stress she and Ray had been through a year before. She wanted to help, but didn't know how. And, as she walked down the hall and into the living room, she knew there was nothing she could do. Dylan needed to work through this on his own. They—Dylan and Alexandra—needed to work through this together. She could be there for them—to answer questions, to help when they needed it, to listen—but she couldn't make them work it out.

2. Bear. April 30. 5:25 pm

Bear Wyden sat, frustrated, staring at the piles of paper on his desk. Despite the masses of information they'd collected into two days, despite the physical evidence, the background files, he still had far more questions than answers.

Why had Tariq Kouri and his still unidentified confederate kidnapped Andrea Thompson? Motives that made sense were in limited supply. Were they somehow involved in human trafficking? Sex slavery? If so, there were far more likely targets than the daughter of the Secretary of Defense. Bear was ready to rule out coincidence or unrelated motives. Andrea Thompson was kidnapped because of who she was, or who her father was.

Which raised the second question.

Who was her father? Richard Thompson claimed he was. But he looked nothing like two of his daughters, both of whom towered over him. He also didn't act like it. Fathers—even Cabinet level fathers—rushed to the hospital to protect their sixteen-year-old daughters. The fact that Thompson hadn't was the first clue he had an unusual relationship with his daughter. But it went downhill from there. He'd had little contact with her in the three days since she'd arrived in the United States. He'd taken no time away from work. He hadn't spent evenings with her. Something was just wrong there. Everything he saw indicated to Bear that Richard Thompson bore no paternal feelings at all toward Andrea Thompson.

Bear thought through the limited facts he knew:

Richard Thompson had spent his career in the CIA, with the State Department as cover.

Tariq Kouri—the Saudi national who had kidnapped Andrea—had worked as a contractor for the CIA and the Pentagon. Richard Thompson knew him.

Mitch Filner—who had turned up dead—had worked for CIA, until he was fired after a rape accusation in Singapore.

Bear leafed through Thompson's file, returning again to the photograph from thirty years before. His eyes fell on a Leslie Collins in his early thirties. Collins was now the Director of Operations for the Central Intelligence Agency. Why was he at the meeting at the White House yesterday? What did the CIA have to do with investigating the kidnapping of an American girl?

Collins and Thompson had been in the CIA together, but there was little information publicly available about Leslie Collins. He'd maintained an almost invisible public profile until he reached his current position. Bear knew that if he started inquiring about Collins, it would be an immediate dead end.

What about the others who were present that night? Roshan al-Saud was the head of the Saudi Arabian intelligence agency. Wyden had access to his State Department file. He opened the file on his computer.

A grandson of King Abd al-Aziz ibn Saud, Prince Roshan was one of several hundred potential third generation claimants to the throne of Saudi Arabia. He had served his career alternately as a diplomat and a spy, with periods in the embassies to the United States, Indonesia, the United Kingdom and Pakistan, among others.

Bear narrowed his eyes as he scanned through the file.

Roshan was in Pakistan in the early 80s. Bear checked the dates. Roshan was in Pakistan at the same time as Richard Thompson.

A quick Google search established that Leslie Collins was also in Pakistan at the same time, and also established that the other party attendees—Chuck Rainsley and George-Phillip Windsor— were not.

Was there something between the three of them? Had Tariq Kouri also worked for the Saudi intelligence agency? What about Mitch Filner? How did he fit in? Bear checked through the files, but there was little or no information about Filner. They obviously needed to correct that.

What else did he know?

The other kidnapper: they knew nothing about him at all. No identification. His fingerprints and DNA had turned up no matches in any database. A dead John Doe, driving a stolen vehicle. No one of similar appearance had been reported missing in the last forty-eight hours. He was a mystery, and a deep one, and that screamed intelligence agency as well. People left behind footprints. They carried identification, they had fingerprints on file, and they were reported missing when they went missing. Whoever this guy was, he either worked for an intelligence agency or he'd never had any brush with the authorities at all. It didn't add up.

And then there was the British connection, in the form of Charles Frazier, a British tourist who just *happened* to have been shot directly across the street from the Thompson sisters last night. Frazier had been in the United States for less than twenty-four hours on a tourist visa and was now being treated at George Washington University Hospital for his gunshot wound.

Was Frazier actually an intelligence agent? And if so, what was his connection to all of this? Why would the British be interested in the Thompson sisters?

None of it made any sense. Something connected all of this, but he didn't know what it was. And that missing piece of information was the vital piece.

Bear sighed and began to review the file again. The answer was out there somewhere.

The phone on his desk rang.

"Bear Wyden," he said.

"Sir? I'm calling from the classified documents desk. You've received a secure fax from the San Francisco police department."

Bear sat up. That would be the police report. Which contained... who knew what? It was time to find out.

3. Adelina. April 30th. 3 pm Pacific Time

Sister Kiara sat down in the chair facing Adelina. At a right angle to them both, completing the triangle, was Jessica, whose heavy eyelids and posture spoke of her exhaustion. Jessica had slumped deep into the cushions of a couch and looked as if she was having difficulty staying awake.

Tired she may be. But she still looked so much healthier than she had ten days before, when she'd come home in the morning after staying out all night, puking all over the kitchen. Adelina had packed her in the car without hesitation and driven here.

"So," Kiara said. "First, thanks for sitting down with us. The reason I wanted to have all three of us talk—you two are headed home in a few hours. I wanted to talk over plans for the next few weeks, and also see if there are some things we could talk about. Is that okay with both of you?"

Adelina nodded and looked to her daughter. Jessica's eyes went to her mother, then back to Kiara. She nodded, her expression dull.

"Okay, then. First of all, I understand Jessica's going back to school starting next week so she can graduate with her class?"

"That's right," Adelina said. She looked over at Jessica. "It's really up to you. You'll have a lot of catching up to do—but I thought you'd be happiest not being set back a year."

Jessica nodded. "I'd like that, if it's possible."

Adelina swallowed, hard, struggling to contain her emotions. Jessica's voice sounded incredibly sad.

Kiara said, "I think that's a really good idea. But I'd like to talk about a couple of things. First, I've made arrangements for you to meet with a psychiatrist, Jessica. Doctor Ralph Foreman. He's a specialist in addiction and grief counseling. For now, I think twice a week would be a good idea, and he's made the space available. Is that okay?"

"Of course," Adelina said. But in her head, she thought, *Grief counseling?*

"Jessica? You're eighteen years old, so it's your decision."

Jessica nodded.

"I'm going to recommend that the two of you go into therapy together for at least some of those sessions."

Adelina took a deep breath. She'd had so many secrets, for so long. But maybe it was time to let some of them go.

"Yes. I think that's a good idea," Adelina said.

"Finally, Jessica. I think it would be a good idea, now, while we're in a safe space, for you to talk with your mother. About Chrys and Marion."

Jessica's eyes widened, and Adelina felt her heart thump. *Who were Chris and Marion?* She watched carefully as Jessica said, "Do you think..."

Her voice trailed off. Then she looked at her mother and said, "I didn't tell you because I thought you'd hate me."

Adelina's voice was broken as she said, "I'd never hate you."

"Mom, I'm a lesbian. And I fell in love. And she died."

For just a second Adelina felt shock. Her daughter was gay? Reflexively, she fell back for an instant to her upbringing, and she wanted to correct her daughter and tell her that no, she was not a lesbian, and no, she had *not* been in love with a woman.

But then she thought about how alone Jessica must have been. *Alone.*

She pictured her daughter. All alone, her twin injured in the accident. Everyone she could lean on was gone. Her mother gone.

"You...fell in love? And she died?" Adelina's eyes watered, and her breath began to move in and out quickly. "Oh, God, and you had no one to turn to. Baby, I'm so sorry. I'm so sorry I wasn't there."

Jessica was shaking now, her eyes wide, her face twisted in fear. "Mama, you're not mad?"

Adelina reached out and took her daughter's hands. "Come here," she said. Then she sobbed. "I'm so sorry I haven't been the mother you needed. Oh, God, I'm so sorry."

Jessica collapsed into her arms, and Adelina pulled her close. "Baby, I'm so sorry," she whispered. She thought about all the times she'd failed her children. But she wasn't failing this time. She wasn't losing *this* daughter. She pulled Jessica tighter and whispered, "I'm here, baby girl."

In halting steps—a few words at a time, and punctuated by many tears—Jessica began to tell her mother the story of how she fell in alive with, and lost, Chrysanthemum Allen. They cried together, and finally Jessica fell asleep in her mother's arms, as Adelina slowly brushed her daughter's hair.

Adelina whispered, "I wish we could stay here longer."

"I know," Kiara said. "But she has you. And you're a good mother."

Adelina closed her eyes, trying to hold back a sob. "I wish that was true. I'd give anything for it to be true."

CHAPTER TWENTY-TWO
On that day I will punish

Crank. April 30. 2:45 PM Pacific.

The Richmond district of San Francisco was blanketed with fog when Crank pulled the rental car to a stop in front of the house on Cabrillo Street. After the morning flight, it had taken nearly ninety minutes for them to get their car arranged, and then drive into the city.

As he parallel parked the car, the three of them stopped talking. Julia leaned forward, resting her hand on the dashboard and looking up at the house. It looked the same as always. Four stories, light blue brick with white ornamentation, it was one of the most striking houses on the block.

"I don't know why," Julia said, "but I'm actually nervous about this."

Crank looked over at her. It was out of character for Julia to ever admit weakness on any topic. "We'd better head in, then?"

She looked back, meeting his eyes. "Right." Her eyes darted to Anthony, in the back seat. "Tell me again why you're along for this?"

Anthony smiled. "I'm here to help you."

She shook her head then opened the door of the rental car. "Let's go."

Crank opened the driver's side door and stepped out, walking up to the door beside his wife.

After twelve years together, he knew her moods well. But this was unusual. She was pensive and withdrawn in a way he'd rarely seen.

"Hey," he said, his voice quiet. He touched her arm and raised an eyebrow.

"I'm okay," she said.

"You sure?"

She nodded, brushing him off, and rang the doorbell to the house. Crank knew she had a key. But Julia had never actually *lived* in this house, so whenever they visited, she was scrupulous about knocking.

Today, however, there was no answer. They waited, and she rang the bell again. And again.

Crank coughed. "You've got your key on you?"

"Yes," Julia said. She sighed. "I don't like using it." She opened her purse and rooted around in it for a minute. Then she fitted a key to the deadbolt and carefully turned it. Crank heard the lock slide, then click, and she opened the door.

"Well, then," she said, her voice low. She paused for a moment more. Then she pushed the door open. It was immediately apparent no one had been home in some days. The mudroom at the foot of the stairs was cluttered with junk mail. Magazines and catalogues, bills and other mail had grown into a small pile behind the door. A rank smell radiated from somewhere inside—spoiled milk or worse.

Julia looked at the pile of mail, then at Crank.

"She's fine," he said. "Just out of town or something. She told your dad she was going to some retreat center."

"For how long?" she said. "I spoke with her on Friday, and this is a lot more mail than that. And that smell..."

She started up the stairs. Crank followed, leaving a bewildered Anthony Walker behind.

The house was quiet, empty. Eerily so. As they looked around the ground floor, with all the lights out and not a soul in the house, Crank realized that he had never once been in this house by himself. It was dark inside, and the quiet was eerie and uncomfortable. It was almost as if the fog outside had seeped into the house, rendering it cold and dark.

Crank thought back. The last time he'd been here was the fall of 2012—Thanksgiving night. Andrea had been in Spain, but the rest of the Thompson clan was on hand, and that night, at least, they were full of drama. Jessica and Sarah were fighting. Alexandra had revealed her sexual assault at school and then Dylan Paris showed up on the doorstep after a cross-country flight. An altogether satisfying night.

The house was very different now.

Cold.

Crank followed Julia into the kitchen. She froze at the door to the kitchen.

"What is it?" he asked, coming up behind her. Then he saw and heard it.

The floor on the far side of the kitchen table was covered in... vomit? Days old. Maybe weeks. Dried out, but crawling with ants and flies. This was the source of the smell. Julia stared for one minute, and then her shoulders shook. Once, twice, then she ran, covering her mouth, for the bathroom.

Anthony came up behind Crank.

"I don't get it," Anthony said.

"I don't either. Adelina would *never* leave her house in this condition unless it were a real emergency."

Crank met Anthony's eyes. Then he said, "I don't know what's going on here. And I don't know why Julia's trusting you. But you better not screw her over."

Anthony said, "That's not how I do business."

"I'm cleaning this shit up," Crank replied.

"Don't. In case—in case the police need to get involved."

Crank sucked in a breath. Anthony was right, of course. You didn't fuck with the scene of a crime, if that's what this was. He'd absorbed that much and more from his father, a retired Boston cop, over the years.

With that in mind, Crank tiptoed around the kitchen. More signs of an abrupt departure. The coffee pot was full, but cold, and it had a spot of mold floating on top of the liquid. Two glasses, dirty, in the sink. On the kitchen floor, near the vomit, a half-gallon of milk in its plastic container, laying on it's side and bloated from expanding glasses. That wasn't going to smell good.

Crank didn't touch anything. "Let's go," he said. "We leave everything as it is. Whatever the fuck happened, Adelina and Jessica left in a hurry."

As they stepped out of the kitchen, they found Julia sitting at the dining table. She had her hands on her laps, her posture straight, staring straight ahead at the wall.

"Julia?" Crank asked.

She looked up at him. "They've been gone a week. At least. How the hell didn't we know? What kind of family are we? My mother and one of my sisters has been missing for *a week* and no one even knew?"

Crank put a hand on her shoulder. "You talked on the phone with her on Friday."

"She sure as hell wasn't here."

"So, maybe she's at that retreat your Dad talked about?"

"Why wouldn't she say anything? Why leave the place such a disaster?"

Crank sighed. "I don't know. I...I don't know. My suggestion... let's take a look around. If we don't see anything, we call the cops."

She swallowed and nodded. "Yeah. Yeah. All right. Check her bedroom and bathroom. Maybe there's some clue there."

She stood and led the way, down the hall, past the closed door to Richard Thompson's office, and up the stairs. The second floor had two bedrooms, Adelina and Richard's.

"Mother's first," Julia said.

"Wait," Crank said. "They have separate rooms?"

"Well—yeah."

"Weird."

Julia nodded. "I guess. It's been that way a long time." She turned the doorknob.

The room was spare. A queen sized bed, a small bookshelf, a bureau and a desk/vanity combo. Adelina had a large walk-in closet, hung with dresses on both sides.

"She didn't pack much stuff," Julia said, looking in the closet. The desk and vanity told the same story. Adelina's laptop was still on the desk, along with a charger cable for an iPhone. Did Adelina have another charger? Impossible to know. Julia walked to the desk and tentatively pressed the power button. The computer, a relatively new MacBook, began to boot up.

"Who leaves for a trip without their laptop?" Anthony asked.

"And without cleaning the kitchen floor?" Julia asked.

They watched the computer boot up, and Crank felt a sick fascination. What would they see when the screen finally appeared? Possibly nothing. Possibly, Adelina's computer would be password protected. Or infected by viruses. Or wired to a bomb which would explode when they finished inspecting it. Who knew?

The computer finally booted to a password prompt.

"Damn," Julia muttered. She slid into the chair, chewing on her lower lip. She reached out and attempted a password. No good. Then she tried another. Nothing. "I could do this all day," Julia said. She tried three more passwords in quick succession. Nothing.

"What have you tried so far?"

"Variations on my Dad's name and birthdate. Her birthday. Her hometown."

Crank's eyes darted across the hall to Richard's bedroom. "Somehow I don't think she's going to use anything of his as a password."

Julia frowned. "Yeah, you're probably right."

"Your parents aren't close?" Anthony asked.

"They're WASP iceboxes," Crank said.

"Not my mother," Julia said. "She's no WASP."

"Fair," Crank replied. She tried another password. Crank wandered across the room. He opened the top drawer of the bureau.

Crank frowned. Half a dozen prescription bottles. Buspirone. Three times a day for anxiety. Amitriptyline for panic disorder. Risperdal for bipolar symptoms.

Crank said. "Your mom is on some serious meds. Take a look at this?"

Julia stood and walked over. Her eyebrows scrunched together. ""Panic disorder? Bipolar?" Her eyes darted to Crank's. Then she pulled the drawer out further.

A battered and frayed Bible. Notes were stuffed in the Bible, her mother's dense handwriting on them. She opened the Bible up to one of the well-worn notes.

A verse had been underlined several times and circled in pencil.

Zephaniah 1:9:

> *On that day I will punish*
> *all who leap over the threshold,*
> *who fill their master's house*
> *with violence and fraud.*

Julia frowned, confused, and flipped through the Bible again. Another heavily underscored verse.

Psalm 37:

> *For the wicked shall be cut off,*
> *but those who wait for the Lord shall inherit the land.*

"My Mom was always devout. But this is…I don't know." Julia lay the Bible down.

"Wait—" she said. She bent down a little, peering in the top drawer. At the very back, another book. She pulled it out.

It was a journal. Her eyes went to Crank's. "I don't know if I…"

"She's missing," he said.

"Right." She took a deep breath then opened it up.

It was in Spanish. Densely written in barely legible handwriting that covered every square inch of the journal's pages. No margins. No paragraph marks. A solid block of text.

On every single page.

"Oh, my God," Julia said. "I feel like I don't even know who she is."

"Can you read it?" Crank asked.

"I hardly know any Spanish," she said. She flipped through. "Some of it I recognize, or…maybe." Her eyebrows furrowed. "This can't be right."

"What is it?" Crank moved closer to her.

"I swear it says, *He raped me again today*. Or violated? I'm not sure, I don't really know Spanish!" Julia swallowed and looked up to Crank. "I'm reading this wrong. It can't be."

"Bring that with you," Crank said.

She began to pace back and forth. Finally, she marched across the hall, shoving open the door to her father's bedroom.

The room was spare. Clothing hung in the closet. Julia began to pull open drawers. Clothing. Another one. Then another. The fourth drawer, she pulled open and dumped out, tossing clothing across the bed. Her face was oddly frozen, confused. She pulled open another drawer.

"Nothing," she said. Then she looked up at Crank. "The office."

He raised his eyebrows. "Your Dad's office?"

Julia nodded. She turned and walked out, then down the stairs.

The office door was closed and locked. Unlike the rest of the doors in the house, this one had a relatively new doorknob, modern, with a metal plate.

Julia let out another curse. Then she said, "Wait...stay here." Then she ran downstairs.

"I don't get it," Anthony said.

"I don't either," Crank replied. "But—she's onto something."

Two minutes later, Julia was back. And she was holding a small axe.

"I'll handle that," Crank said. "If we're doing breaking and entering, let me handle the breaking part."

She snorted. "All right. Have fun."

Anthony said, "Are you sure this is a good idea?"

Julia shook her head. "If you don't think so, go on without us."

Three minutes later, Crank had the door open. Mangled, broken to shreds. But open.

The office was much as Crank remembered it from his one visit in here. Ten years ago? More? A large bookshelf extended from the ceiling to the floor, an entire wall covered in books. The wall with the door was covered mostly in photographs and plaques. Pictures of Richard Thompson with various Presidents: Bill Clinton, Ronald Reagan, George Bush. A photo showed a much younger Thompson in military fatigues, his arm around another man, both of them standing in a desert.

On the desk, a single family portrait with all of the daughters. No pictures anywhere else in the office of Adelina, but each of the daughters had a portrait somewhere on the wall.

Except Andrea.

"That stings," Crank muttered.

Anthony was looking at one of the photos, the one of Thompson in the desert. He said, "That's Vasily Katatygin."

"Who?" Julia asked.

Anthony shook his head. "Highest ranking Soviet defector to the Afghan rebels. He was a Spetsnaz Major—that's the Russian Special Forces, like our Green Berets. He ended up joining Ahmad Massoud's militia."

"I haven't a clue what you're talking about," Crank said.

"I'm sure it doesn't matter," Anthony said. "That was thirty years ago."

"My dad was never posted to Afghanistan," Julia said.

"Well, nobody officially was back then," Anthony said.

Julia wandered around the office, a frown on her face. She began to open desk drawers.

"What are you looking for?"

"I don't know," she said.

Crank slid open another drawer. Files. He pulled one out randomly. It was labelled Wakhan/Badackshan. Idly, he flipped it open, then his eyes widened. He dropped the file. "Jesus Christ," he muttered.

"What is it?" Julia asked.

She reached for the file, but Crank put his hand on it. "You don't want to look at that."

"The fuck I don't," she replied, grabbing the file away from him. She laid it open on the desk and gasped.

The first thing in the file was the photo Crank had seen. A dozen or more bodies, most of them children. Bloated, blackened. Crank winced and looked away.

Anthony moved forward and picked up the file. "Holy fuck, that's Wakhan. Why does your father have this?"

"Wait. What?" Crank said as Anthony flipped through the file.

Anthony said, "Back in December 1983. A group of rebels got their hands on nerve gas and used it on a village they felt was collaborating too closely with the Soviets. As a matter of fact it was Ahmad Massoud's militia, or at least they were implicated."

Julia's eyes darted to the picture on the wall. "Was that guy involved? Karatygin?"

"Nobody knows for sure," Anthony replied.

"Whatever it is, it doesn't tell us where Julia's mom is," Crank said. "Let's keep looking."

He pulled another file out of the drawer. Credit card bills. Another file contained what appeared to be a copy of Richard Thompson's personnel file. Crank dumped those on the desk and kept looking.

"Huh," Anthony said, as Crank continued to rummage through the drawer.

"What is it?" Julia asked.

"Look at this," he said. "I think your dad may not have been State Department at all. I'm starting to think CIA."

"What? Dad? No way."

Anthony said, "You never know. Take a look at this." He laid the file on the table in front of her and pointed at something in it.

Crank had frozen, looking at another file. He didn't say anything as he looked at it. His heart was beating heavily.

The file was a police report. February 13, 1990. From the San Francisco Police Department.

The photos made it all too clear what had happened. Someone had beaten Adelina Thompson nearly to death. Swollen face, bloody lip. *Jesus Christ*, he thought, when he saw the sentence, *Victim refuses rape examination.*

Crank looked up at his wife. She was having a lively debate with Anthony about the likelihood of her father being in the Central Intelligence Agency. Laughing a little.

Then she saw Crank's face.

"What is it?"

He shook his head. *Shit.* She reached out and grabbed the file. Then her eyes widened, and she gasped, covering her mouth.

"Oh my God," she whispered.

A lab report fell from the file. Julia picked it up with shaking hands. Her eyes scanned it, then she handed it to Crank.

It was from the DNA Diagnostic Center. The first paragraph read:

Dear Mr. Thompson. Thank you for your recent examination at the DNA Diagnostic Center. At your request, we have examined the samples provided, and can rule within 99.9% probability that the individuals tested are not related.

The lab report was dated February 12, 1990.

"That *son of a bitch,*" Julia whispered. Her eyes scanned the file. The photographs of her mother. Beaten and raped. "It says...it says in here that she refused to press charges. The police referred her to the battered women's shelter."

"Fuck," Crank muttered.

"That's not it," she said. "Alexandra was born November 9." Julia began to breathe heavily. Hyperventilating. "She was born exactly nine months after this police report, Crank. Oh, my God. Oh my *God*, and do you know how badly I've treated my mother?" Julia's voice sounded desperate as her eyes swiveled to Crank.

"There's no way you could have known," he whispered.

"She's my *mother*," Julia cried. "Look what he did to her! Is it any wonder she couldn't be there for me? Can you even imagine what she went through?"

She stood up, her fists clenched. Then she cried out. "We have to find my mother, Crank. We *have* to!"

Crank looked up at the sound of brakes out front. His eyes darted to the window. A car had parked out front, and two men got out. Both of them had short, closely cropped hair and muscular builds. Both wore open suit coats.

"Trouble," Crank muttered.

CHAPTER TWENTY-THREE
Those are drugs

1. George-Phillip. 10:35 pm GMT

As was his habit, George-Phillip stopped in to check on Jane when he arrived home a few minutes after 10 pm.

Jane, of course, was fast asleep in her bedroom, her tiny hand curled up, touching her lips, her knees drawn up to her chest under the blanket. She breathed in and out quietly, her raven hair spread out evenly around her head in a fan.

George-Phillip was troubled. He didn't like coming home after Jane's bedtime, regardless of the reasons.

Unfortunately, today at least he had good reasons to be so late. The news from the United States had been increasingly grim as the day went on. George-Phillip spent the day on the phone, his number one focus the shooting of Charlie Frazier. The good news was that Frazier was going to recover—the gunshot wound was serious, but not critical. He would be out of the hospital in a few days.

But not on his way home, most likely.

George-Phillip hadn't received any official enquiries yet about Charlie's status, but he knew it was coming. At some point, the United States government would formally ask the British government if Charlie was an intelligence agent, if only because of the circumstances of the shooting. When that moment came, the British ambassador wouldn't have to lie, because he wouldn't know.

George-Phillip had been called to speak with the Prime Minister, who wanted an explanation of why a British citizen—and employee of the Secret Intelligence Service—had been shot in Washington, DC. That discussion had been unpleasant, but George-Phillip made it absolutely clear. Charlie Frazier's employment was and must remain a secret. He was fairly certain the American government would jerk them around for a few days, asking a lot of questions and delaying Charlie's departure. But in the end they would let it go. As friendly nations, the United States and the United Kingdom maintained a polite fiction that they didn't spy on each other. But everyone in the intelligence community recognized that for what it was—fiction.

In practice, in the years since the September 11 attacks on the United States, intelligence budgets for both the United States and the United Kingdom had ballooned, with each government employing tens of thousands of intelligence employees, military, civilian and private contractors, often in overlapping roles. The United States was clearly worse: George-Phillip had read a report indicating that the US had more than 800,000 individuals with secret clearances, most of them employees of private companies. Undoubtedly some of those were employed spying on the United Kingdom. And, George-Phillip thought, no doubt some of them were using their access to secret funding and information to further their own personal aims rather than their government's.

George-Phillip shook his head. Even here, in the doorway to his daughter's room, he couldn't clear his head of work. He straightened himself, stretched a little, then walked out of the room, gently closing the door behind him. He walked down the hall to his office and mixed himself a whisky and soda.

For a minute or possibly two, he looked out at the square. The trees and shrubbery at the corner were overgrown, obscuring the center of the square with its garden and tennis court.

He sat down at the desk with his drink and began to scan through the evening's accumulated emails.

Five minutes later he sat up, alarm bells ringing in his head. Now *that* was interesting. A report indicated that Vasily Karatygin had turned up in Kabul. The former Spetsnaz major had defected from the Soviet Union in the early 80s and later became a deputy leader in Ahmad Massoud's militia in Afghanistan. It was unclear where his loyalty lay now, if any—but it was clear that he ran a huge opium smuggling operation centered in Badakhshan Province.

Karatygin had been on George-Phillip's radar for thirty years because of his involvement in the massacre at Wakhan. He wasn't one to show up in the Afghan capitol for any reason. It was too dangerous, too many competing interests, not to mention the fact that the Americans had a price on his head.

Was it connected?

George-Phillip had to assume it was. Someone—possibly Leslie Collins, possibly Prince Roshan, possibly even Richard Thompson—was making an aggressive move. But who? And why? Why now?

The phone rang. It was O'Leary.

"George-Phillip here."

"Sir, news."

"Go."

"It looks like our player is Leslie Collins. Surveillance picked him up giving orders. He's going after all of the Thompsons, anyone who can even potentially give information on Wakhan."

George-Phillip muttered a curse. "All right. Even Richard Thompson?"

"As far as we can tell, yes, sir. And—you, sir. I've already mobilized an extra protective detail, they'll be on their way shortly."

"I don't need a protective detail, O'Leary, we've been through this."

"Beggin' your parson, sir, but you do, and they're on the way whether you like it or not."

"Fine. O'Leary, you know what to do? Start making arrangements."

"Yes, sir."

George-Phillip hung up the phone and looked out at the square. Adelina Thompson and her daughters were likely in a great deal of danger. They were the wild card, and in some ways that was his fault. He shook his head, and reached for the phone again.

He didn't hear the gunshot in Belgrade Square before the bullets hit the glass.

2. Dylan. 6:26 pm

Dylan Paris leaned back in his chair and closed his eyes. Carrie, Sarah and Alex had all left the condo about forty minutes before.

It was the first time he'd had any peace in days. He felt as if he might pass out any second, but for the moment he wanted to just rest his mind. Sarah's words the day before had been weighing on him. His best friend weighed on him.

Ray would have said something like, *Man up, Studmaster, and tell her. Ask her for help.* He would have. But asking for help, that was the hardest thing in the world. The thing was, he was stuck. He remembered the moment he'd decided to do it. It wasn't that night in the dorms. It wasn't even at the funeral. It was before Ray had even died. He'd been at the hotel with the rest of the Thompson clan. Alex's dad was there, and he had a gin and tonic, and Dylan couldn't keep his eyes off that drink.

He wanted one so badly right now he could taste it.

You're turning into your dad, Dylan.

Fucking asshole.

But it was true.

"Dylan? Can you come here a second?"

Dylan's eyes popped open. Andrea was standing in the hallway, a confused look on her face. He stood and walked toward her. "What is it?"

"This..." she said, pointing in her room. "I went to check out some of the clothes Carrie loaned me, and..."

Dylan frowned. Inside the closet, underneath the pile of clothes, was a cardboard box. Several plastic baggies were in it, filled with white powder.

"What the fuck?" he asked. He walked closer, and picked up one of the bags. Underneath the plastic bag—money. A lot of it. Twenty-dollar bills, stacked.

"Something's wrong," he said.

"Those are drugs," she said.

"Yeah."

"A lot of them."

"Yeah," he replied.

Her face was pale. "Those weren't in here yesterday, or this morning. I know—I went through the closet before I left to get the blood test this morning. Who was in here?"

Dylan tried to think back. That morning, he and Alex had gotten breakfast at the corner diner while Andrea went with Sarah to get the blood test and Carrie went to the Pentagon. The condo was empty except Rachel and the nanny. And their guards.

"I don't get it," he said. "I think we need to call the cops."

"What? Are you sure?"

"I don't know what's going on, Andrea."

Both of them froze when the phone rang. Neither of them had ever heard it before—it was the house landline.

3. Adelina. 3:30 pm Pacific

delina knew exactly when they drove into cell phone range again, because both of their phones started to ring with message after message.

Jessica said. "We're popular, aren't we?"

"It was like this when I drove to town last Friday to talk to Julia," Adelina said. "Sometimes I wish I could just get rid of the damn thing." But of course, she knew she couldn't.

"I got like fifty text messages from Sarah," Jessica said. She frowned as she scrolled through the messages then sat up straight. "Mom!" she said in a squeal.

"What is it?" Adelina said, alarmed by the sudden note of urgency.

"Pull over, Mom. Check your messages!"

"I'm sure there's nothing that urgent—"

"Mom! Do it!"

Adelina didn't argue. She pulled the car to the side of the road and pulled up her messages.

Julia had sent her two dozen text messages. Carrie just as many. One message from Richard. It simply said, "Call me."

"Oh my God," she said, when she saw the message from Carrie: Andrea kidnapped. Call. Now. She looked over at Jessica and said, "Call Carrie now. I'm getting us home. I'll call Julia."

She put the car in gear and began to drive, too fast, out of the mountains. She reached for her phone again to dial Julia's number, when it rang.

She stopped the car again as she recognized the beginning of the incoming number.

She answered it. "Hello?"

"Adelina Ramos, please."

Adelina *Ramos*. Of course he wouldn't use her married name.

"This is she." Her voice shook. She hadn't heard that voice in years except once or twice on television, and it shook her to her core. A yearning she didn't think she was even still capable of washed over her, along with fear, because this phone call could only mean one thing. He'd said he would never call again, unless it was the end. He'd said—to forget about him. To forget about what could have been.

"You need to get them out," the voice said. *Them* meaning her children.

"Are you sure?" she said.

"We intercepted some calls. You need to act right now, you're all likely in danger."

Adelina gasped. "All right. Where do I go?"

"Try to make it across the border. I may be able to get you more help there."

She sobbed. Then she threw caution to the wind and whispered, "I still love you."

There was a long pause. Then the response.

"Always, Adelina. Always."

The phone disconnected. In the seat next to her, Jessica was talking too rapidly. "Yes, of course I'm okay, I've been up in the mountains with Mom. Yeah, at a retreat. It's...complicated. But Andrea...she's okay?"

Adelina dialed Andrea's phone without hesitation. She would be the first and most in danger, followed by Carrie.

Andrea's phone went straight to voicemail. She tried again. No good. Was she back in Spain?

No. The text messages from Carrie were clear. She leaned toward Jessica. "Who are you talking with? Is Andrea with them?"

"No," Jessica said. "Andrea's at the condo. I'm on the phone with Carrie, she's out to dinner with Sarah and Alexandra."

Adelina nodded. "Tell Carrie to make sure she's in a public place with lots of people. Tell her she's in danger."

Jessica's eyes widened in confusion. "What?"

"Just *do it*."

Jessica started speaking rapidly into the phone again. Adelina dialed the condo.

It rang. Three. Four. Five times. Six.

A moment later a voice answered, a male voice with a voice bordering on a Southern accent.

"Hello?"

"Dylan Paris? This is Adelina Thompson."

"Mrs. Thompson? Everyone's been looking for you!"

"No time for that now. Is Andrea there with you?"

"Yeah..."

"Get her out. You're in danger. Do you understand me? Whatever you do, you need to get her out of that building."

"I don't understand—"

Dylan's voice cut off suddenly. At the other end of the line she heard something terrifying. A loud crack.

A gunshot.

CHAPTER TWENTY-FOUR
Trouble

1. Julia. 3:30 pm Pacific

"**Trouble,**" Crank said.

Julia looked up from the file. Crank was standing against the window, his face looking tense and alarmed. "What is it?" she asked.

He shook his head slightly then raised a finger across his lips. *Quiet.* Then he whispered. "Two guys. Suit jackets. They're armed. I don't think they're cops."

Julia stopped breathing. It never occurred to her that they might be in danger. But the last forty-eight hours had changed a lot. Andrea had been kidnapped. Her father worked for the CIA. Her mother had been attacked.

She didn't move. A drop of sweat rolled down her forehead. She whispered, "Crank, I'm worried."

"Out the back door," he said. "Grab the file."

She scrambled to gather up the police report describing her mother's assault. Crank grabbed her hand, pulling her toward the door. A deep anxiety lined his face like nothing she'd ever seen before.

He paused at the door to the office, listening. Anthony also stood stock still, face frozen.

"They're messing with the front door," Anthony whispered.

"Go. Back door," Crank replied, his voice urgent.

They moved quickly, Crank in the lead, pulling Julia by the hand, Anthony following behind. Julia winced at the sound of boards shifting and creaking under Crank's boots.

They heard a loud crack downstairs, and a male voice muttering.

Crank didn't say a word, moving now through the kitchen to the back door. Anthony eased the kitchen door closed behind them.

Eyebrows narrowing, Crank twisted the knob, but the back door didn't budge. The deadbolt, which required a key inside and out, was locked.

"Shit," he whispered. He looked desperately toward Julia.

Footsteps up the front stairs. Hands shaking, she got her keys out of her purse. She only had one key to the house and had never tried the back door. Did it use the same key? She had no idea. She got the key out, and tried to fit it in the lock.

It didn't fit.

The intruders had made it up the stairs. Julia imagined them at the landing, trying to decide whether to move toward the office, the stairs, or the kitchen.

Then she heard a man, cursing, and rapid steps toward the other side of the house. Office it was.

"Block the door," she hissed. She turned toward the kitchen window and unlocked it, then tried to raise it. It didn't budge. Damn it. She had to get it open, and get the bars open, quickly.

While she tried again to raise the window, Crank and Anthony lifted the kitchen table and slid it to the door.

"That's not going to hold them long," Crank whispered.

Footsteps in the dining room. Julia grimaced and let out a groan as she tried again to raise the window.

"Oven," Crank said.

Anthony looked at Crank, then to the oven, and nodded. The two of them raced to that side of the kitchen, then slid the oven out, away from the wall. A loud squeal rose from underneath as the metal scraped against the stone tiles.

Julia heard a shout, then footsteps pounding through the house. At that sound, Crank let out a loud cry as he and Anthony lifted the stove in the air. The gas line stretched to its length, then cracked and broke away from the wall at one of the joints.

"No!" Julia cried.

It was too late. They dropped the stove, blocking the table, just as the intruders tried to open the kitchen door. Julia waited for an explosion, a hissing, but nothing came. Instead, Crank dove for the wall and disconnected the gas.

The kitchen door banged against the table, once, then twice, then again.

"Let's go," Crank said. He lifted a chair, and swung it, wide and fast, at the window. With a crash, the glass shattered, just as a hole was blown through the door. A bullet! Julia let out a scream.

"Fuck me fuck me fuck me," Crank said, fumbling for the lock for the barred windows.

"Got it!" he said a second later. The cage lifted wide, and he lifted Julia off her feet and to the window.

"Go!" Anthony yelled.

The three of them tumbled out the window and onto the stairs, then ran for the gate in the back yard. Beyond was the alley going half a block down a public street. Crank held Julia's hand the whole way, tugging her along behind him.

Less than a minute later, they were out onto the street. Crank led them to the corner and stuck his head out for just a second.

"Gone. They're already gone." He sagged for just a second. Julia collapsed against him.

Five seconds later, with a loud crash, an explosion blasted the house, spewing flame and debris out into the street.

2. Leah Simpson. 6:31 pm

One minute later and three thousand miles away, Leah Simpson stood at the door of the Thompson condominium, a frown on her face. Mick Stanson sat at the desk twenty feet down the hall, cleaning his service weapon.

"What? Who is here?" she asked over the radio again.

John Lochlear, the agent at the front desk, said, "Our relief."

She sighed. What kind of fuck up was this? "They've got valid ID?"

"Yeah."

She frowned in frustration. They weren't supposed to have a relief team here until midnight. "Hold them there," she said into the radio. "Let me call Bear. This is bullshit."

She didn't wait for an answer, instead reaching for her cell phone and speed dialing Bear. The phone rang once, twice, a third time.

"Yeah, Bear speaking."

As Bear answered the phone, she saw the light appear above the elevator. She tensed, even as she said the words, "Bear, is there supposed to be a relief team here?"

His response was instant and vociferous. "No! Keep your guard up, someone just tried to assassinate the head of MI-6."

Leah's first response, before she could even think properly, was to crouch and reach for her weapon. The crouch saved her life—when the elevator door opened, a tall man stepped out and sprayed the hallway with bullets. The burst missed her, but took the top of Mick Stanson's head off, spraying the hallway with his blood.

She ducked back, squeezing her body into the alcove across from the Thompsons.

3. Dylan. 6:31 pm

The sound of the bullets from a light machine pistol, probably a MAC10 or an Uzi, were unmistakable. So was the panic in Adelina's voice over the phone.

Dylan didn't have time to deal with Adelina. He let the phone drop and shouted, "Andrea!"

Without thought, he moved as quickly as he could toward the front door. He didn't have a clue what was going on. But he knew that *someone* had put a great deal of both cash and drugs in Andrea's room. He knew that, for reasons he didn't know about, Adelina had chosen *that moment* to call. And now someone was shooting in the hall?

Coincidences were one thing. This was something else.

"What are you doing?" Andrea shouted as he moved toward the front door.

"Finding out what's going on. Stay down."

She didn't need to be told twice. Instead, she crouched down next to the couch, where she had a line of sight to the front door.

He put the chain on then cracked it open.

Across the hall, Leah Simpson was in the alcove, her weapon out. Twenty-five feet further down, another one of their guards was down, blood splattered all over the wall.

Christ. They were pinned in place. No way to escape. Only one defender with a weapon, and that was a lousy automatic pistol with maybe fifteen shots.

Without looking at him, Leah shouted, "Stay inside."

"I am! How many are there?"

"Three!"

Fuck. There was no hope of holding them off. Dylan left the chain on the door and marched directly to Andrea. His eyes scanned the condo, trying to figure out options.

The balcony. Christ. It was eighteen floors down. But if he could get her to the floor directly below—

"Stay," he called, then ran into Carrie's room, the first bedroom after the living area. He yanked the blanket off the bed and carried it out to the living room.

Five shots in quick succession. Loud. That must be Leah.

"Shit. Andrea—they're after you. You're going over the side. Get into the condo below us, then meet me...in thirty minutes. At the war memorial on Norfolk. If we miss each other there, then the Metro station at midnight. Got it?"

Her eyes were wide as saucers. He shoved the blanket at her. The shooting started again.

"Go! You can do this!"

4. Andrea. 6:33 pm

ndrea crouched on the floor, holding a useless sheet, her heart pounding. Four more shots outside shook the entire floor, the glass sliding doors to the balcony shaking and rattling.

Dylan was in the kitchen, pulling back drawers, an unreadable expression in his face. He strode from the kitchen carrying a butcher knife in one hand and a cleaver in the other. As he passed into the living room, then the front hall, he switched the light out, stationing himself in the darkness, knives at the ready.

"Go, damn it! I'm only going to be able to stop one of them, if that many!"

At Dylan's command, she jumped to her feet and slid the balcony door open. The wind was blowing, warm, from the Potomac River half a mile away. She rushed to the edge of the balcony then sucked in a terrified rush of air.

It was eighteen stories down. The cars at street level looked like toys.

She heard a voice cry out, and Dylan said, "Damn it, Leah's down. You need to go *now*."

Tears began to run down Andrea's face freely. As quickly as she could, she wound the blanket up and knotted it around the balcony railing.

Before she could give it even a moment's thought more, she grabbed the knotted blanket, wrapping it twice around her right wrist. Then she looked back at Dylan as she swung a leg over the edge of the balcony.

He stood, ready, in the darkness. His legs were spread shoulder width apart, knives at the ready. His expression was savage. She met his eyes.

Dylan nodded, his expression an inscrutable mix of love and resignation. His hands tightened around the knife handles. She dropped down over the side, just as the front door of the condo burst open. Dylan crouched, huddled in the darkness behind the door.

Andrea gasped as she swung down and the blanket tightened. Immediately she heard a tearing sound, the fabric not strong enough to hold her weight, and she screamed, unable to see anything but the ground two hundred feet below. Flailing, she reached out and grabbed the rail of the condo below Carrie's, gripping it as tightly as she possible could and pulling herself in.

Tears ran down her face as she got purchase for her feet. Her heart beat in her chest so hard that she thought she was going to die of a heart attack then and there, and as she raised her leg and scrambled over the side, she heard more gunshots upstairs.

Shit!

The balcony door down here was locked.

A man was crouched in the kitchen, clearly in view of her, holding his wife and a small child. He watched her with terrified eyes, but made no move to unlock the balcony, even though he'd seen her come over the side on a fucking sheet.

Andrea didn't hesitate. She picked up one of the cast iron chairs on the porch and swung it.

The glass sliding door shattered inward.

She strode into the condo, her feet crunching on the broken glass. She looked at the man who cowered on the floor with his family and said, "Sorry about that."

Andrea let herself out the front door.

Epilogue

1. Carrie

"**W**hat the hell?" Alexandra said as half a dozen uniformed police officers, accompanied by their Diplomatic Security detail, burst into the restaurant. They were accompanied by Bear Wyden, the head of the investigation.

Carrie shifted position, her body tensing up. The sudden change alarmed Rachel, asleep in the sling across her chest. Rachel began to stir, then cry.

Sarah stood, alarm on her face.

"What is it?"

"Can the three of you come with us, please?"

Alexandra went pale. "Dylan? Is Dylan okay? What's going on?"

"Ma'am, please," Bear said.

The three women stood. Carrie felt an awful sense of dread. Bear didn't say, *Dylan's fine*. He didn't say, *Don't worry, Dylan will be okay*. Unconsciously, she reached out and took Alexandra's hand.

A moment later, the three of them were in the back of a giant SUV. Bear sat in the front passenger seat as a uniformed DSS agent drove. "Go!" Bear said. "The rest can catch up."

Carrie leaned forward and said, "Where are we going? What's going on, Mr. Wyden?"

Bear rubbed a hand across his forehead.

"Mr. Wyden? Where is Andrea? And Dylan?"

Bear shook his head. "We don't know."

Alexandra gasped. "What do you mean you don't know?"

"Exactly that. At least three men bearing apparently valid IDs attacked the condo. They killed the security guards. It appears, as best we can tell, that Andrea got away. It's...less clear...about Dylan. Two of our agents are dead, and at least three of theirs."

"Who are *they?*" Carrie said.

"We don't know. But whoever it is...your family home in San Francisco has been...destroyed. There was a bomb."

"*Shit!* Julia and Crank?"

"They're being questioned by the San Francisco Police Department now, and we've got agents on the way."

Carrie looked back at Alex, who was sitting, stunned, her face pale. She looked...terrified. She looked like Carrie must have looked in the hospital last August, not knowing if Ray was going to make it or not.

He hadn't. And she...did. And some days, some moments, if it hadn't been for Rachel, she might have wished otherwise.

Alexandra didn't have a baby girl to worry about. Carrie reached out and squeezed her sister's hand. Sarah had Alexandra's other hand. They'd be there for her. She was going to need it, if anything had happened to Dylan.

She slumped back to her seat. She still had no idea what had prompted all of this. She didn't know why Andrea had been kidnapped, or who had attacked them. But whoever it was, whatever it was, it was serious enough they were willing to kill. Whoever *they* were.

"What are you doing to find Andrea and Dylan?" she asked.

"We've mobilized every police department in the region, Miss Thompson."

"Mrs. Sherman, please. Or Carrie. But not...that," she corrected.

"Right. We're on it, Carrie. I promise you, if they're out there to be found, we'll find them."

2. Adelina

The sun had long since set over the Pacific Ocean. Adelina glanced over at her daughter. The one daughter she was in a position to take care of.

Jessica was asleep in the passenger seat, curled up in a near fetal position. She'd been asleep most of the drive, her body still recovering from the drugs which had ravaged her system. When she wasn't sleeping, she was eating. The good news was, she'd gained 15 pounds in the last ten days.

The bad news was, she still hadn't made it back over a hundred pounds.

Just one more score to settle with Richard.

Her phone was off. She'd made one stop, at a bank, where she'd withdrawn ten thousand dollars in cash from her savings account. After that, there would be nothing, because she had no plans to leave an electronic trail until they were across the border, and not even then if possible.

For thirty-two years she'd kept his secrets. To protect Luis, and later to protect her daughters.

But now her daughters were in danger. Her home was gone—she'd seen that much. She didn't wake up Jessica as she drove past the smoking hulk of their house. Nor did she spare a moment's regret for the building that had been a prison for much of her adult life. Instead, she kept on going, turned the car around and got on the highway headed north.

Traffic on 101 North was light. It was going to be a much slower route than the interstate, but she wanted to stay off the main highways. She would take it slow, use pay phones, and keep a low profile until she had Jessica out of the United States. Once her daughters were safe, then she could worry about the rest.

Starting with the unfinished business in that phone call, and the chill those words evoked.

Always, Adelina. Always.

3. Andrea

From the War Memorial on Norfolk Avenue, Andrea Thompson could just make out the mass of police and emergency vehicles crowded around the condominium four blocks to the south. Flashing strobe lights in blue and red illuminated the windows of buildings on both sides of the street, and cars were stuck in heavy traffic on Wisconsin Avenue, angry commuters blocked and unable to get around. Horns honked and angry voices cried out.

As she watched, she could just make out EMTs, not in any particular hurry, wheeling a body out of the building.

Andrea knew she looked like any other teenager in the area, though perhaps not dressed as well. Blue jeans and a pajama top. She had no money, no passport, and no phone. She had people trying to kill her who had the resources to gun down federal agents in a highly secured building. She had a father she'd never met, and a not-father who she wished she'd never met.

She had a mystery for a mother, who—for reasons unknown— knew something was going to happen and called a warning. Too little. Too late.

She fished in her pockets, but found nothing but lint.

Meet me...in thirty minutes. At the war memorial on Norfolk.

Far longer than thirty minutes had passed since Dylan said those words. But she'd hung around, just in case. Hoping Dylan might show up. Hoping he might still be alive, even though she knew she'd left him armed with nothing but kitchen knives, as gunmen came down that hallway.

Gunmen intent on killing *her*.

She sighed. Then turned to walk away. Dylan Paris had sacrificed himself so she could live. She wasn't going to waste that sacrifice.

27517644R00207

Made in the USA
Charleston, SC
14 March 2014